Second Chance Rose

SALLY GLOVER

Second Chance Rose

Copyright © 2023 by Sally Glover
Print Edition

ISBN
978-1-7386620-0-5 (ebook)
978-1-7386620-1-2 (paperback)

BOOKS BY SALLY GLOVER

The Farthest Star

Second Chance Rose

The Drop

Dear reader,

Welcome to the Pacific Northwest, where the trees are tall, the air is salty, and the romance is steamy.

Thank you for taking a chance on *Second Chance Rose*! Please note that while Orcas Island is a real place, the towns and landmarks mentioned in the book are the work of my imagination.

I hope you love Rose and August's story.

Happy reading,
Sally

Orcas Island
WASHINGTON
MOONSTONE BEACH
GRANGE HALL
THEE MOUNTAIN
WINSLOW
BAYVIEW
COTTLE'S

CHAPTER 1
Rose

"I won't do it!"

My voice reverberated through the hotel kitchen. A hush descended on the staff, interrupted only by the tinny sound of the radio shoved on a shelf in the corner. I threw my hands in the air and pushed through the back door to the parking lot behind the inn. Leaning against the side of the delivery van, I forced in a few deep, calming breaths. When I closed my eyes, the look of hurt and surprise on Bluebell's face repeated in my mind, and my hot anger quickly melted into shame. Bluebell was becoming a frequent recipient of my frustration these days. It was hardly fair. She knew just as much as I did how difficult operating Big Oak Farm was, how important it was to me and Pappy.

The insistent cawing of a seagull echoed my ire. I waved a fist at it. "You said it, Mister!" The bird stared back at me, stark white on its window perch against the building's weathered gray clapboard.

Bluebell wasn't the first to suggest I should sell the business, and I was sure she wouldn't be the last. We were fighting tooth and nail to keep Big Oak Farm. No way would I allow all Pappy's hard work to be in vain.

I huffed out a breath and gathered the last delivery crate from the van, using my elbow to shove open the door to the kitchen again, where normal activity had resumed like a movie released from pause mode. I unloaded the fruits and vegetables from the crate, then scurried to peer through the little square window inlaid in the door that separated the kitchen and dining room, surprised to see the dining area full to capacity, every chair in use. Bluebell practically ran from one table to the next, furiously scribbling orders. It wasn't an ideal scenario for an apology, but I needed to tell her I was sorry for snapping.

"Hey, Fern," I called to Fern Russo, who co-owned the Driftwood Inn with her brother, Forest. "It's Wednesday, right? Why is it so busy in here?"

"You didn't hear?" Fern barely glanced up from a row of cocktail glasses. "Movie. They're all here for the shoot." I slapped a palm to my forehead. Right. Superstar actress Domino West had chosen our sweet little island in the Pacific Northwest to film *Shore Thing*. I'd been so busy with the farm I'd lost all awareness of life beyond its fences. Fern began lining up drinks on the bar. "Think you've calmed down enough to get these to table four?" She stuck a hand on her hip and smiled.

"Oh god, you heard that?" I shook my head, regret heating my cheeks anew that I'd shouted at Bluebell. "Can't imagine yelling is good for business. Sorry. Lemme help." I loaded a tray with cocktails and a jug of water and headed for table four, doing my best to catch Bluebell's eye.

At the table I set down three rhubarb mojitos and a G&T. Fern managed the bar and kitchen at the Driftwood Inn, and she loved using local ingredients in her specialty cocktails. This week's drink was no exception. I was bringing her as much rhubarb as I could grow. "Here you go. Sorry about the wait. It'll be worth it, promise," I said, holding the empty tray against my leg. "You all working on *Shore Thing*?" A round of nods lapped the table. "Tell me what—"

"Hey, girlie!" A shout erupted from the table next to us. An older man, who appeared to have over-enjoyed the rhubarb cocktail, judging from the number of empty glasses in front of him, put his fingers between his lips and readied to whistle. Horrified, the man next to him pushed down his arms as I rushed over. Bluebell looked up in alarm from where she stood by the big fireplace at the far side of the room.

"Can I help you, sir?" I focused on the would-be whistler, forcing a pleasant smile despite the outrage at his rudeness simmering in my chest.

"There you are. I ordered a steak. Where the hell is it?" Spittle seeped from the corners of his mouth. His face was tomato red—whether from the warm June sun or the mojitos, I couldn't tell. "An hour I've been waiting. And I don't like waiting!" He slammed his fist on the table, sending the empty glasses clinking into one another.

"I'll check on that right away for you, sir." I nodded curtly and turned to face the bar, working desperately to maintain a neutral expression in front of all the customers watching the commotion. Then a familiar sight entered my field of vision. A little older, a little weather worn, but there was no mistaking him: August Quinn.

I felt the blood drain from my face. I stood stock-still, and the world around me seemed to do the same.

"Rose?"

An interminable moment passed between us. I shook my head, unable to believe I was staring into the sharp green eyes that had haunted me forever. He looked the same—but different. Wounded somehow. But still handsome as a hundred-dollar bill.

Suddenly self-conscious, I reached up to brush a nonexistent strand of hair from my eyes, and the world swirled back into motion.

"August."

"I— Gah, let me apologize for Arthur here." He jabbed a thumb in the direction of the big red man seated at the table, and we both turned to look where he pointed. "He doesn't mean to be rude. He just…is. Anyway, what are you doing here? You don't still live here, do you?"

My hackles jumped to attention at the derision in his tone. I didn't have time for judgment, from August or anyone else. "You bet I do. Not everyone runs away from their problems, you know."

He pinched his mouth in a tight line, quiet for a beat. "But, Rose—"

I didn't let him finish, just spun on my heel and stalked toward the bar, grabbing Bluebell's hand and pulling her into the kitchen.

"I'm sorry for shouting at you." I dug my fists in my pockets to stop them from trembling like they always did when my emotions ran high.

She laid a hand on my arm. "It's okay. I get it. I won't men—"

"Did you know he was here?" I interrupted.

She dropped the pen she was holding into the pocket of her cocktail apron. "I did, but I never got a chance to—"

"I gotta go." I reared around abruptly, grabbing the empty produce crates and stomping to the back door, leaving my friend openmouthed.

I slammed shut the rear doors on the van and scrambled behind the wheel faster than Bluebell—or anyone else—could follow. I floored it off Water Street and onto Elison Road as though I was being chased, and in a way I was. Memories of ten years ago flooded my mind as I sailed past towering redwoods and Morning Glory Farm like I'd been shot from a cannon. As much as I'd tried all these years, I'd yet to escape the deep, aching hurt of August's disappearance from Orcas Island a decade ago. He'd been an anchor, a constant in the chaos of my life back then that had grounded this place as home. One day I was riding around shotgun in his old truck, my fingers entwined in his, head on his shoulder, and the next he was gone. No call, no email—no explanation.

His family's vanishing act and the discovery of the fraud they had perpetrated had rocked the whole community. Winslow was a tight-knit little town on the east side of the island, where the number of year-round residents hovered near three thousand. For me, their departure had also marked a distinct change in who I was. In one rise and fall of the sun, I'd gone from a wide-eyed, trusting farmer's daughter, grieving the death of her mom, to a young woman determined never to be hurt again.

August

I was quiet for the rest of the meal. No one took much notice, especially not Arthur, whose behavior went from bad to reprehensible as the evening wore on. I tried to get Bluebell's attention each time she passed the table, but she avoided me. A familiar tingle of shame crept along my spine—for the ninth time since I'd arrived this morning—at the ridiculous notion I'd held that I could avoid everyone from my past while I was here. Especially Rose Hardy.

Despite that, I'd been imagining what she looked like now for a decade. In my mind she was still eighteen, the prettiest girl on the island, her whole life ahead of her. I'd loved everything about her back then: the way her long blonde hair, bleached by salt and sun, fell to her waist like spun gold, her round brown eyes, the scent of wild roses that followed her everywhere, the crooked tooth that showed when she smiled.

But when I'd left she was overwhelmed with grief after the death of her mom. The light in her eyes had dimmed, and she'd smiled so rarely I'd missed seeing that tooth. I'd wondered, over the years, if she'd had it fixed.

So it was a shock to come face to face with a fully grown woman in place of the girl I'd pictured for so long. Her hair, pulled back from her face, was darker now, though still streaked with gold. Her cheeks were slimmer, more angular, her once-round face oval. She was strong and lean where she'd once had soft curves, and half-moons shadowed her big brown eyes. But she still made my heart skip like a stone across water.

Then there was Bluebell and Fern. I'd known them the minute I stepped foot in the Driftwood Inn this morning, Bluebell's brown curls still wild as the sea. Fern was just as bright and energetic as I remembered. Growing up on an island the size of Spokane meant a tight group of kids who experienced everything together, from kindergarten to prom and everything in between.

Coming home to Orcas Island wasn't exactly top

of my life goals, and if I'd learned anything tonight, the feeling was mutual. But I was here for the next five weeks, alongside my partners, Sam and Noah. I'd been reluctant to say yes when a friend of Sam had offered us work as underwater cameramen on *Shore Thing*—and for good reason. I doubted my being here was a happy thing for anyone. Fern had been gracious, but that was her job, wasn't it? You couldn't run a hotel and be rude to your guests.

The guilt of what my family did haunted me more than I'd feared now I was here. Eyes squeezed shut, I breathed in deeply, reminding myself why I was: I had a commitment to Sam and Noah, the friends and partners who'd stood by me when I needed them most. The movie was an opportunity too good to miss, and I hadn't had the heart to ruin it for us with my past. I knew now I'd have to.

A firm elbow to my side drew my thoughts back to the table.

"Let's get this guy upstairs." Sam gestured to a finally silent Arthur, whose head was flopped back against the red-leather booth, his mouth open wide, as if he'd passed out mid-diatribe. He clutched a half-eaten bread roll in his fist. It would almost be funny if this man wasn't my boss for the foreseeable future.

I looked at Noah, who shrugged as he stood from the table, rising like a Douglas fir. Noah was six five, a sandy-haired Viking from Norway.

"First day on set tomorrow, boys. The sooner we get this guy to his room, the sooner we can get some shuteye ourselves. I'll take this side—" Sam indicated Arthur's right arm "—Noah, you hoist the left. Quinn, you're in charge of finding his room card once we get him vertical." He bent to heave-ho position next to the snoring director.

With Noah in place, too, I counted them down. "Three, two, one—up!"

Arthur mumbled incoherently as I fished around in his shirt pocket for the hotel key card.

"We're good. Room 412."

Noah and Sam shuffled Arthur toward the elevators as I followed behind, picking up the coins and toothpicks and bits of paper that fell from Arthur's pockets. After so long sitting in the booth, I limped the first few steps, flinching through the nerve pain that shot from my ankle to my knee. By the time we got to the three stairs that led up the lobby, the pain eased, but not before I saw Bluebell watching me from behind the bar, twirling a finger through her curls. I hurried to catch up with Sam and Noah at the elevator before she could voice the concern that flashed in her eyes.

Rose

I was out fixing a sprinkler valve before the sun hit the horizon the next morning. Pappy would have insisted on doing the job himself, but I'd rather he didn't work outside when the weather got hot. Besides, I'd lain awake most of the night, jumping from bed when the sky finally lightened enough for work. Pappy and I had been converting Big Oak to organic, and the certification agent's inspection was scheduled for next month. The process had been long and exhausting, but we were counting on it setting us right. Organic certification meant we could apply for government grants and subsidies—and avenues to market our crops to organic sellers all over Washington State. It *had* to work. I couldn't bring myself to think of the alternative. I surveyed our little parcel of land, its colors and shapes so familiar they felt like part of me.

Bluebell's red hatchback stuck out like a fly on a wedding cake, bright against the side of the old estate house on the property. Poking the wrench I'd been working with into the worn canvas apron around my waist, I set out across the farm to where it was parked.

Cupping my hands around my eyes and peering in through the passenger-side window, I spotted her mop of hair spilling from under a camp blanket in the back seat.

"Bluebell, honey? You want breakfast?"

My friend bolted upright. The blanket fell away to reveal her work clothes from the night before, dotted in grease stains and red splotches, the telltale sign of last night's special: pasta with red clam sauce. Her shiny brown curls were even more wild than usual.

"Ooh, breakfast in bed? I do live glamorously," she joked once she'd squinted acknowledgement at me. She reached for her purse and fumbled around. "Ta-da!" When she'd used the elastic to wrangle her hair into a topknot, she climbed over the center console and exited through the passenger door, which I held open majestically.

"My lady," I said, gesturing the path in front of her. We burst out laughing. Through thick and thin—mostly thin, of late—me and Bluebell had been each other's rock for much of our lives. The going could be tough for year-round residents of Orcas Island. In the winter our work lives slowed to a crawl. Most of us had to make hay when tourist season hit in spring and summer to earn enough money to last through the year. In some ways I was better off than Bluebell: at least I knew I always had a bed in the two-room cottage on the farm I shared with Pappy. To make extra money, she often gave up her apartment during the busy months. There were always seasonal workers willing to pay more than market value for a place to stay in town, and Bluebell was eager to take it from them. Which sometimes meant she ended up here, tucked up in her little car. No matter how many times I offered, though, she refused to take the bed upstairs in the old house—whether out of respect for me or to avoid feeling like a burden, I wasn't sure.

"Ready to talk about him?" she asked as we trod the worn dirt path to the cottage. The sun was well above the horizon now, the shadows of apricot and cherry trees growing shorter as the morning fog burned away.

"No. Yes. Oh god, do we have to?" My jaw clenched and unclenched. "When did you know?"

"Not much sooner than you did, promise. I didn't really get a chance to tell you after we—"

I held up a palm. "I'm sorry I shouted at you. But I won't leave Pappy, the farm, any of this. It would break his heart. It would break mine. After he fought so hard to keep it going, to give me a home." The three-acre hobby farm on the east side of Orcas Island was all I'd ever known. I could fix sprinklers and oil tractors and plan intricate crop schedules, but if you dropped me anywhere else, I wouldn't survive a week.

I wasn't going anywhere.

"I hear you, Rose, I do. It's just so hard to watch you struggle. We could leave this place. Go somewhere easier. Without all the history—and hardship."

"There's nowhere else for me. This is it, for better or worse."

Bluebell threw up her hands. "Well, I'm not leaving without you, so I guess we're stuck here."

We continued along in silence, broken only by the sweet birdsong of skylarks as they flitted through the orchard. "I can't believe he's here. It was like seeing a ghost," I finally said.

"I know. It was the weirdest thing, walking into that dining room to find him sitting there, like no time at all has passed."

"Did you talk to him? Why is he here—now?"

"Must be the movie. That's all anyone was talking about last night. The hotel is booked solid for five weeks. Some of our regulars even got the boot. If last night was any indication, we're gonna need more servers, fast. Thanks for helping, by the way. I'm only sorry you were faced with such a shock when you did." She stuck her hands in the back pockets of her work pants, elbows pointing behind her like wings on a sparrow.

"Anyway, no, I didn't talk to him beyond taking orders at his table. He tried to get my attention a few times, but I sort of brushed him off." She turned to face me and wiggled her eyebrows. "Can't say the years have been bad to him—at least not in the looks department. Kind of like Clint Eastwood in *A Fist Full of Dollars.*"

"Can't say I noticed." I focused my eyes ahead and schooled my lips into a straight line, but I knew Bluebell wasn't buying it. "Okay, okay. Looks were never his shortcoming. Doesn't give him the right to strut back into Bayview, high on the hog, order steak, and drink too much with those Hollywood people. What does he think, he *is* Clint Eastwood?"

I grew more infuriated with each step, so I got a start when my beloved pappy, known to others on the island as Felix Hardy, stood from his chair on the cottage's tiny front porch to greet Bluebell. Fig, his brown border terrier, didn't budge from where she lay sprawled in the sun next to him.

"Well, aren't you two a sight for these old eyes," he said, springing forward. He may have been nearing seventy-six, but his eyes still sparkled brightly, his movements birdlike on his wiry frame.

"Felix, I was here last weekend! You act like I've been away for ages." Bluebell leaned in to kiss his wrinkled cheeks.

"When you get to my age, everything does feel like ages," he said. "You two sit. I'll fix eggs." He disappeared through the screen door before either of us could protest. Fig raised her head, her eyes following Pappy until he was gone from view before she let out a groan and fell back on the warm wooden slats of the porch.

Bluebell shook her head, finding it hard to reconcile Pappy's energy with his age. "Does he ever slow down?"

"I wish he would. He's always surprising me. This week I've been getting up early to beat him to the big chores. He's on to me, though. I've had to set my alarm earlier and earlier to foil him. Soon neither of us will sleep at all."

She giggled. "Well, I'm just glad he agreed to convert Big Oak. Not many people his age would be so willing to change. You never said how you did it, anyway."

I let out an uncomfortable laugh. "Honestly? Neither of us can say it, but we both know how close we are to losing this place. How real the possibility is we might lose everything he spent his whole life building. Everything my mom worked so hard for." Hearing the words aloud made my throat clog with panic. Blinking back tears, I looked away, at the big oak tree rising from a gentle hill at the edge of the farm. When I turned to Bluebell, her eyes were shiny, too.

"Anyway. I started by showing him stuff on

YouTube, poking holes in any justifications against it, and within no time I would come home to find him doing research on his own." I paused, wistful. "I can't do it without him. That's a lot to carry on those pokey little shoulders of his."

The screen door creaked open, and Pappy began bringing out fried eggs, crispy bacon, baked tomatoes, and thick slices of sourdough bread from Pies & Otherwise, the baking pride of Winslow. We ate it with gusto, both hungrier than we'd realized, and I reflected on the unconventional family I'd surrounded myself with. After my mom died, it had taken years to fill the enormous hole in my heart. At first I'd had August to lean on, but when he'd disappeared from the island three months later like dew on a May morning, I'd had to mourn his loss just the same. It had been like two deaths, really. Bluebell had buoyed me at every turn. And my pappy—well, if Bluebell was the beacon that kept me from drifting out to sea, Pappy was the anchor that moored me to this little island in the Pacific.

CHAPTER 2

August

The first two movies I worked on with Sam and Noah were filmed at a lake in rural Ontario, Canada, miles from any town. This time I knew it was a privilege to walk from our production headquarters to a local coffee shop. I hit the bull's eye with Grind House on Water Street, where I scoffed down a vanilla-glazed doughnut and took my coffee to go so I could digest some of the changes that had come to Bayview in my absence.

With each step the stiffness in my leg eased a little more, the warmth of the morning sun calming my bones. Time had been good to Orcas Island's main town. Tourism seemed to be driving the economy here now, with upscale galleries and boutiques in spaces once occupied by seedy tobacco and souvenir shops. Even the coffee was about the best I'd had, although things always tasted better in the fresh sea air.

I made my way back to the dockyard in Bayview marina that was *Shore Thing*'s production office for the next five weeks. The building's quiet exterior belied the bustling activity happening inside. Arthur Dagon's two production assistants were glued to his side like imprinted ducklings, zigging right and zagging left to follow his lead around the cavernous space normally used for boat repairs. The director and script team were huddled around a desk on one side of the space. Domino West's costars would be arriving on Saturday, and the next two days would be hectic in the lead-up to the director's first shout of "Action." Scanning the space, I spotted Sam and Noah on the other side, unpacking the diving gear we had sent to Bayview ahead of us.

"Hey. How's it going?" I set my coffee cup on a paint-splattered old workhorse.

"It all looks good so far." Bent forward, Sam carefully lifted underwater lights from a hard case and checked them over before setting them back against their protective foam. Where Noah was tall and lanky, Sam was compact and muscled. He had the energy of a sprinter about to burst from the blocks.

Noah sat in a folding chair, inspecting his wetsuit seams. The water in the Pacific Northwest was notoriously cold, even in summer months, and we'd be spending much of our time immersed in it, filming the two lead characters in *Shore Thing* as they searched for treasure in the ocean's depths.

"We should get these on and jump in. I'd like to be confident we have everything we need when it's go time," Sam said.

Noah whooped and raised a hand for me to high-five. "I'll take that twenty anytime, Auggie."

I shook my head and tsked. "I shoulda known better." Of the three of us, Sam was the one who dotted every *i* and crossed every *t*—sometimes twice—so much so we often teased him about it. I dug into my jeans pocket to cough up the bill.

Sam looked between us, his dark eyes observant. "All right, all right. But one of us has to be the hard ass." He hung three wetsuits on a rolling rack set in place by the production team. "Seriously, though, what time do you want to suit up?"

"How does the saying go? You can take the man out of the FBI, but you can't take the FBI out of Sam," Noah said. He and I eyed each other again, laughing.

I clapped Sam on the shoulder. "Okay, you're on. How about we check in with Arthur before we do a trial run." I leaned on the workhouse and rubbed my knee. They watched me with concern.

"All right, Auggie?"

Shit. I stood straight and shoved both hands in my pockets. "Right as rain." An injury had ended my career with the FBI, and even though I was healing—slowly—I hated showing weakness to anyone, even Sam and Noah. "Hey, Arthur," I called loudly as the big man crossed the floor in front of us, production assistants in tow.

The director stopped his agitated pacing and pinned us with a stare. Up this close, it was easy to see the effects of his overindulgence last night. His eyes were bloodshot, his hair greasy and sticking up at odd angles.

"You guys better be ready to go," he growled. "If I have to deal with one more thing—"

Seeing the production assistants cower behind Arthur, Noah interrupted quickly. "All good, boss. Just seeing if you need us this afternoon." Noah pointed to the dive gear and wetsuits. "We'd like to test all this before principal shooting starts."

Arthur grunted approval before stalking off, his assistants scurrying behind.

We loaded a rolling shelf with all the equipment we'd be using for the movie—fins, tanks, masks, lights, dive computers, and underwater camera gear.

Next we began the process of getting into our wet-suits, first turning them inside out, stepping in one leg at a time, and slowly rolling them up and over our bodies. Once I was zipped into mine, I reached up to tighten the velcro fastenings at the neck. Taking a few steps, I rotated my shoulders and bent my arms to check the fit. Sam and Noah did the same. While they did jumps and squats, I did a few gentle kicks. I wondered if my knee would ever heal to the point of squats.

We rolled the shelf across the plank floor to the entrance and swung open the barn-style doors. The sun shimmered brightly off the water, a startling contrast to the building's dark interior. Arthur had ordered the removal of the fishing boats and cruisers that normally filled the slips of the marina, and the *Redemption*, the large boat that would be featured in *Shore Thing*, was the lone vessel docked today.

The water was deep enough at the end of the docks for the purposes of our mission this morning. Hoods up and flippers on, we each secured dive masks and tanks, tested our buoyancy devices, checked our air sources, and made sure one another's shoulder and chest clips were secured. Sam flashed the okay signal and waited for me and Noah to do the same before stepping to the edge of the dock, the balls of his fins on the edge. Holding his mask and regulator, he took a giant stride forward into the Pacific. Counting to three, Noah followed behind. I waited for them to surface, then leaned down to pass them their cameras. Sam grabbed his with both hands and attached himself to it with a lanyard. Noah fastened his the same way, and after Sam flashed me another okay sign, I stepped forward into the ocean to join them.

We dove beneath the waves and into the eerily silent world below, exploring the barnacles and anemones that carpeted the underwater rock formations not far from the dock. My years on the FBI dive team had been purely mission-based—and usually dangerous. I'd been too focused on combing the ocean floor for evidence, dismantling explosives, and making risky rescues to spare attention to the creatures that made the ocean their home. I tried to savor the moment.

Forests of bull kelp hung like balloons, their tales dancing in the currents like silky green streamers. Despite growing up in the Pacific Northwest, I hadn't learned to dive until my training with the FBI Underwater Search and Evidence Response Team— USERT—in Miami. This was my first time exploring the rugged shore of Orcas Island from this perspective, and I was awed by the endless array of soft corals and the huge beds of sea urchins. Since the accident I had developed a renewed appreciation for the weightlessness of swimming. It was a great equalizer, the one place I felt just as capable as my teammates.

Noah swam up beside me, pointing with his index and forefinger first to his eyes and then to his left. I held my breath in awe as a pod of orcas appeared from the depths. Sam focused his camera on the giant mammals. After a few moments circling our trio, time suspended, the huge whales carried on their journey.

Transfixed in the presence of these marine giants, a memory flashed through me like a bolt of lightning: Rose and me as teenagers, my gangly arm around her waist as we leaned over the railing of the Orcas Island ferry to watch a group of enormous black-and-white whales swim alongside the boat, taking turns dancing in and out of the water, their shiny black fins glinting like diamonds in the sun. We had skipped out of school, and I remember how grown-up I felt that day, taking the ferry on our own. It didn't matter where we were going; what had mattered was we were together. It was the memory of Rose that lived closest to the surface for me, one filled with the exuberance and joy of a first love.

A short while later, when I thought we could be satisfied with the test run of our gear, I flashed "up" at Sam and Noah to signal the end of the dive. At the surface I swam to the ladder, slipped off my fins, and climbed out of the water. Sam unclipped the camera from his lanyard and carefully handed it up to me before following the same definning procedure. Noah came up behind.

"Whooo!" Noah hollered and raised a fist in the sunshine. "What a rush."

"Never seen an orca before. They're massive! They must be old news to you—being from around here, huh?" Sam asked.

"I only ever saw them once, from a boat. Sometimes people see them from shore if they're really lucky. Actually it's not that common to spot them, even in this area." Gazing out at the expanse of blue before me, I thought again of that day on the ferry, how Rose and I had taken for granted that we shared our world with such magnificent mammals—and with each other. If only I'd realized how precious that moment was, how often the memory would get me through hard times in the years to come.

When I returned my focus to the dock, Noah and Sam were loading up the rolling cart with their gear. At least, Noah was loading equipment on the cart; Sam was moving each piece into just the right place. "Want to hand me that mask?" Noah reached a hand toward it.

"Sorry, man. Here you go."

"Everything cool? You seem distracted," Noah said.

"Yeah, I'm cool. I dunno, I guess it's just being back here. It's weird, you know? I figured it would be different. Well, it's different, but it's the same, too." I thought of Rose again but didn't say more. I'd been meaning to tell Sam and Noah how—or rather why—I'd left Orcas Island when I did, but somehow I couldn't find the courage.

Sam straightened up and clapped my shoulder. "If there's one thing we know about you, Auggie, you're always on the move. Never known you to get attached to someplace. You're not feeling nostalgic, are you? Didn't know you had it in ya."

"Of course not. Let me tell you, I couldn't wait to get off this rock when I was a kid. Nothing here but run-down old barns and sub-par hotels. Hell, you needed a train, boat, or plane just to see a pretty girl." I blew out a breath. It was a lie. Rose had been the prettiest girl in the state back then—still was, from what I'd seen yesterday—but for some reason I felt the need to bluster. "So what do you think? We ready to shoot some awesome footage?"

As we walked barefoot across the docks to the production office, the talk turned to *Shore Thing* and how we planned to capture the scenes we'd been hired for. It was a big-name movie with big-name stars, and all three of us knew what a coup it was to be part of it. Noah had been on every mission I'd run with the USERT, with Sam joining our crew for the last four years. We were all the same age, and our experiences with the FBI brought us together in a way not many people understood. The accident meant I could never return to USERT. Noah and Sam made a huge sacrifice in leaving their posts to join me in the film business. It was an idea we'd come up with late one night, fueled by whiskey and bravado, an escape from the stress and high stakes of the FBI. I was proud of how far we'd come.

The rest of the day was a blur of prepping for our first scenes, consulting with the script team, and staying out of Arthur's path. Five o'clock rolled by, then six. Close to six thirty, when we could no longer ignore the rumbling of our stomachs, we left the marina and walked the short block to the Driftwood Inn, swapping notes about what snacks we were most looking forward to when craft services set up in the coming days.

We parted ways to shower before dinner. When I headed back downstairs to the busy dining room on the main floor, the same gang as last night was running the place. Pretty blonde Fern Russo tended bar and ran food out to patrons, while Bluebell, Rose's closest friend when we were all at school together, took orders and answered questions. A tall young kid—maybe eighteen or nineteen—cleared and wiped tables.

Had I expected no one from the old days would

still be here? Naively maybe I had. Seeing familiar faces again tonight sent prickles of remorse across my chest about what my family did to this community. I waited by the entrance to be seated, nodding meekly at Bluebell as she passed with a tray of cocktails. She halted in front of me on her return to the bar. "Table for one, August? Or will your charming friend be joining you?" she asked, referencing Arthur's regretful behavior the night before.

"Party of three, actually, thanks. And no, Arthur isn't in on the party tonight. Or any other night, hopefully."

Bluebell grabbed three menus and led me to a booth by the bar.

"He, uh, isn't my friend. He's the director. Of the movie we're shooting," I clarified. I took a seat.

"Don't worry about it. Not the first asshole to come through here." She began placing menus on the table, but when I reached up and touched her arm, she stopped. Really looked me in the eyes for the first time. She seemed to soften a little, which I didn't deserve.

"Listen, can I talk to you? I want to explain—"

"There you are, Auggie." Noah shoved into the seat next to me, his hair wet from the shower. Sam filed across the room next.

"Sam Fox. Nice to meet you." Sam stood next to

Bluebell and stuck out his hand in greeting.

She paused for a moment before shaking it. "Bluebell. Your server tonight."

"Bluebell, I hope August here apologized for what happened last night. Our director—he's a big...dude."

Bluebell waved him to sit. "Arthur. I heard. No big deal, but thanks. Now, what can I get you? The gin basil smash is our drink special. Fresh basil leaves, simple syrup, real lemon juice, and Tanqueray on ice." She pulled a pad and pen from her apron pocket and held them expectantly.

Noah sat up straight and squared himself to Bluebell. "I'll take anything you're selling," he said, flashing a charming grin.

Sam rolled his eyes at me. Noah was as true to his playboy self as Sam was to being prepared. Bluebell was unfazed.

"I'll take one, too," Sam added. "But hold the syrup."

Noah elbowed my side. Sam was forever careful about what he put into his, as he called it, "temple."

Bluebell looked to me expectantly, pen poised. "Just water," I said. She nodded and retreated to the bar. I'd have to watch for a chance to pull her aside later.

Soon we were digging into salmon steaks, roasted and served on cedar planks, with generous scoops of mashed potatoes and garlicky green beans. When I left Orcas Island, the Driftwood Inn had a reputation among locals as dated and run-down, but I was impressed with what I'd seen these past few days. Domino West had bought a stake in the place. In fact, it was on a location scout for *Shore Thing* that she'd first come to Orcas Island from Hollywood. The story went that she fell in love with Fern's brother, Forest, and never went back to LA. The Russo family had operated the hotel for over a century, and alongside Domino, Fern and Forest had really made the place thrive after their parents retired to Arizona.

We stayed longer than almost all the other diners in the place. I couldn't help but think it had something to do with the way Sam kept looking over at Fern. With her bright blue eyes and bubbly personality, I had no doubt Fern regularly had to deflect the attention of men at the inn. It was good for business, I guessed, and she seemed to be really digging the attention. She returned every look Sam threw her way with a flick of her ponytail and an easy giggle.

"Something catch your attention tonight?" I heard Bluebell tease Fern as she loaded a tray of empty glasses into the washer. Sam and Noah were deep in conversation about a new camera Sam wanted, oblivious to the conversation at the bar.

"Helloooo, earth to Bluebell, you'd have to be

blind not to notice Mr. Hold the Syrup over there."
Fern looked at our table again with a smile.

"Hellloooo, earth to Fern, doesn't Forest have a strict rule against dating customers?"

"He's one to talk." Fern stopped loading glasses and pointed a finger at herself. "It's not something *I* want to do, though." With another flick of her hair, she resumed what she was doing. "But flirting—that's a whole other story."

"It's your funeral, kid." Bluebell laughed and walked away to clear another table.

Bellies full, we stood up to leave. As Sam and Noah headed to the lobby, I lingered under the arched doorway that connected it to the dining room, waiting to catch Bluebell's attention.

She stopped in front of me on her way to the bar. "Look, I know it's a surprise to see me here. And I know it's an even bigger surprise for Rose. The way she looked at me yesterday... She looked right through me, like I don't exist or something. Can you tell her—"

She held up a hand. "Whatever it is, tell her yourself."

"Even if I had her number, she'd hang up the minute she heard my voice. She hates me—I know it. If you'd seen the way she looked at me..." I stared at the floor, hands clenched at my sides, then looked back up at Bluebell. "I owe her an apology. I owe you an apology, too. I can't—" My breath hitched at the look in her eyes. Was that…pity? I hated pity.

"Tell you what. Me and her meet every Friday at Cottle's. Call it a late lunch. Remember the place? The old fish market in Winslow? We'll be there tomorrow. Three o'clock."

"I remember. I'll be there." I pressed my palms together in a prayer sign. "Thank you. So listen, maybe don't tell her I'm coming?"

"What do you take me for, a ninny?" She rolled her eyes and poked her index finger into my shoulder. "Don't mess with her, Auggie," she warned, her curls bouncing as she shook her head.

"That's the last thing I want to do."

CHAPTER 3

Rose

Every Friday morning I prepared for the Winslow Farmers Market, a Saturday tradition at Grange Hall going back nearly fourteen years. It was often the highlight of my week, a chance to visit with friends and neighbors and catch up on news. Particularly in the summer months, I cherished this time connecting with the community when the island was crowded with tourists.

I piled a canopy tent and folding table into the back of the van, leaving space for the crates of fruits and vegetables I needed to harvest later and store in the cool parlor of the old estate house until morning.

Shutting the rear doors, I looked down at my worn jeans and work boots, deciding they would have to do for lunch with Bluebell. There was no one to impress at Cottle's Fish Market, a casual little spot in Winslow with picnic tables and counter service. I ducked into the cottage to wash my hands and tell Pappy I was leaving.

He sat in a sliver of afternoon sun at the kitchen table bent over Jean-Martin Fortier's *The Market Gardener*, a book I had ordered on small-scale organic farming. I'd dog-eared the pages, too, soaking in everything I could about biointensive farming and how to make it profitable. Seeing the stack of invoices piled next to his teacup sent a prick of worry through me.

"Heading out to Cottle's, Pappy." I ran my hands under warm water at the kitchen sink.

His eyes lit up. "See if you can't find me some of those littleneck clams, would you?"

I smiled to myself. We had the same exchange every week, but I would never grow tired of it. I would do anything to make him happy, especially indulging his favorite local delicacy. Fig's scruffy tail flopped twice as I bent to scratch her tummy.

It was a perfect day for a bike ride, so I pulled my old ten-speed from the side of the cottage, fixed up with a crate bungee-corded to the rat-trap I'd once crammed my backpack into for the commute to and from high school. I'd refused many offers over the years of a hand-me-down car when friends or neighbors upgraded or moved away. I had all I needed with my bicycle and the delivery van. Besides, another vehicle would mean extra costs: insurance, gas, upkeep. We needed every penny we made to keep Big Oak alive.

With the ends of my jeans tucked into my boots, I stepped a foot on the pedal, swung the other leg over, and pushed off down the gravel path to the road, tires kicking up dust behind me. I treasured these Friday lunches at Cottle's as the one hour of the week I allowed myself not to think about the farm.

The squawking of gulls called me to the end of Larsen Road, where a two-story building was perched near the edge of a pier. Opened in 1969 by Louis and Mary Larsen, Cottle's captured all that was charming about Winslow, with its weathered cedar shingles and beautiful views. Picnic tables and makeshift chairs made of wooden crab traps dotted the pier.

"Hiya, Louis," I called, propping my bike against the side of the building, where old yellow-and-orange fishing buoys hung like Christmas ornaments against the gray shingles. Decades of salt air had faded and peeled the paint.

Louis turned from the task of clearing a picnic

table. "How's my favorite farmer?" With a twinkle in his eyes, he added, "Don't tell Pappy I said that."

"Never." I wrapped an arm around him and squeezed. Louis and Pappy had been close their whole lives. They were among the longest-lived residents on Orcas Island, particularly in Winslow. They'd grown up on the very same land they lived on today, had swum together every summer as kids, and supported each other for a generation. "How was your week?"

"Aye, it was good," he said. "I can set my clock to the ebb and flow of tourist season around here. Right about now we're hitting our flow. Quite a few folks from Bayview been coming around—something about a movie? 'Spose it ain't the first time. Did you hear Orcas Island was one of the places they looked at for *Jaws*?" He chuckled, gazing off the pier over the flat blue water in the sound. "That'd have been the death of us, I think. A giant, man-eating shark?" He was still chuckling when he turned and walked away.

I'd heard this urban myth before. Whether I believed it was another story, but I supposed it was possible given the sheltered bays and shallow waters on the west side of the island. Orcas Island's only movie connection I knew of—besides *Shore Thing*—was when neighboring San Juan was pictured in the opening scene of *Free Willy*. I guess that counted as location-adjacent.

My stomach grumbling, I left my helmet on an empty picnic table and headed to where Mary Larsen was talking to a young couple at the order window, her long braid of gray hair slung over her shoulder. Bluebell wouldn't mind if I ordered without her.

"Hi, Mary!" I said when my turn came. "How are things?"

"You mean besides this lot?" She indicated the galley kitchen behind her, where Freddy, her twenty-three-year-old son, was mixing gallons of beer batter and Louis was stocking a refrigerator case with some of the littleneck clams I would take home to Pappy later. Freddy had been trying to get his parents to update their dine-in menu for the past few months. I'd heard wonderful things about his ideas.

"You might not think it, but dreams do come true, my girl," Mary said. "Nothing like working alongside your nearest and dearest. Speaking of, Bluebell not here yet?" She poked her head through the window and scanned the pier.

"Not yet, but if I don't order now, I'll eat my hand, I'm so hungry."

"How would you keep Pappy in line with just the one?" She raised her hands in front of her, giving them a razzle dazzle, and laughed. "What'll it be, then? One of Freddy's new items?"

I scanned the chalkboard menu nailed to the right

of the order window. "I'll try some of the tacones, please. With wild salmon. Bluebell would like that, too. Make it two orders."

"You bet, my love. Take a seat."

"Thanks. Here—" I handed Mary a twenty. "She never lets me buy. This time she doesn't have a choice." Lunch at Cottle's was the only extravagance in my life these days, but I loved supporting the Larsens.

Back at the empty picnic table, I pulled the phone from my pocket.

You OK? I tapped and hit send. Bluebell couldn't always get out of the restaurant on time, but she usually texted if that was the case.

Ten minutes later there was still no sign of or word from Bluebell. Mary pushed through the double doors out to the pier, two plastic baskets with red-checkered paper clutched in one hand and two Coronas in the other.

"Grilled flour tortillas with wild salmon, coleslaw, pea shoots, house-made sauce, and lemon-pickled onions," she said as she set the baskets on the table, one in front of me and the other across the table. "And a couple of Coronas. On the house." She put her hands to her hips and cocked her head. "Anything else, love?"

My mouth watered at the sight of the tacones and

beer. "If it tastes as good as it looks, I'll eat Bluebell's, too, by the time she gets here."

"You wish," Mary said, waving behind me to the pier entrance, where Bluebell rushed toward us.

As Bluebell scrambled into her seat, she tucked a wayward curl behind her ear. "Sorry I'm so late!" she said breathlessly. "These movie people are something else. What is *this*?" she exclaimed, her eyes widening at the salmon tacones. "Mary, these look delish."

Mary smiled proudly. "I'll tell Freddy. They're his creation."

"Told you he had it in him," Bluebell teased. Freddy had apprenticed with the chef at the Driftwood Inn last year. Bluebell had been impressed with his ability to combine flavors and come up with inventive ideas—something she'd mentioned every time she'd seen Mary since.

"That's an I told-you-so I can take," Mary said over her shoulder on her way inside.

Tacone in hand, I couldn't hold myself back a second longer. "You weren't kidding," I said between bites. "That kid knows his way around food."

We inhaled our lunch. When I finished, I took a swig of beer and noticed Bluebell looking furtively behind her—for the second time since she'd arrived.

I plonked the beer on the table. "Expecting someone?"

She hesitated, as if trying to decide the correct answer. "N-no. I mean, yes. Maybe. Look, don't be upset, okay? He just wants a chance to apologize."

"Are you kidding? That statute of limitation is over. Done-zo." I stood abruptly, but as I reached for my helmet, Bluebell laid a hand over mine.

"Just sit, please. I'm sorry to ambush you. I just feel for the guy, okay? Something in his eyes looks... I dunno, sad. I mean, we're adults now, right? The way I see it, what his parents did—that's not *his* fault. And he's walking with a limp—did you notice? As much as he's trying to hide it." She let go of my hand.

Still standing, I turned to my left to look across the sound, willing the calm Pacific to assuage my anger. I sighed and sat again.

What explanation could he have for leaving his best friend, his high school sweetheart, without calling, or texting, or emailing—ever again? For disappointing me so deeply? For changing the course of my life so profoundly? I pressed my fingers to my temples, frustrated. "I don't blame him for what his parents did. I blame him for discarding me like some old shoe." I huffed out a breath at Bluebell's pleading expression. "Fine. I don't promise to be kind." He was going to be here for a while whether I liked it or not. The sooner he knew where he stood, the better.

"I get it, believe me. But remember what your

mom used to say? Everyone deserves to be heard." Bluebell took a sip of beer.

"Oh, sure, tell that to Pappy, who counted on August's dad to deliver fertilizer every week. Or to my mom, who saw Mrs. Quinn at every hospital appointment." *Or tell it to my eighteen-year-old self, who lived and breathed the guy.* None of this was new information to Bluebell. No one knew better how drastically I changed after August left. My mom's death had marked a profound shift in who I was, and when August left, too, I'd felt even more adrift. I'd waited—too long—for him to reach out, to tell me everything was okay, that he was coming back for me. But the call never came. "Don't think you're going anywhere, though. I'm only staying if you do." I folded my arms over my chest.

Bluebell nodded. Sensing my nerves, she squeezed my fingers in hers. "Imagine what it would be like to let go of all that anger."

Even through the bitterness that simmered in my belly whenever I thought of August Quinn, I knew she was right. Forgiving him would give me freedom from the hurt I'd been carrying around for ten years. I'd always put it off, figuring I'd examine my feelings at some point—resolve the emotions of that chapter in my life. His being here only meant I'd have to forgive him in person rather than just in my heart. "Yeah.

You're right, I know you are."

We sipped our drinks in the sun, my stomach twisting in knots at the prospect of confronting him.

August

The dashboard clock in the cargo van I'd borrowed from the production team read 3:49 as I made a right on Larsen Road. Much had changed in my absence from the island, but I found myself navigating as if by autopilot on the drive from Bayview. Being born into a place did that to you—sights and smells and landmarks were just part of you, and you didn't have to give it much thought. I hadn't expected that, coming here. I'd been prepared for resentment, sure, and definitely regret, returning to this place that loomed so large in my past. But fond familiarity? Not so much.

I parked in a spot near the top of the hill, unable to shake the uneasiness that settled in my chest at the thought of seeing Rose again. As much as I'd tried to rush through the workday, I hadn't left Bayview on time to make it to Cottle's by three. Now I found myself hoping I was too late, that Rose and Bluebell were gone. Phone in hand, I walked the rest of the way down the road to the old clapboard building on the end of the pier, picking up speed as my muscles loosened. The place looked exactly as I remembered. I wondered if Louis and Mary would know me now.

Rounding the corner of the building, I spotted the women right away. Sitting sideways on the benches of a picnic table, the remains of their lunch between them, they faced the sparkling water in the sound. I paused where I was, doubting my decision again. Seeing them made real what I'd come here to do: apologize. Would Rose even care? Before I could change my mind, though, Bluebell noticed me. She lifted a wave.

Rose turned to look at me, her expression blank. Despite my smile, her face didn't change. She averted her gaze quickly as I approached.

Bluebell climbed out of the picnic table and stood. "Hi. Nice to see you again. You look like you could use one of these." She pointed to the empty Corona bottle in her hand. "Be right back."

I studied Rose, trying to get a read on how she felt about me being here. "Mind if I sit?" I indicated the bench Bluebell had vacated.

"Suit yourself." Her shoulders were taut, her back pin-straight. Her hair was bound in a bun at the nape of her neck. Her jeans and T-shirt were streaked with dirt, and a wrench poked out from a canvas apron around her waist.

I sat across from her, balling my hands into fists so tight my fingernails imprinted in my palms. "Look, I'm sorry to crash your lunch with Bluebell. It's just—" I thought for a minute, trying to figure out the best way to say it. "I'm going to be here awhile. We're bound to run into each other, and I don't want to make things awkward for you." *Say you're sorry, you idiot*, I cursed silently.

Rose looked straight at me, and my heart stuttered in my chest. Her face was so familiar yet different. Matured. I saw her notice the crinkle above my nose, once visible only when I smiled but now more permanently etched in my forehead. Then her eyes went to the scar on my cheek, and I wondered at the emotion that flickered in her eyes.

"Mm-hmm" was all she said, continuing her assessment of me.

Bluebell broke the awkwardness. "So, what's new?" she asked, placing three cold bottles of beer on the table and climbing into the seat next to me. I was surprised, actually, at how nice she was being. "What do you think, Auggie? You can't tell me you expected Cottle's to still be standing, right? Pretty amazing what the Larsens have done. If you're hungry, I highly recommend the tacones. Like, so good."

I took a long sip of beer, letting its cold bubbles fizzle down the back of my throat. "Yah, cool. Funny how much things change." I looked pointedly at Rose.

"What do you want?" she said.

"How about a coffee sometime? I need to—"

"Not a chance."

"But if you'd just let me—"

"Nope." She crossed her arms. She felt no compunction to fill the silence that followed.

My shoulders sagged. I was dejected but not surprised. I didn't blame her; if I couldn't forgive myself for the way I'd left, how could I expect her to? How had I managed to convince myself anyone on Orcas might welcome my presence here? I chuckled bitterly, wishing like hell I'd turned down the job on *Shore Thing*, told Sam and Noah it was impossible.

"This was a mistake." I stood. "I came here to tell you I'm sorry. To apologize. To both of you. Hell, I probably owe this whole island an apology." I scanned the tables around us, my cheeks burning. "But that doesn't matter, does it. Thanks for the beer, Bluebell. I'll keep out of your way while I'm here." I spun around and weaved through the picnic tables, my leg aching.

I felt Rose's eyes on my back, sure she was clocking the hitch in my step.

Before I was out of earshot, I heard Bluebell say,

"Hey, what happened to hearing him out? At least give the guy a reason you won't talk to him. He didn't even get to finish his beer."

Why was Bluebell taking my side? I couldn't make out Rose's reply.

"Go on, you can still catch him."

Footsteps thudded behind me. I looked over my shoulder at Rose but didn't stop.

"August. Auggie!" she called. She quickly caught up to me, although I kept moving toward the road that led to the van.

"I'm sorry you came all the way out here. Bluebell thought I was ready for it." She slowed into pace alongside me, her blonde hair shiny in the sun. "I appreciate the thought—I do. But I just don't trust you. Whatever explanation you have or story you want to tell—that won't change my mind."

I stopped and faced her. But before I could say a word, she held up a finger. "You're here for work, right? So maybe we'll bump into each other. Fine. But I have no room in my life for anything right now. Not a trip down memory lane, or some excuse or apology, or even a friendship. I have two priorities. Pappy and the farm. That's it. You left. You have no idea how hard it's been—how hard it *is*—to keep going, year after year. Season after season! I know everything looks rosy to you now. We're coming up on summertime, and the hotel and Water Street are full of tourists and you film people, but come November, it's a different game."

"I remember—"

She interrupted me again. "Things change, as you said. Whatever you remember of Orcas, it's different now. Back then we had nothing to worry about. Nothing real, anyway."

I considered her words carefully. "Whatever you say," I said quietly. I realized how asinine it was to imagine she might be open to an apology—a second chance at friendship. It was obvious she wasn't. "We can agree to be civil." I held out a hand.

"Civil," she said. As her palm hit mine and my fingers curled around hers, a zing of electricity raced through me. I fought to keep my expression neutral but held on a second longer than the shake warranted. Recognition dawned in her eyes, too.

Leaving her standing there, I took the last steps to the van and climbed in, willing myself not to look back. Much as it killed me, I started the engine, backed out, and drove to the main road. So much for second chances.

CHAPTER 4

Rose

I cast a long shadow over the vegetable field in the early morning light as I pulled several rows of new potatoes from the ground and dusted the dirt from them. Next came the beets. Chioggias were popular at the market, with their cheerful candy-cane stripes. We also grew deep purple ones as well as orange and glowing cerise-pink, and this year we'd added an heirloom white variety that was crisp and sweet as sugar.

My thoughts were stuck on August. I dropped an overflowing crate close to the estate house and moved on to the neat rows of kale, their deep green leaves standing straight like soldiers in the soil. Where had he *been* for the past ten years? What was that scar from? I floated down each row deep in thought, grasping at the stems of outer leaves and pulling down and out, away from the new growth. It was important to leave a handful of leaves at the center of each plant so they could continue to produce. I liked using my fingers rather than gardening shears where I could, enjoying the connection that afforded me to the land.

As a teenager I'd found real joy pitching in to help Pappy and my mom with chores. In those days I'd looked at everything with joy and wonder, oblivious to the stress and uncertainty that came with farm life. Pappy always made it look easy, never voicing a worry or doubt the farm would survive another year. It was a happy time in my life; we'd had no idea my mom was staring down the barrel of a cancer diagnosis, a year filled with appointments, needle jabs, and surgeries ahead of her.

My life had been interwoven with August's since we were kids. Toby and Emma Quinn, his parents, had run Bayview Soil and Landscape, a feed and fertilizer business, and worked with Pappy and my mom practically their whole lives. Toby had made deliveries to Big Oak as a teenager working part-time, taking over the business when his own father retired. The progression was obvious: August would helm

Bayview Soil one day, too. He hadn't minded the idea. He'd loved being in nature and wanted to work outside as much as possible. Buried somewhere in all the anger I'd felt at him leaving, I knew it must have been hard for him to give up that dream.

No one had thought twice about trusting Toby Quinn when he'd approached a group of farmers in Winslow about a new tractor supplier with rock-bottom prices. At that time folks around here didn't use the internet much—but even if they had, they wouldn't have questioned Toby's offer. They'd happily made cash payments toward new tillers, blades, utility tractors, and more, believing their equipment would arrive in two weeks' time as Toby promised. But when two months went by, then four, without so much as a fence-post driver arriving on the island, Pappy and a few others knew something was wrong.

They'd confronted Toby one Friday night, cornering him in the dining room at the Driftwood Inn. Before the group could get the police involved, though, the Quinns disappeared. I'd never seen Pappy so angry.

Later, we'd learned Toby covered his tracks well. There was no trace of the money—and no signed agreements between him and the farmers. Without actual evidence of the crime, the police had no grounds to arrest him.

I continued filling my crate with flowery leaves as memories of August played in my mind. How one spring day, an afternoon like any other, I'd caught him watching me press seedlings into the soil and felt a lightness in my stomach I'd never noticed before. We were fifteen then, gangly and awkward, our bodies coursing with hormones. Later, after Pappy and my mom went to wash up, August wrapped a hand behind my head and kissed me under the big oak tree at the edge of the farm. I didn't resist. I kissed him back, pressing against him, feeling his hot fingers around my waist. He moaned quietly as the wind rustled the leaves above us in the dusky light.

Crate brimming over, I stood from my knees and lifted it next to the beets and potatoes. As I grabbed an empty one from the stack, I shook my head free of the memory. I had too much to do to be reminiscing about August Quinn.

I turned my attention to the kohlrabi. Along with the white beets this year, I'd convinced Pappy to give this unusual vegetable a try, hoping to differentiate Big Oak from our peers at the Saturday market. The first crop was crisp and tender, and I couldn't wait to show off the Sputnik-shaped Brassicas this afternoon. I pulled shears from my apron and cut each root off at ground level, tossing the bulbs and stems in the crate.

In our journey to organic certification, Pappy and I had learned about the importance of making good "neighbors" for our plants. Mixed among the kohlrabi's blue-green leaves was the ferny foliage of carrots that would be ready in the coming weeks. Pansies and wild roses dressed up the edges of each row, their flowers bright and cheerful. Also nearby was the start of Big Oak's tomatoes. We'd learned that by the time the tomatoes needed more space, we'd be ready to pull the aging kohlrabi plants from the soil. At the left side of the plot, a thicket of raspberries grew next to the split-rail fence.

Eighteen-year-old me would never have imagined my life would one day revolve around carrots and kale. But after my mom died, Pappy had stepped in to care for me full-time. It couldn't have been easy for a sixty-four-year-old farmer to take on a grieving, lost girl on the verge of womanhood, especially after August left. We'd stuck it out together, though. The work on the farm kept us just busy enough we didn't drown in our grief.

But four years ago, when it became impossible to ignore our dwindling savings while the cost of everything climbed, we started the process of organic certification. We threw ourselves into it as though our lives depended on it, and in so many ways they did. Lucky for us, our customers had started to ask about it, too. The more I learned, the more passionate I became about reducing the farm's impact and improving the health of our soil. It had been a long road. National Organic Program standards dictated organic crops be grown on land free from pesticides and synthetic fertilizers for at least three years before it could produce organic growth. This was the year we hoped to complete certification.

I still lay awake at night, worrying over past-due bills, but today I let myself feel proud. I stood from the kohlrabi and surveyed the crates of colorful vegetables piled at the edge of the garden. We were doing good work here.

"I'll pick the strawberries," Pappy called from the little porch at the front of the cottage.

I shielded my eyes from the sun to see his wiry body bounding toward the raised beds of berries. He'd filled a dozen cardboard pints three days earlier and stored them in the cool of the estate house. This time of year I knew we could pick another dozen this morning.

Two hours later, after another of Pappy's big breakfasts and a cool shower to wash away the dust of the morning, I arrived at Grange Hall and parked in my usual spot, under the cover of a chestnut tree bursting with leaves the color of moss. I began hauling crates out of the back of the van, then the folding table and canopy tent. In mid June the weather was usually mild, but today was sweltering. Though the tent was a pain to haul around and set up, I knew I'd be grateful for the shade.

I dragged each of its spidery legs into place as Ida Pease arrived to take the spot beside me. It was a badge of honor to be next to her every week. Pies & Otherwise had been a staple on Orcas Island for nearly fifty years. Though the eighty-one-year-old had eased back production from what I remembered as a kid, Ida still baked for all the local restaurants, plus a few on the mainland, and did a roaring business every Saturday.

I left my spot to help her get organized, a routine we'd established a few years ago as she found it harder to move around. Together we unloaded a dozen pies made with Big Oak rhubarb and strawberries, six loaves of sourdough bread and six whole wheat, and five dozen thumbprint cookies filled with her legendary raspberry jam.

"No tent today?" I asked as we displayed the pies on her table. Usually Ida's husband, Bob, loaded a tent similar to mine into her Ford Explorer.

"Nah. Bob's back is out again. I'll be fine." She shooed away my concern and pointed at the crates of produce set on the ground under my tent. "Haven't you got some work to do?"

"Don't I always." There was *always* work to do.

Ida wrapped an arm around my shoulder, pulling me in for a hug. "Go on. I'm fine here."

I looked around, taking in the vendors setting up their stalls in neat rows, the impossibly blue sky, the happy sounds of friends and neighbors greeting one another. "We have everything we need here, don't we?" I asked Ida. "And the weather is perfect." Sun dappled through the arms of the chestnut tree.

"Bit hot for my liking. But you're right—I'll never tire of this. Now, stop wasting time with this old lady. Get to work."

Locals always arrived at the market early, eager to stock up on everything on their list and escape the crowds that appeared in the afternoon. Soon the field was bustling with activity, folks weaving between the stalls set up in three long rows. There was Mount Constitution Sausage Company, named for the highest peak in the San Juan Islands; Winslow Soap, run by a couple new to the area; produce stands filled with fruits and vegetables from neighboring farms; pear and apple brandies from Orcas Island Distillery; meat from Morning Glory Farm; tables filled with homemade crafts; a coffee truck run by Grind House; and even a tarot card reader.

At a break in the crowd, I refilled the display baskets on my table and brought out another six pints of strawberries. It really was a good day. I glanced to my right to check on Ida, concerned to see her flagging a little, her shoulders drooping, her brow wet. I didn't blame her. It had to be—what?—seventy-five degrees?

"Can I get you some water?" I called across to her. Without waiting for an answer, I grabbed the gallon jug from under my table and hurried to her side.

"You're a love," she said as I filled her empty bottle. "I swear I don't know how I managed to drink mine so fast." Her complexion was pale, her silver hair damp with perspiration.

"Why don't you sit? I'll bring you my stool." Before she could protest, I whipped away and returned with it. "Look, see? It's high enough you can deal with your customers and everything."

"Oh, stop your fussing," she protested, but she was grateful to sit. "It's just I didn't eat breakfast this morning, that's all. Pass me that lunch bag, will you?" She indicated a blue bag in the back of her open SUV.

I grabbed it, peeking inside on my return. Seeing an apple, a sandwich, and a little zippie bag of almonds, relief washed over me. "Here it is. People won't mind if you munch while they browse."

A line of customers had formed at my stand, so I scurried back to help them. And it kept on going. It was another hour before I lifted my head to look around again.

When I did, I was a little stunned to see August approaching, flanked by the two men from the hotel the other night, one tall, the other small and fit with impeccable posture. My heart skipped a beat, and my fingers felt clammy against my sides. As my vision tunneled at the sight of them, questions flooded my mind. Was I angry they were here? Or proud August wanted to show off Orcas Island to his Hollywood friends—colleagues—whatever they were?

"Hello."

"August. What can I do for you?" I jammed my fists in the pockets of my shorts, suddenly hyperaware that I was leaning side to side, shifting my weight from one foot to the other.

"Thought I'd show these guys around while we have a break." He waved to where his buddies stood slightly behind him. They weren't paying attention to August and me, just peering around, taking it all in. They probably weren't used to small-town events like this one. Likely talking about how podunk it all seemed. "Listen, I—"

He stopped talking when a customer next to him picked up a kohlrabi and began turning it over in her hand, confusion on her face. "It's called kohlrabi," I told the woman, focusing my attention on her. "Isn't it cool?"

"Funny-looking," the woman said. "Feels like a

baseball. What the heck do you do with it?"

"Pretty much anything. Boil it, steam it, roast it, fry it, toss it on a salad. You can even eat the leaves."

She didn't look convinced.

"Think of it as a cross between broccoli, radish, and apple. Crunchy. Fresh. A bit peppery." Her eyes brightened a bit. "Sounds interesting, doesn't it? Worth a try?"

I continued serving her without another glance at August, feeling my heart resume its usual steady pace. A few other customers had lined up behind as well. When I looked up again, he was retreating toward his friends. He could take a hint, at least.

August

Rose was busy. Which was a good thing, I reminded myself. But I was determined to speak with her, even if it meant crashing her afternoon at the farmers market. She deserved to know why things happened the way they did—why I never contacted her after I left.

For now, I rejoined Sam and Noah, who'd discovered the Orcas Island Distillery tent. As we sipped on apple brandy, I realized what the nagging sensation I'd felt in my gut since we arrived at the market grounds was: pride. My heart swelled seeing how the island had evolved and grown. To know I'd ruined my chance to be part of it left me feeling tender. They had it all here: strong community, togetherness, inclusion, respect for the land. A lifetime had passed since I'd belonged to a community like this. That was the old August, the boy who didn't know he was about to be yanked from this paradise and forced to confront who he really was: a man who could turn his back on everything he loved.

Familiar faces emerged from the river of marketgo-ers streaming past us: Forest Russo, arm-in-arm with his new wife, Domino West. Juniper Eliot and Poppy Willoughby. Poppy's mom, Georgia. Leo Wolff. River Black, arms full of brown-paper bags overflowing with produce. Writer Angela Fletcher, whose mystery novels I'd seen for sale in almost every country I'd visited with the FBI. She looked at me with interest, her eyes wide, her head tilted in thought. I nodded politely, and she nodded back.

The noise of the event roared in my ears, and I felt the sudden urge to disappear. "Hey, guys, I need a coffee. I'll be back," I told Sam and Noah.

I headed to where the crowds thinned out and wandered into Grange Hall, the traditional post-and-beam building that'd held agricultural fairs and community gatherings when I was a kid—and long before. It had housed the farmers market in fall and winter when the weather turned, I remembered. The old floors creaked under my feet as I took in the rough-hewn beams and wavy glass windows. Standing at the center of the old space, the dust and age of the place filling my senses, I took strength from the fact it had stood here, strong and mighty, while decades of people came and went, through rain and snow, sunshine and wind.

Emotions rushed through me: sadness for what could've been, sorrow for what my family did, this strong, unexpected connection to the landscape—and then there was Rose. I wasn't sure how to label what I felt seeing her again. How could I put words to the way my pulse kicked up when she was near, the exhilaration that skittered through my veins when she looked at me? She made me feel alive in a way I'd forgotten to be.

And I was angry, too. The rage I'd felt at my parents for uprooting my life came flooding back. The move to Seattle had been nothing short of disastrous. Within six months of leaving, Mom and Dad had moved into separate houses. My mom worked as many overtime shifts at the hospital as she could. Dad couldn't keep a job. And I'd withdrawn more and more, distancing myself from them. The week I finished high school, I'd signed up for the military, and within a month I'd moved to the Naval Amphibious Base in Coronado, across the bay from San Diego, and never looked back. Until now.

A cry for help and the sound of shouting outside drew my attention. I rushed back to the rows of farm stands to see a crowd gathered near Rose's tent. I jogged over, pushing through the stiffness in my leg.

"I called 911!" a teenage boy said, holding up his phone.

"Give her some water," yelled another bystander.

"Is there a doctor here?" shouted a woman's voice. Shoving through the onlookers, I pinpointed its source: Rose, who sat on her knees, an older woman's head on her lap. "Ida?" she said, her thumbs gently gliding over the woman's cheeks. "Can you hear me?"

CHAPTER 5

August

I knelt down beside Rose, ignoring the pain that fired through my knee as it hit the grass. "Here, let's get her legs lifted up. You, toss me your bag," I told a bystander with a large carry bag. I propped it under the woman's knees, lifting them up a foot, then loosened her collar. "Did you see her go down?" I asked Rose. "Did she hit her head?" I recognized the woman immediately as Ida Pease.

"I—I don't think so, no," Rose said. "She fell sort of sideways, off her stool. Do you think she's okay? Is it... Is it a stroke?" Her eyes were wide with fright. "Where's that ambulance? Come on, Ida. Can you hear me now? It's me. Rose. Ida?"

Ida's eyelids fluttered for a second before they opened. She looked first to Rose, then around at all the faces peering down at her. She scrambled to get up, but I held her back.

"Ida? You're okay. Looks like you fainted. Just stay back and rest awhile—help is on the way."

Confusion creased her forehead.

"I'm August, ma'am. How are you feeling?"

"I'm fine, I think," Ida croaked. She cleared her throat. "Yes, I'm right as rain. Better than ever actually. Help me up, would you? Who's at my stall? I have to get back—"

"Let's not worry about that for now," Rose said, her hands on Ida's shoulders. "Let's just sit here for a bit." She stole a glance at the Big Oak Farm stand, though. A few bystanders had gathered around her produce.

I searched the crowd, my eyes stopping on Sam and Noah a few feet away. "Boys? Can I get a hand?"

I stood and spoke to them quietly. On a mission the two separated and moved to Rose's and Ida's tables. Each took a spot behind one of them and, after orienting themselves to their stations, took over operations as though they belonged there. I knelt again next to Ida and Rose.

Ida clasped my hand. "Thank you, dear. I suppose

I could take a few moments." Her eyes searched my face. "I know you, don't I?" I nodded. She seemed satisfied with that.

When I glanced up at Rose, she was staring back at me. "Thank you," she mouthed.

The people around us parted to make way for the EMTs, who laid a stretcher next to Ida and began asking her questions. They waved to Rose and me, indicating they could take it from here. We backed away to give them space, Rose's attention lingering on her friend.

She looked worriedly again at her table, where a smiling Noah seemed to be enjoying himself chatting with customers.

I touched her shoulder. "Don't worry about those two. They got it."

"But what about—"

I interrupted her. "Nah. Like I said, they got it. I think you could use a break, don't you?" Rose's fingers were clasped tightly in front of her, her knuckles white. "How about that coffee?"

I sensed she wanted to protest, but instead she closed her eyes, inhaling deeply. "What the hell. Sure."

I reached for her hand, but when she jumped at my touch, I dropped it immediately. The tips of my ears burned with embarrassment. "Sorry. Coffee's on me.

Let's go." I pointed to the Grind House truck.

We set off, strolling through the busy market in silence, jittery energy making my insides float. "So how—" I started at the same time she said, "Quite a way to—"

We looked at each other and laughed. It felt good, the sudden lightness between us calming my nerves.

"Quite a way to get me to coffee, after all," she finished.

"Yah, well, I was determined, wasn't I?"

"I'll say." She walked with her arms folded in front of her but let them fall when she almost tripped over an electrical cable that ran behind the Grind House truck. Wait, was she nervous, too?

"Hi, Ginger," she said when we reached the window of the old VW bus Ginger had converted. "August, remember Ginger Kidd?"

"We've already gotten reacquainted," Ginger said. I smiled. "How are you, Auggie? We missed you this morning." After the shock of seeing me that first morning at Grind House, Ginger and I had been chatting on my daily coffee runs. Not today, though; I'd grabbed an espresso from the dining room at the Driftwood, where Fern, too, seemed to be over the initial surprise at my presence here. Neither had mentioned my parents yet, but I knew it was coming.

"Just fine, Ginger, just fine. Cool truck." I ordered

and paid for two iced Americanos, and we moved to the side to wait for them.

"I hope Ida's okay," Rose said, fiddling with the neckline of her T-shirt.

"She will be." I'd been in enough emergency situations to know when things were going to be fine. "You were great back there, by the way."

"No, *you* were great. How'd you know what to do? So calm and methodical."

When Ginger called my name, I stepped forward and grabbed two Grind House–branded cups filled with ice and rich, brown coffee. Rose sipped hers as we wound back through the market stalls toward her table. "You learn a thing or two as the son of a nurse," I said. "And a thing or two more when you join the FBI."

She stopped walking. "What? But you were going to…" Her voice trailed off when she remembered my plans were thwarted the moment my family left Orcas.

Suddenly unable to meet her gaze, I took in our surroundings. We'd stopped in front of a tarot card reader's stall, where a table and a few chairs were set up in front. "Can we sit?"

Rose blinked in the direction of her farm stand, shaking her head.

"It'll be okay for a few more minutes. Please?"

She watched as I pulled out a chair. "Oh, all right.

But only for a minute." She blew out a breath and took the seat across from me.

I adjusted my position on the folding chair so I could straighten my leg. "That's what I wanted to talk to you about. Where I went."

Rose sat, willing now, it seemed, to hear me out. Maybe it was the shock of Ida's incident; whatever the reason, I needed to take advantage of it.

"I had no idea it was coming. I didn't," I insisted when she raised her eyebrows. "My mom woke me early that morning, must have been after a night shift at the hospital. It was still dark. Told me to pack a bag and be ready to go in a half hour. I kept asking where we were going and why, but every time I did she just shook her head. My dad was away for the weekend, at a trade show in Seattle. So I guess I assumed we were joining him for a few days." I stared at the ground, shame burning the pit of my stomach. "I had no idea it was forever."

How quickly her expression changed, from curious to furious in an instant. Her cheeks flushed red. "You should have called me." She said it quietly, but it wasn't a good quiet. It was the kind of quiet that was worse than a shout.

I scrambled to keep explaining. "Mom kept insisting it was no big deal, that we'd be back in a week. I meant to call you when we got to Seattle. But then…"

"Then?" Rose's lips were pinched in a tight line.

"Then... I just couldn't. Once I figured out what he did, how my dad hurt so many people here, I—" I swallowed the lump in my throat. "I was too ashamed, Rose. Too embarrassed to face anyone. Even you." The humiliation gnawing at my chest now was the same one I'd carried with me for ten years, rearing up any time I felt comfortable. I leaned forward in my chair, sweat making the armpits of my T-shirt wet. Coffee had been a bad idea. The caffeine zinged through my body like electricity through a wire, turning my stomach in knots.

"That's ridiculous. No one would have blamed *you*. Your dad, yes. But you were a kid, August." Her voice thickened with frustration, and her foot tapped against the table leg. "I don't buy it. I don't buy it!" Her raised voice brought attention from passersby. "Ten years went by. Ten," she said at a lower volume. "At least be honest with me. You couldn't handle a grieving girlfriend anymore, could you? Oh, I bet I was a real drag to be around back then. How could you do that, when I needed you most? No." She pulled her hand off the table when I reached for it. Did she really believe that's why I hadn't contacted her? Because I couldn't handle her grief? All the times I'd played this scenario out in my head, that thought had never been part of it. "You can't—"

"Hi, Rose!" A tall woman with long black hair approached the table, oblivious to the emotional confrontation unfolding in front of her. A scruffy black dog followed and leaped onto Rose's lap, tail wagging. Rose looked like she wanted nothing more than to shoo the woman away, but the anger in her expression melted a little at the ball of black fur licking her face.

"Zoe." Rose nodded, her lips pinched again.

Without asking, the woman sat down and placed a stack of tarot cards on the table, her bracelets clanging. She brushed a long lock of hair—the same black as the dog's—away from her face, although there seemed to be more of it in her eyes after than there was before. "Well, you're new and handsome," she said to me. She held out a hand. "I'm Zoe. That's Coco." She pointed to the dog in Rose's lap. "I heard we were expecting some movie stars around here. I just didn't expect Clint Eastwood's son!" She batted her eyes.

Her flirting made it even more obvious this woman had no idea of the tension simmering between me and Rose. What did she want?

Rose

Oh god. Trust Zoe to make everything awkward. August blushed, which made the scar on his cheek stand out against his flushed skin, and I made the connection. That scar, his limp—he must have been injured on duty! I felt a pang of regret about the strip I'd just torn off him but quickly brushed it aside. It didn't change the fundamentals: I didn't trust him, and he needed to know that.

"August Quinn, ma'am." He shook Zoe's hand politely, although she'd presented him with a hand to kiss rather than one to shake.

"August is here for the *Shore Thing* shoot," I said. Maybe Zoe would be satisfied with that information and walk away. "But he's not an actor. Wait, are you?" I realized I had no idea what he did.

"Why don't we let Zoe tell us?"

Zoe ran her fingers through another tangle in her hair. "That's not really the kind of thing I can read with my cards. But I do like a challenge." She sat still as a statue for half a minute, then closed her eyes and kept them closed for so long August and I exchanged a glance, eyebrows raised. We waited while she inhaled a long breath, held it, then blew it out through her nose before she opened her eyes again.

She faced August. "Ask me a question."

His expression turned nervous, glancing left and right, as if trying to decide how honest he should be. What did he want to know?

"Am I lovable?"

That hit like a sucker punch to the heart. Is that what he really thought of himself? That he wasn't lovable? I might not trust or believe him, but I knew deep down someone else could. I thought about what Bluebell had said about forgiveness, how it would free me of my anger. Maybe August needed to forgive himself, too. I tried to catch his eyes, but he avoided looking at me.

Zoe nodded. Gathering another deep breath, she shuffled the deck of cards, split the pile in two, and moved them from one hand to the other. Once she was satisfied, she fanned the cards out with both hands and surveyed them quickly before choosing one, which she placed facedown on the table. She put the deck to the side.

"Why that one?" August asked.

"It's the one that felt right." She turned it right side up. On the card was a giant wheel with symbols inside. The corners of the card each depicted a winged creature: a bull, an eagle, a lion, an angel. A snake slithered down the left side of the wheel. "The Wheel of Fortune," Zoe said. "This card reminds us the wheel is always turning. Life is in a constant state of change." She laid her hand on it and focused on August, lines framing her eyes as she squinted. Then she nodded. "Good luck and good fortune will make their way back to you. This card is telling you to cherish the blissful moments in life and make the most of them while they're in reach—because they could be gone in a flash."

I inhaled sharply. If anyone at this table knew how quickly your whole life could change, how much you might long for things once they were gone, it was me. But didn't this card pertain to every person, all the time? Zoe hadn't actually answered August's question.

"Good advice, for sure. But what does that have to do with my question?"

She held up a finger. "I'm getting there. Tell me, are you open to love?"

He let out a *pfft* sound. "Of course. Who isn't?"

"No, I mean really *open*. The Wheel of Fortune is also the wheel of karma. You know the expression 'what goes around comes around'? Think of the energy you put out. If you're kind and loving to others, they'll be kind and loving to you. Be nasty and mean, and you'll get nasty and mean back. So if you want love in abundance, make sure you're sending out positive juju. What you send into the universe comes back to you." She lifted her hand from the table, bracelets jangling, and held it in midair in front of her chest. "Your life is about to turn in a more positive direction if you're willing to grow," she said, eyes closed. "Keep your mind open to the signs of the universe. The magic of fate is behind you. Miracles are happening."

August's eyebrows shot high on his forehead as Zoe's explanation turned mystical.

"You like to be in control." She opened her eyes again and focused on August. He nodded, which she took as encouragement to continue. "Sometimes this card is a shock to people like you. By its very nature it suggests factors outside your control are influencing your life. It's like the universe is dishing up whatever it pleases, which can be very unnerving. No matter which way the wheel turns, though, it's impossible to change it. You need to accept what is happening and adapt." She waved her arms high in the air, looking up at the sky, bracelets clanging. "Go with the flow! This is an invitation to make a significant change in your life. The more you tune into your intuition and allow the universe to guide you, the better the out-come will be."

Although what she said sounded like it could hit a

few notes of truth for August, I just didn't get the whole karma thing. I doubted he did, either, but he smiled politely anyway.

"Interesting, thank you." He shifted on his seat, bending then straightening his leg.

Zoe patted his hand, sensing his reticence. "I know it's a lot right now, but believe me, the Wheel of Fortune is part of your life. Remember—be open to what comes your way." Satisfied with the message she'd delivered, she turned to me. "Well, Miss Rose, can I answer a question for you today?"

"This stuff is nonsense. No offense, Zoe." Zoe's lips curled up at the sides. We'd had this conversation before. I had nothing against her personally; I just wasn't one for make-believe. At least that's what I told her. If I let myself examine that feeling, I knew I'd find something deeper: fear, perhaps, that I might hear something I didn't want to know. "I should be getting back to my table, anyway." I looked at my watch. "There's no way your friend is selling anyone on the finer points of striped beets," I told August. "Come on, let's—"

"Aw, be fair, Ro." *Ro.* No one had called me that in ten years. "If I can ask a question, so can you. Can't she, Coco?" He petted the scruffy little dog, still perched on my knee.

I could've sworn Zoe's eyes twinkled. She'd been

waiting for this moment. "Oh, all right," I said. *At least she'll stop pestering me every time I see her.* "If it means I can get back to my stall, fine. Lay it on me."

She shuffled her cards again. "Ask me anything. Got boy troubles? Boring old farm questions? A mystery I can solve?"

"I've got a mystery for you, all right. Will our little island—and the farm—survive this film shoot that's filled our town with strangers?" I looked pointedly at August. He'd been here less than a week, and already it felt like a tornado had swirled my life upside down.

"Hmm. I wondered that myself. Let's see." Again she went through the routine of closing her eyes for a long time, almost too long once again, inhaling a deep breath, holding it, then letting it out through her nose, all the while continuing the shuffle. Again she fanned the cards out in her hands and made a selection that seemed to make sense only to her.

She placed it facedown on the table, then laid down her deck of cards. She turned the card over.

"Death."

The word reverberated through my whole body. I rubbed my face, looking anywhere but at the card itself. "How dare you!" I burst. "My grandfather is healthier than you are. Just who do you think—"

"Hold on, hold on," Zoe interrupted, wagging a finger side to side in front of her. "It doesn't mean someone's going to die. In fact, the Death card is one of the most positive cards in the deck."

"Hmph." I finally let myself look at it. On it was a skeleton in black armor riding a white horse. "Sure looks like the Grim Reaper to me."

Zoe shook her head, her earrings swinging like pendulums. "You're hanging on to something that no longer serves you," she said. "This card is telling you it's time to close that door and open another. The Death card is a sign transformation is coming. You need to put the past behind you and part ways with it, so you can embrace new possibilities. It's hard to let go, but you will soon see the promise of renewal."

I let out another "hmph."

"If you resist letting go of whatever negative thing you're holding on to, know you will experience pain. But if you imagine a new possibility, you allow new patterns to emerge. Change is always coming. It's up to you to welcome it as a positive, cleansing process. The death of limiting thoughts opens the door to life." I ruffled my fingers in Coco's tight curls, letting Zoe's words sink in.

"Death is also a sign you need to learn to let go of unhealthy attachments. This is a perfect card to break a bad habit. Let in the new! Purge the baggage in your way."

"Not much room in my life for anything new," I

said resolutely. Between the farm and Pappy, even the idea of change was impossible to imagine. I lifted Coco from my lap and placed her on the ground next to Zoe, then stood. "Maybe some people have time to fantasize these cards mean anything real, but not me. Oh, and if anything happens to Pappy, I promise I'll hold you fully responsible. Now, I really have to get back. August, let's go." I faced away from the table and the Death card on its surface, leaving August seated there with Zoe.

"Uh, what do I owe you?" August asked her.

"This one's on me," she said. "You did me a favor, really. I've been dying to do her cards for three years. Hear that, Rose?" I heard her loud and clear. "She's always busy, always stressed, always seems to have a lot on her mind. She's a tough nut to crack, that one. Say, how do you two know each other, anyway? I only ever see her with Bluebell Price. And that blonde from the hotel. And how come so many of you folks here have plant names?"

"No one's told you?" August chuckled. "We grew up together. I used to live here. Believe it or not, Rose wasn't always so tightly wound."

I spun back around to see him grinning. He wasn't wrong, but I folded my arms over my chest again, tapping my toe in the grass.

"Ha! I'll have to take your word on that."

"As for the names—our parents, before they all had kids, wanted to strengthen their connection to the island. Solidify their legacy in some way. They were a bunch of hippies, really." He laughed again. "Anyway, they decided to name any daughters they had after the wildflowers of Orcas. A couple of them even choose nature names for their sons, too. Heard of Rocky and River Black?"

"As in the mayor of Bayview Rocky Black?" Zoe asked. Rocky was the older of the two brothers.

Back in high school, none of us would have pegged Rocky as a politician. August looked at me questioningly. "Yep," I said.

"Oh, and Forest Russo," he added.

"Mr. Domino West, you mean," Zoe said.

"That's what I hear." August shrugged. "Anyway, this was…interesting, but I have to be going, too. See you around, maybe." I watched as he stood, straightening slowly, favoring his right leg.

"Wait, you never did tell me. *Are* you a movie star?" Zoe collected her cards in a pile on the table.

"Nothing quite that glamorous. I'm a cameraman. Underwater, mostly."

"Wasted opportunity not to have you on the big screen." Zoe smiled, exposing the gap in her two front teeth. "If I were a few years younger…" She let her words trail off.

Blushing, August grabbed my arm and steered me in the direction of my farm stand. I flinched again at his touch. I didn't like the heat it sent through me, the way my body betrayed my brain. He dropped his hand quickly.

"You're quiet now," I said as we walked through the rows of stalls.

"Just thinking about the Wheel of Fortune." He dug his hands in his pockets. "No matter how much I try to convince myself I'm my own man—one who can do anything I set my mind to, I always come back to the same feeling. Everything I do leads me back here—back to this place where I did the unthinkable. Where I don't deserve love or trust. And now, with my leg…" It was the first time I'd heard him acknowledge his limp, but it wasn't the right time to pry.

He looked at his watch. "Shit. Me and the guys have to get back to Bayview. We have a shoot to-night."

I nodded. We both had work to do. Whatever else had happened here today, I felt less fearful about his presence on the island. I guessed that was a good thing. Was it forgiveness? I didn't know, but at least I could put my focus where it was needed: Pappy and the farm.

August, too, seemed more at ease. His hands were no longer clenched at his sides, and his shoulders relaxed as we walked.

When we reached my table, I started calling instructions to Noah and Sam. Nearly all Ida's pies were sold.

Sam checked his watch twice within the first few minutes of our return. He and Noah looked relieved to see their friend. Sam looked at his watch a third time. "T minus an hour fifteen. Time to go."

"Will you be all right here?" August indicated the space between the stalls. "Is there someone you can call to help?" Just as the words left his mouth, I spotted Bluebell hightailing it toward us.

"Got it," I said. "Your work here is done, boys. Thank you. Hollywood's calling." I wiggled my eyebrows. But looking at the empty baskets on my table, I really was grateful for their help. "I don't know what I would have done if you weren't here."

"Sorry it took me so long," Bluebell panted, moving around to Ida's table. "Thought the lunch rush would never end. How's Ida? Looks like she still sold everything, even from a hospital bed." Only two loaves and a handful of cookies were left.

"She'll be fine," August volunteered. Sam and Noah waited impatiently behind him, Sam still checking his watch at regular intervals. "Bye, Rose," he said.

I was already busy helping a customer. "Bye now," I said without looking up.

CHAPTER 6

August

The first week of photography on *Shore Thing* was hectic and exhausting. We shot some decent footage but not without a few hiccups. Two windy days caused a delay in filming some of the above-water scenes, and then there was the issue of ships and other vessels passing by in the background. Murmurs went around set that we were doomed to be the next *Jaws* after one of Arthur's assistants read *The Jaws Log*, a book that detailed all the things that went wrong in the making of the classic movie. All I knew was Arthur Dagon was no Steven Spielberg. I hoped like hell the problems were behind us.

I spent several hours in the water on shooting days with Sam and Noah, trying to capture what we needed of Damon Mann diving. The actor had insisted he didn't want a stunt double, having spent several months learning to convincingly dive to play a marine archaeologist.

At night in my room, and during breaks in the day, my thoughts kept returning to my afternoon at the market. I'd surprised even myself by being so open in front of Rose and Zoe, a total stranger. It was as if I knew something deep inside had to give. I'd retreated into myself after I left Orcas Island and never really came back out of my shell. Concepts like intimacy and vulnerability were foreign to me. The accident had only compounded the feeling I was in this thing called life on my own.

Except for Sam and Noah. Our shared experience on USERT had bonded us like brothers. They each had interesting backgrounds of their own, too. Despite his easygoing manner, Noah of the three of us had the most to hide. Born to a wealthy oil family in Norway, he'd moved to America and joined the FBI in part to have a "normal experience"—one where people didn't treat him differently because he had money or befriend him just for that reason. FBI life put everyone on the same footing. I understood completely his instinct to act cool and calm at all times. Having money in the family didn't mean there wasn't also chaos; in fact, there was probably more. Noah fought his instinct to control by letting go.

Sam was the opposite. He was rigid, and careful, and liked everything in its place. His parents were respected members of the San Diego military community, and Sam had been expected to follow in their footsteps. Having grown up on the water, a career as a diver was a natural fit. His folks had been thrilled when he joined USERT, relieved it would tick the boxes of his desire to see the world and do one of the things he loved most in the world: be on the ocean. Whenever we had a break, though, Sam disappeared to New York or LA. At first no one on the team knew why. He'd confided in us along the way he was studying to be an actor.

He loved the challenge, loved being someone else. Acting was his one release of control. Noah and I knew that as soon as Sam could make a name for himself—and a living—acting, he would dedicate his life to it. For him, this project was a foot in the door of the film industry and a way to support his acting classes. With his strong jaw, classic proportions, and thick brown hair, he might just make it, too. I admired his dedication to doing something so different from his military background. His dream came first.

Despite all we'd shared, though, I hadn't found the

guts to be honest with them about my family. They knew I'd left Orcas Island as a teenager and finished high school in Seattle, but they didn't know why. It'd been on the tip of my tongue to tell them twice this week. Both times I'd allowed fear to stop me, and I was still reckoning with why. Maybe I didn't want to alter their perception of me. Maybe I couldn't afford to lose their trust. Trust was the most important part of being on a dive team, where our lives depended on trusting each other if something went wrong.

Or maybe I was scared to hurt them. I'd hurt enough people on Orcas Island. I wanted to do everything in my power not to hurt others.

I'd gotten a brief glimpse through Rose's prickly exterior on Saturday, and I wanted more. Walking down Water Street Friday morning, coffee and doughnut in hand, I made up my mind: I would leave the set early today, no matter what. Destination? Cottle's at three o'clock. I was desperate to set eyes on her again.

It wasn't a dive day, anyway. Just a day of going over footage and planning for our next scenes. We met with Arthur's assistants over lunch, who told us a local had agreed to rent us the use of his narrowboat barge so we could film from another angle. When the clock hit two, I beelined for the crew member who'd loaned me the van last week.

"Need this for the rest of the afternoon?" I knew they didn't. Sam's organizational skills applied beyond our own team to helping anyone on the crew who needed it get ahead of schedule with prep.

"All yours, man," he said. "Key's on my desk."

I spent the twenty-five-minute drive to Winslow going over Rose's words. When I left ten years ago, I never imagined she'd hang on to the hurt as long as she had. I figured she'd be over me fast and better off without me—better off without a guy whose dad was a con man. I realized now how wrong I was, and a feeling began to take root in me: I needed to prove she could trust me again. Maybe it was the only path to forgiving myself.

Parking next to a little red hatchback, I caught sight of Rose on her bike rattling down the hill to the pier. It couldn't be the same bike, could it? I chuckled and shook my head. We used to ride from one end of the island to the other as kids, the perfect way to spend a summer afternoon. Looking back, it was everything we'd needed: sunshine, the wind in our hair, laughter, and love.

Dismounting at the bottom of the hill, she propped her bike against the side of the restaurant. She unclipped her helmet and shook her hair free, then disappeared around the building onto the pier.

I followed behind, watching her take a seat at the

same picnic table as last week, her back to me. Bluebell looked up and saw me, surprised. She leaned in and said something to Rose, who turned around, not overly thrilled I was there.

"Crashing the party again, huh." She hadn't phrased it as a question.

"Never mind her," Bluebell said. "Come on, sit. I'll get us a drink." She climbed out of the bench seat and moved to stand in line behind an older couple at the order window. It was even busier here this week. Two tables over, Angela Fletcher peered at me over her glasses, pen poised above a tattered-looking notebook.

"The food looked so good here last week, I had to try it." It was a weak excuse for showing up uninvited again. "So what do you recommend?"

I attempted an earnest expression and watched Rose battle with her emotions. After a moment she huffed out a breath. "All right, I give. The littleneck clams are always good," she said. "Pappy practically waits by the door every week for me to bring him some. Although lately Freddy's specials are to die for, too. Remember him? Mary and Louis's son? He's all grown up and training to be a chef. You probably want to look at today's menu over there." She pointed to the chalkboard sign hanging next to the order window.

"Cool," I said, glancing around the bustling tables, where diners ate from red-plastic baskets lined with checkered paper. I stood as Bluebell returned with three Coronas and a basket of her own. "Can I get you something?"

"No, thanks. Late breakfast." Rose put a hand to her stomach.

At the order window, Mary beamed brightly. At least one person was happy to see me here.

Rose

I looked around the busy pier, debating whether to leave while August was at the order window or stick around and finish my beer. People looked happy. It was Friday afternoon, the sun was shining, and a cool breeze floated in off the Pacific that seemed to lift everyone's spirits after a hot, dusty week. It was unusually dry on Orcas for this time of year. We hadn't had rain in twenty-seven days.

I could sit here for an hour, I decided. I needed a break from worrying about the farm, and I wasn't going to let August ruin that for me.

Watching him stride to the table, red basket in hand, it occurred to me it was kind of nice to see him. For the first time since his return, I allowed myself to feel something I'd been ignoring up to this point: affection. Despite the anger and betrayal I'd felt every time I thought of him for the past ten years, underneath it all I couldn't help but remember a bit of the good stuff, too. The way his jeans hugged his body. The strong line of his jaw and the glint in his sharp green eyes. The butterflies that danced in my belly when I looked at him.

He was back at the table before I could examine that thought.

"How's Ida?"

I watched him set his food down before climbing into the picnic bench, lifting his right leg up and over. "Clean bill of health," I said. "The doc at the ER said she fainted from the heat."

"It's been hotter here than I remember."

"Honestly, it's hard to tell what's normal anymore." I thought of how little rain we'd had—and how high our water bill at the farm would be this month—and shuddered.

"So tell us about the movie," Bluebell said, changing the subject. "So exciting to have Damon Mann here—he seems like the nicest guy! Domino is really putting Orcas Island on the map. But all I keep hearing is how it's already behind schedule, and people are running around the hotel scratching their heads with worry. What's it about, anyway? And what do *you* do?" She poked a finger in August's shoulder.

"I'm an underwater cameraman." He held up a hand at the surprise on Bluebell's face. "It's only my third movie, so I'm not sure what to expect, to be honest. But yah, it's not going exactly as planned."

"Underwater cameraman, hey?" Bluebell eyed him thoughtfully. "You still haven't said what the movie's about."

"You know, your basic underwater rom-com." He laughed. "Sort of. Damon plays a marine archaeologist who lives on this backwoods island."

"Hey, that's not fair," I protested.

He clarified, "Backwoods *fictional* island, I mean. Anyway, he can't catch a date, so his friend comes up with a plan to get him one and posts an ad on the internet. You know, 'Wanted: One gorgeous, water-loving bride,' that sort of thing. Enter Domino West. But the catch is she's a marine archaeologist, too—one who's secretly searching for the same buried treasure as he is."

"*You've Got Mail* meets *Fool's Gold*," Bluebell said between bites of crab cakes. Freddy's special today looked delicious, served with a few pinches of watercress and a dollop of tartar sauce. August had ordered the same thing. "How did you get involved?"

"Noah and Sam—they're underwater cameramen, too. We went into business together after—" He trailed off, and a beat of silence followed. "After we left the FBI," he said simply. "We've worked together for years, so we have a kind of shorthand. We come as a package deal, a team. Our job is to shoot all the underwater stuff."

"You're filming stunt people then, obviously." Bluebell phrased it as a statement, not a question.

"Actually Damon's doing all his own diving. Trained for three months, apparently. But there's a stunt diver for Domino."

Bluebell swooned. "Is there anything that hottie can't do? What's he like?" A dreamy look entered her eyes. "You know he broke up with Ana Chase, right? So he's single." She wiggled her eyebrows.

I let myself enjoy fun watching August deflect Bluebell's pleas for an introduction to Damon Mann while trying to learn as much about the handsome actor as she could. It was a reminder of his old playful self, a side I hadn't seen of him for a decade.

I stopped myself before I went too far down the path of nostalgia, though. This was the guy who left without so much as a glance back ten years ago. No matter what he presented himself to be now—more mature, slightly wounded, still achingly handsome, and maybe a little lonely—the movie shoot would end at some point, and August would be out of my life again. My focus was the farm and always would be. I couldn't pretend anything otherwise, not with everything hanging so precariously in the balance.

Orcas Island was my home. It was the one constant that never let me down. It was with me every morning when I awoke and every night when I laid my head on the pillow.

I simply didn't have time to care about anyone but me and Pappy. Caring cost, and I didn't have the capital to spend on it.

CHAPTER 7
August

Our 4:00 a.m. call time came early. Today was all about capturing Damon and Domino above water, and the plan was to film spots for several scenes in the movie, not necessarily in order. Arthur's assistants had been watching the weather for days and decided now was our best chance at a windless day on the Pacific.

Sam and Noah were waiting for me in the hotel lobby, and together we trudged down to the marina in the dark. Some other crew members were already there, set dressing the *Redemption*. In the first scene on the call sheet, Damon's character would take the boat out to where he knew a shipwreck lay beneath the water—one rumored to have diamonds aboard. Later in the morning, Domino would join the crew to film scenes on the boat with him, on their first "date," where she had to pretend to know nothing about diving. In the final scene of the day, Domino would take the boat out alone after Damon's character ended up in hospital with the bends.

A narrowboat barge was floating next to the *Redemption*. After I left Cottle's yesterday, I'd learned all I could about this type of vessel. I'd read online that narrowboats were mainly used in canals due to their long and narrow shape and shallow draft.

But when its owner appeared in front of me, my stomach sank. Chip Thurlow had worked at Bayview Soil and Landscape when I was a kid, doing odd jobs for my parents. He was the kind of guy who always had a scheme on the go, and I'd always wondered if he'd played a part in my father's bad business dealings. We scowled recognition at each other. What was he up to now? No way would he have agreed to rent out his boat if he didn't have some ulterior motive.

He told Noah he was living aboard the narrowboat and rarely took it out from the marina, but since the weather was good, I had no recourse to voice any concern with Arthur. I checked my phone to be doubly sure: no wind in the forecast. The barge, even though not designed for use at sea, should float comfortably for our purposes—Chip or no Chip.

We boarded as the rising sun streaked the sky red and purple. It stole my breath with its beauty, although I couldn't help but murmur, "Red sky in the morning, sailor's warning," under my breath as I stepped down into the boat's forward cabin. Was the old adage about a red sky at sunrise a harbinger of bad weather for us? I hoped not.

Chip had cleared enough room inside for Sam, Noah, and me to set up our equipment—waterproof housing for the camera, since we'd be shooting through an open window on the boat, battery packs, and some clamps and straps that would keep the camera steady in the window frame.

By 6:00 a.m. day had broken, and Chip got us out on the water, following the *Redemption* to our first location. He and I exchanged several glares as we taxied into place, a silent agreement passing between us to pretend we were strangers. I was nothing if not professional. I wasn't about to drag my family's shameful business affairs from a decade earlier into what I hoped would be a successful job.

A third boat on the water contained Arthur and his assistants; Domino's co-producer, Trudi; and the principal cinematographer, who would be filming a different angle. We all kept in touch by walkie-talkie. Once Arthur was satisfied with our location, we dropped anchors.

The first scene rolled as smooth as butter. Damon lived up to his reputation of being an affable guy, keeping us entertained between takes by miming jokes to the narrowboat crew when the bigwigs on the third boat argued over light and angles. We did fourteen takes before Arthur deemed it okay to move on to the next scene, and I heard him walkie-talkie to the dock that we were ready on set for Domino.

Around that time, Chip started to behave oddly. He moved back and forth on the boat, scratching his head and muttering to himself. At one point he disappeared into the bedroom, and we heard him on the phone, sounding frantic, but I couldn't make out any words. As we were setting up for the first shot of the next scene—the one where Damon's and Domino's characters embarked on their first date—Sam finally couldn't take it anymore.

"Hey, man," Sam interrupted when Chip approached on another pace back and forth. "Everything okay? We're just gonna start shooting this next scene. Anything I can do for you?"

Chip scratched his head again. He'd done it so many times it was standing straight up. "It's just that..." Chip looked from Sam to Noah and me as if assessing what to tell us. "Nah, it's nothing," he said, shrugging. But he went right back to pacing and muttering.

Sam being Sam, he needed his surroundings to be calm and quiet before he could shoot. He grew increasingly frustrated. "Look, Chip—"

Chip kept walking—this time right through the door that led to the small deck at the front of the boat, closing the door behind him.

"What the…?"

"Of all the locals we could've asked." I rolled my eyes. I should have warned them.

Before I could say a word, though, the door flew open again, Chip looking wild eyed and nervous. "Mayday! Mayday!" he shouted into the cabin. "We gotta get off this thing! She's going down!"

"What?" Noah and I said in unison, at the same time Sam shouted, "Are you fucking serious?"

"Of course I'm serious! Pass me that bag!" Chip gestured wildly at a blue waterproof bag on the shelf behind the bench seat next to the kitchen table. "And if you're smart, you'll get that camera gear off this thing, too."

Unaware of the urgency of the situation, Noah casually grabbed the bag and tossed it to Chip, who whirled out the door again and started waving his hands in the air and shouting to the other boats.

The narrowboat tilted to one side then, jolting Noah, Sam, and me into action as water began surging in from all sides. The cabin quickly filled with seawater to the height of our knees, and it rose rapidly as Sam and I struggled to unlatch the complicated series of straps we'd used to stabilize the camera in the window.

"Forget that thing and let's go!" Noah shouted, straining to keep the door open against the gushing water. "Come on, come on!"

I grabbed Sam's arm, and together we pushed through the now waist-deep water to the door Noah stood against. Outside, the people on the other two boats were waving and calling to us.

"Jump over!" shouted the speedboat driver who'd ferried Domino out to the set. He edged closer to the sinking narrowboat, ready to pull us aboard. Chip had already made it and sat with his head in his hands next to a startled, but gorgeous, Domino West, her dark hair smooth and shiny in the sun.

The water was freezing. It was a shock to my system that took my breath away when I jumped from the narrowboat to make the short swim to the speedboat. The speedboat driver pulled me aboard, and together we reached down to help Noah and Sam up as well. Once safely in the boat, we all turned back to watch as the narrowboat submerged in the Pacific, taking all Chip's worldly belongings, and one of our best cameras, with it.

Domino patted the spot between Chip's shoulder

blades. "It'll be okay. That's what insurance is for."

If I didn't know better, I would have missed the slight smile on Chip's face as the narrowboat dropped below the surface.

All three boats of onlookers stared in silence, stunned by what we'd just seen and how quickly disaster had happened. The speedboat bobbed gently in the waves. I shivered next to a gorgeous movie star. *How the fuck did I get here?* I thought, my teeth chattering.

Arthur pierced the quiet with a barrage of shouts at Chip, who executed a near-professional acting job of being in "shock." Truthfully I was in a bit of shock myself. I tuned out Arthur's diatribe, instead focusing on the rugged shoreline of the tiny island I'd once called home as the speedboat driver ferried us to shore.

A crowd had gathered at the end of the dock. Word must have spread about the chance to see Damon and Domino make movie magic, but they'd witnessed something entirely different. The group parted to let Noah, Sam, me, and Chip past. We were trembling in our wet clothes in spite of the warm sunshine. A few people reached out to high-five us, which Noah, leading the way, was happy to oblige, but I couldn't meet anyone's eyes. I kept my gaze on the dock, a little embarrassed and a lot uncomfortable.

Just as we passed the last cluster of observers, I felt a hand on my arm. My first instinct was to shake it off, but I looked up instead and saw a familiar face beaming up at me. Felix Hardy.

"Come for dinner?"

Rose

The farmers market was even busier this week. Ida was back by my side, tent in place above her and an enormous jug of water on her table. Every half hour or so, I hustled over with a reminder to make sure she ate. In her usual no-nonsense way, she waved me off each time, but I could tell my consideration was appreciated.

At the close of the market, exhausted and happy, I packed my wares into the back of the van. "I could use a cold drink," I told Ida as I slammed the doors shut. "Bluebell's working. Want to join me at the Driftwood?" I asked, even though I knew she wouldn't.

"Oh, you go on, dear. Bob will be here any minute, anyway."

Satisfied she would be fine without me, I climbed into the driver's seat and steered out of the Grange Hall grounds in the direction of Bayview. Though I'd told Ida—and myself—that I was in pursuit of a cold drink and Bluebell's company, I hoped I'd see August, too. His question to Zoe last week had haunted me for seven days.

Am I lovable? Was that really what he wanted to know? Eighteen-year-old me could've answered that in a heartbeat. Twenty-eight-year-old me wasn't so sure. And part of me wanted to find out.

I parked behind the hotel and tugged open the door to the kitchen, where Chef George and his assistant Tommy were prepping for dinner service. "Bluebell out front?"

George held up a thumb without lifting focus from where he stood at the grill.

I pushed through the swinging door into the busy dining room. Bluebell was at a table by the fireplace at the far end of the room. I pulled out a stool at the bar to wait for her.

"Hi, Rose." Fern poured a pint from a tap and set it on a tray beside two sophisticated-looking cocktails. "Are you delivering today? Unusual for a Saturday."

She had on a cobalt-colored belted jumpsuit with puffy sleeves that made her blue eyes glow. I looked down at my chino shorts and T-shirt, smeared with dust, and slid the beat-up Mariners cap from my head.

"It's pleasure, not business today." I ran my hands over my hair in a feeble attempt to smooth it. "Came by to see my gal." I waved at Bluebell, who turned from the table she was serving and headed in our direction, her curls bouncing.

"Hey! How was the market today?" She entered orders in the restaurant's computer system, her fingers flying over the screen. "Any interesting encounters?" She raised an eyebrow. I'd told her about last week's experience with tarot cards—about August's question and Zoe's answer. I shook my head no.

"Let Fern make you a drink—on me. Back in a flash."

"Orchard Catch Cooler," I read from the fresh sheet Fern put in front of me. "One of those, please."

"Good choice on a hot day." She grabbed a cock-tail glass from where they were lined up on the counter. "I wanted to use the strawberries you dropped off this week." She quartered two berries and muddled them with two basil leaves and a half ounce of simple syrup in a tall glass. Next she squeezed the juice from two lime wedges, dropping them in as well. She filled the rest with ice, eyeballed an ounce of vanilla vodka and four of cider, stirred, and set the drink on a coaster in front of me.

I picked up the glass, already sweaty in the warm

air, and took a long sip. "Ooh, that's fantastic." It was delicate and satisfying without being too sweet. "I have to tell you, Fern. Before you took over the bar, the most interesting thing to drink was Jack and Coke. Now I can't wait to try all the new things you come up with."

She flicked her blonde ponytail and smiled. "I'll take that." She filled two pint glasses with pilsner from San Juan Island Brewing and set them on the bar for Bluebell. Then she leaned back on the counter and stuck her hands in the pockets of her apron. "That's some excitement they had at the marina today." She cocked her chin at the wall of windows that looked over the docks.

"How do you mean?"

"You didn't hear? Oh, the market was today, wasn't it. One of the boats they were using for the movie sank! Weird, right?"

"What? That is weird. Do they know why?" My stomach did a dive bomb. "Wait—was anyone hurt?"

"Not that I know of. A few of them traipsed in here dripping wet from head to toe. A pack of drowned rats, they looked like." She giggled.

Bluebell eyeballed me as she returned to load her tray with drinks. "Lemme guess. You heard about the sinking ship."

I nodded and attempted a smile but couldn't ignore

the worry settling into my chest.

"Not to worry. He's fine." She twirled around and disappeared among the diners again.

"Who's fine?" Fern asked. "Oh, of course! I can't believe I forgot you used to date August. I almost didn't recognize him when he walked in here."

"I guess we're all getting older, huh."

"Did he always have that limp?"

I winced at her description. If I knew one thing about August, it was how much he would hate to know people noticed.

Instead of answering, I sipped my drink and told her again how delicious it was. She wiped down the bar and refilled her ice bucket. "Those guys been by tonight, by the way?" I asked, trying to sound casual.

"One of them—Mr. Tall, Blond, and Handsome— poked his head in an hour ago, said it'd just be him and...Sam, I think he said the other guy's name was? Anyway, just him and Sam for dinner tonight and asked me to save them a seat at the bar."

That feeling of worry turned to fear, especially when Fern launched into details about what had happened on the water. It sounded pretty scary. I hoped August hadn't hurt his leg again—not that I knew what was wrong with it in the first place. But if he wasn't joining his friends for dinner, something must be wrong.

"I always did get bad vibes from that Chip guy," Fern said. "He's from Winslow, right? You know him?"

I shrugged. What little I did know wasn't great. "I think so, yah. Worked with the Quinns I think. I lost track of him after they left."

"Guy's an asshole," said a gruff voice behind me. Fern's brother, Forest, rested a worn boot on the brass rail that ran the length of the bar and leaned forward on his palms. "Hand me those invoices, would you?" Like mine, his T-shirt was marked with dark spots from working all day. He glanced at me, his eyes the same blue as his sister's. "Tried to rip off our parents a few years ago in some scam."

"Forest had him shaking in his boots, didn't you, big brother?" Fern beamed as she handed him a pile of papers.

"All I know is I better not see his face in my hotel ever again." He took the papers from Fern and nodded before stalking off toward the lobby.

I made a mental note to ask Pappy what he knew about Chip Thurlow.

Bluebell bounced between the bar and the tables of diners, apologizing every time she picked up drinks that she couldn't join me. I savored my Orchard Catch Cooler, hoping to bump into Noah or Sam, but when they still hadn't shown a half hour later, I resigned myself to the fact I'd have to pester Bluebell tonight for an update. Pappy was waiting for me at home. I looped my bag over my shoulder, scanning the room for my friend.

"See you soon," I told Fern, pushing through the swinging door to the kitchen. I swept past George and exited to the back of the hotel. On the drive home to Winslow, glimpses of the Pacific whipping by me, I consciously steered my thoughts away from August and the accident on set to all the work I needed to do before for the organic inspection agent came in a few weeks.

When I arrived at Big Oak, I headed straight for the kitchen, where I knew Pappy would be fixing dinner, as he always did on market days. I beelined to the sink to wash my hands. Standing there, warm water sluicing over my fingers, I heard him talking in the cottage's living room.

"Hello?" I called.

"In here."

I picked up a dish towel and walked toward his voice, drying my hands on the towel as I went. But when I turned the corner into the living room, I promptly dropped it.

"Hi, Rose," August said.

Pappy jumped up to grab the towel, kissing me on the cheek when he handed it to me. "Are ya just going to stand there? You remember August." Pappy winked, then sat down again as August stood in greeting. My heart stuttered at the sight of his sharp green eyes. Whatever had happened on the water this afternoon, he looked fine. Relief swept through me.

"I— Sure. Hi, August. Actually we've seen each other a few times," I said, clasping the dish towel tightly. "But I didn't expect to see you here."

"Sorry to startle you," he said.

"So why are you here?"

The glimmer in his eyes dimmed a little. "Felix invited me."

"Aye, I did," Pappy said. "Saw him today at the marina. Thought it might be nice to catch up. Don't you? Now, I'll just get the charcoal lit." He jumped to his feet and bounded past me through the kitchen to the front porch, where we had an old kettle grill that had seen better days.

My discomfort was obvious. I hadn't moved from the spot in the doorway. I just stood there, wringing the dish towel, not meeting August's gaze.

"Well, this is awkward. Look, I can go—"

I shook my head. *What's the big deal? He's had dinner with my family dozens of times.* So why did it feel like my heart might beat out of my chest? "You're fine. I'm sure Pappy invited you for a reason. He'll be happy to have company with someone other than me."

"What's that, now?" Pappy said as he entered the kitchen, letting the old screen door clap shut behind him.

"We were just— You know what?" I spun around when I heard him open the refrigerator and start fishing around. I moved toward him, holding the fridge door as he reached for a beer. "I got this. Go on, you catch up."

"All right, I'spose that's fine. Another beer, August?"

"Sure, why not." I glanced into the living room to see August tip the last of a bottle of a Summer Haze Wheat Ale. He caught me staring at him as he lowered it. "This is great."

The best approach here is normal, I told myself. *This is just another Saturday.* "Isn't it?" At the kitchen island, I began putting skewers together for the grill. The cottage I shared with Pappy was so small, we could easily hear one another between rooms. "Island Hoppin' Brewery—you heard about it yet? They make beer with wheat from the Canadian Prairies, apparently."

"Island Hoppin', hey?" August mulled over the label on the bottle. "Whatever it is, I like it."

Two beers in hand, Pappy held open the screen door and beckoned for August to follow him to the porch. "Come on out here, Auggie. You can finish telling me about this business with the boat." It was obvious Pappy was happy to see him after all these years. Even at the worst of my heartbreak when August left, Pappy had never blamed him for what his parents did. "He's just a boy," Pappy would say as he wiped my tears or wrapped me in a hug. "He doesn't know better."

I got potatoes ready to bake for each of us and set them in the oven once it was warmed. For the skewers, I had onions, bell peppers, mushrooms, and cubes of beef from Sweetgrass Farm on nearby Lopez Island. When they were ready for the grill, I took the plate out to Pappy, then returned inside to make a salad with radishes and the snap peas I'd brought home from the market. I loved the way crisp, sugary peas balanced out the spiciness of radishes.

"Ready," I called out when the table was set and I'd pulled the potatoes from the oven.

"Perfect timing." August nudged open the screen door with his elbow, balancing the plate of steaming skewers in the other hand. Pappy followed behind, holding two empty beer bottles.

As we sat at the table, my thoughts flashed to all the meals we'd had together at Big Oak Farm—before my mom died, before the Quinns left. Back then we were in the old estate house, its rooms filled with happiness and my mom's easy laugh. August had been an earnest kid, always kind and willing to help—just as everyone in the community was in those days, unaware of the seeds of mistrust the Quinns were planting among us.

I listened to Pappy and August talk, taking note of how Pappy asked gentle questions, never judging, open to learning who August was now. I knew in his heart he believed—what did he always say?—you never lost your connection to the island, just let it rise, fall, and carry you through life.

"What do you all know about Chip?" August used a fork to pull the meat and vegetables from a skewer.

"Didn't he work for your parents?" I asked.

He looked up from his plate and, seeing Pappy and me watching him, set his fork on the table. "To be honest I don't know. He was always around—especially at the end. Seeing him this morning..." He wiped his fingers on a napkin, then closed his hand around it in a fist. "He has something to do with it all. I just know it."

"Hey now, whatever it is, it's done," Pappy said. "It's done," he repeated when August shook his head, frustrated.

"I wish it were that easy—"

"Ah, but it is, my boy. It is. That's all in the past." Pappy rested a bony hand on August's broad shoulders. "I might be long in the tooth, but I've learned a thing or two. Know what the most important one is? Focus on today. It's all we've got. Tomorrow isn't promised, that's for sure. And yesterday—well, it doesn't exist."

"But he's up to something. You didn't see the look he gave me."

"Ah-ah." Pappy lifted his hand from August's shoulder and held up a finger. "It's not your problem to bear, Auggie. Not yours to bear. Now, tell me about this movie that's got everyone in a tizzy. Think there's a part in it for me?" His eyes sparkled with cheekiness.

I listened as August described his work as an underwater cameraman and spoke of his years with the FBI, how he'd trained to be a diver to join something called the USERT program. It didn't escape my notice he skipped over his reason for leaving the Bureau.

I lost myself in the rhythm of their conversation as the sun went down and the cricketsong and katydids signaled nightfall. As much as I tried to force myself to remain closed to August, I felt my heart softening a little, my hard edges smoothing under the spell of memory and shared connection.

"So you stay in the cottage now," August said when I got up to clear the plates.

Pappy and I exchanged a look, and he waited for me to respond. "Yah. It just felt like the thing to do.

We didn't need all that space anymore, anyway." Truth of it was, neither I nor Pappy had been able to shake the grief of the early months following my mom's death, and when August left, it was even harder. Moving into the cottage was the best decision we could've made.

By the time I'd loaded the dishwasher and put everything away, it was nearing midnight. Like Cinderella snapped from a spell, I bit out, "Isn't it time you go?"

"I, uh… Yah. I'll get out of your hair."

Pappy sat with his elbows on the table, chin in his palms, his eyelids droopy with fatigue, but he pinned me with a look of disapproval at my sudden rudeness. "You're not going anywhere, son," he told August. "It's a long way to town in the black of night."

"It's fine, really," August protested. "I know these roads like the back of my hand, remember?"

Pappy tsked and shook his head. "I wouldn't count on it. Tell you what. There's still a bed in the old estate house. There ain't much else, but it's yours."

"I'm not sure Rose…" August let his voice trail off.

I caught a sideways look from Pappy. "Rose is just fine with it," I said. I wiped my hands on my jeans. "Hang on. I'll grab you a sleeping bag." I disappeared from the kitchen, returning a few minutes later with a faded plaid camp bag.

"I'll walk you out there." Pappy stood slowly from the table, rubbing his back, and I felt a pang of regret we hadn't moved to the couches in the living room after dinner. He walked to the door and flipped on the light switch, summoning August to follow him. The porch flooded with light from the main fixture outside, illuminating the start of the path between the cottage and the estate house.

August came toward me, arms out awkwardly, unsure whether to lean in for a hug. As he lunged forward, I veered back, then we repeated the motion in reverse. With an awkward laugh, we finally managed a quick, polite embrace. He grabbed my hands as we separated. "Thank you," he said, squeezing my fingers. "This felt...normal." Before I could respond, he dropped them and went after Pappy.

"Lead the way, Felix. I can't believe that old pile is still standing..."

Their voices faded away, blending with the cricket chirps. August's shadow was a familiar silhouette, with a slight hitch in his cadence, Pappy's steps shorter and sprightly. I waited on the porch for Pappy to return.

"Night, Pappy," I said once we were back inside. One blessing of a late night: he wasn't likely to be up before me, tackling chores better suited to a younger person. I bent to kiss his cheek before he headed to his room at the north end of the cottage.

"Night, Rose." His voice was gravelly from the night of talking. "Apricots tomorrow?" he croaked, holding his bedroom door ajar to hear my answer.

"You bet."

I kicked off my boots and retreated to the bathroom that adjoined my room at the opposite end of the cottage. I caught my reflection in the mirror. A flush of pink on my cheeks and a light in my eyes harkened of the carefree girl I once was. Wisps of hair had escaped the low bun I always wore, softening my features. It was obvious. The night with August and Pappy had been a respite from the constant stress of farm life: staying solvent, getting certified, keeping customers happy. "If you'd told me two months ago I'd have a good time with August Quinn, I would've sent you to the doctor," I told the woman in the mirror.

I brushed my teeth and peeled out of my clothes, slipping into my favorite summer nightie, a voluminous white babydoll dotted with printed strawberries. It seemed silly to make the bed only to get right into it, but I fluffed the pillows, smoothed the cotton sheet, and straightened the waffle blanket over top before slipping in. The sheet was soft and cool against my skin. I reached for the bedside table and switched off the lamp, inhaling deeply, trying to clear my mind of all things August.

CHAPTER 8

August

I had everything I needed at the old house on Big Oak Farm: a belly full of food, a comfortable—though bare—bed, a warm sleeping bag, and cool night air flowing in through the big dormer window. The place had no functioning electricity, so I found my way up the stairs to the front bedroom by both memory and a cell phone flashlight. But sleep remained elusive.

Being on the farm was unexpectedly grounding. Though my memories of it were hazy, they were overlaid with a sense of peace and contentment I hadn't felt since I was a kid. Images flashed through my mind like out-of-focus snapshots, my brain too alive with them to sleep. Most of all, though, I couldn't shake the desire that surged through me knowing Rose was nearby.

She was just as beautiful now as she was then. Where she was once soft and willowy, now she was lean and strong from a decade of work on the farm. The blonde hair she'd worn long and loose was shorter, usually tied back in a bun at the base of her neck. And something else was different about her. She had an air of seriousness I didn't recognize—a seriousness that shadowed some of the light she'd once carried. *Did I do that?* I turned the question over in my mind, asking myself for the thousandth time since the day I left if I should have—could have—done anything different.

No. It'd been enough to keep my own head above water amid all the shame back then, all the while witnessing my parents' breakup and trying to fit into a new world in Seattle. I'd had a sense deep inside Rose was better off without the burden of disgrace my family had brought to Orcas. Little did I know she thought the blame laid with her for grieving the loss of her mother.

A sound pulled my focus. Just a farm noise at night, I decided, rolling over on my back and staring wide-eyed at the ceiling. Then I heard the sound again, more clearly this time, and recognized the creak of a floorboard. I lifted open the flap of the sleeping bag and sat up, placing my feet on the floor.

"Rose?" I listened for a reply as footsteps reached the top of the stairs. Illuminated by the moonlight streaming through the window, she stood in the doorframe, leaning her back against it. "Hi," I said.

"Want to walk?"

I reached for the jeans and T-shirt I'd slung at the foot of the bed. "Can't sleep either?"

She shook her head. Neither of us needed to explain why. I trailed her down the stairs and out to the front porch. Her feet were bare, so I stepped down to the grass barefoot, too. Rose was already off, her white dress billowing down the path ahead of me like a ghost.

"Hey, wait up." The ethereal figure stopped. As I got closer, I saw the dress had a pattern— strawberries—and thin straps down into a V-neck. Her legs were long and brown against the white cotton. "Where are we going?"

"You know."

That's when it hit me. The path we were on was familiar, even by moonlight. We walked in silence through the warm night, bare feet padding across dirt and dry grass as we threaded among the fruit trees and plots of vegetables until we reached a gentle rise at the edge of the property. Here it was: the huge Garry oak tree the farm was named for. I ran my hand along its trunk, the bark fissured with grooves and ridges beneath my fingers.

We'd spent hours here as kids, leaning against the base of the tree, lounging in the grasses under dappled sunshine, dreaming and planning for the future. All those plans had crumbled under the weight of life, but the tree remained, solid, rooted deeply to the earth, connecting not just me and Rose to this place but all the families who'd lived here before us. It brought my hazy memories a little more in focus.

"Thank you," I said into the darkness. Branches of leaves above obscured the light of the moon.

"Did you know the oak is a healing tree?"

"I didn't, but that does explain the feeling I get when I touch it." I trailed my fingers over the bark once more.

"Thought you could use it."

She was right. I closed my eyes, trying to soak in the old oak's strength, willing away the pain being home on the island wrought. Rose stayed quiet, allowing me this space, gently padding around the tree, her footfalls barely audible. Then she was next to me, staring out over the rolling hills of farmland and beyond to an island dotted with lights.

"Rose." I reached for her hand. "Why did you bring me here? Last week you didn't want anything to do with me."

She pulled her hand from mine but turned to face me. My pulse kicked up under her gaze, and my heart seemed to collapse into one tiny speck and explode at light speed. I trailed my fingers along the oak's giant trunk, feeling it ground me again to this time and place.

"I—I don't know. I just thought you needed it. We should go." *What? No. I want to stay here forever*, I thought as she started down the hill. I caught her by the arm, but I sensed a wall slide up.

Couldn't she feel the familiar pull between us? The forever imprint of her heart on mine? To me it was denying gravity to ignore the longing I felt for her. The idea she didn't feel the same terrified me.

So I got desperate. "You know what I think you should do? Try living a little."

I instantly regretted saying it.

She crossed her arms in front of her, a physical manifestation of the emotional wall I'd felt a moment ago. Her bare foot tapped the ground. "Maybe living means different things to different people, August. This—" she spread her arms wide to encompass the farm "—*this* is living for me. I didn't get the luxury of leaving, being selfish, doing what I wanted." She spun on her heel and stormed away. I stood watching as her white dress bobbed between the fruit trees like a specter in the moonlight.

I dragged my fingers along the bark one last time before I slowly retraced the path to the estate house.

Rose

Halfway to the cottage, I threw my hands in the air. "Argh!" *How does he still have this power over me?* Guilt sank like a stone in my stomach for lashing out at him. What had he promised me? Nothing. He was here for a month, give or take. Now was my chance to let him go, get him out of my system. For good.

I altered course for the estate house, where I waited for him on the veranda, leaning my palms on the railing and listening to a northern mockingbird croon. Soft footfalls in the grass alerted me to his approach.

"I'm sorry. I didn't mean to—" I started when he climbed the steps.

He shook his head. "No apology necessary. I deserved it." He propped his foot on the last stair and rubbed his knee.

"You okay?"

"No."

"Want to talk about it?"

He sat on the edge of the steps and rested his head in his hands. After a long pause, he said, "I can't stop thinking about you."

I didn't know what I'd expected him to say, but it wasn't that. "That's...sweet." I was even less sure how to respond. Across the orchard, the cottage was silhouetted like a cartoon house in the moonlight. Who had time for sweetness when the fate of a farm balanced on their shoulders?

"It's not sweet," he said. "It's a problem."

I sat down next to him, tucking my nightdress under my thighs so there was a thin layer of cotton between me and the weathered veranda, which somehow still felt warm from the afternoon sun. Again, I was at a loss for words. "Okay?"

"I can't sleep. I stalk around town late at night, and early in the morning, and I think about you. If I do sleep, when I wake up, I'm thinking about you. When I'm diving, I'm thinking about you."

I felt a chink in my emotional armor. I sighed. "If it makes you feel any better, I think about you all the time, too."

"What are we going to do about it?"

Suddenly the answer seemed so simple, I laughed out loud. "We could just...fuck. Get it out of our systems." I turned to face him, the short skirt of my dress riding high on my thighs.

His eyes wandered over me, gleaming with desire. I sensed a battle warring within him—between the lust that threatened to light our bodies afire and the enormity of what it might mean. "No."

"Just once."

"I don't want your pity."

"What?" I ran a finger along my leg, tracing the edge of my skirt, inching it higher, exposing more skin.

"I don't want your pity," he repeated. "I know how this goes. You'll see my scar, and you'll feel sorry for me."

"What?"

"You heard me."

I did, but I couldn't believe it. Did he really think I cared about some scar? But I saw the way he eyed me hungrily, watched his desire flare like a flame to a candle. He wanted this, too. "I might not remember everything about you fondly, but I know this. You're as perfect today as you were back then. When we were young, and life was easy. Pity, I can assure you—" I dragged a hand across his belly, from one side to the other, feeling his erection jump at my touch "—is the furthest thing from my mind." His bicep flexed against his T-shirt, and my ovaries did backflips against my hip bones.

He reached for my skirt and pulled it all the way

up my thighs, sending chills from my toes to my ears. The sweep of his hand over my legs stopped my world on its axis. In an instant I was in his lap, taking his face in my hands and breathing him in. He smelled of sea salt and sun—of him. We held each other's gaze, tension building like water behind a dam. His cock stirred, and I tilted my hips against him, panting, my lips grazing his jaw.

His resistance dissolved, and he kissed me madly, hungrily, our tongues tangling as we moaned against each other. All rational thought left my brain; the only thing that mattered was the raw, desperate passion coursing through me. I sank into lips so familiar they felt like mine. Gasping for breath now, I leaned back, my mouth swollen with lust.

"I'll never forgive you."

"I know," he said.

"Still want to do this?"

"Yes," he growled, pushing me to stand, his hands around my waist under my dress. He stood, too, never letting the contact between us lapse. Inside, up the stairs, I grabbed at him hungrily, desperate to feel his skin next to mine.

In the diffused moonlight flooding the bedroom, my eyes traced the planes of his body. Standing together, next to the bed, August pulled his shirt up and over his head, then tugged down the straps of my dress. His gaze went to my breasts, fingers brushing my nipples, sending them into peaks. I drew in a sharp breath. His touch sent rivers of pleasure streaming down my body, and I arched my back, longing for more.

I pressed against him, melting into his warm skin as desire bounced between us like an arc of electricity. Grabbing the waist of his jeans, I fumbled to get them undone. He joined hands with mine, and together we unbuttoned the fly, never breaking eye contact, each taking in how the other had changed yet remained the same.

Perched on the edge of the bed, I tugged his jeans down and pushed them off as he lifted first one foot, then the other. There it was—a scar the shape of a crescent that spanned the length of his calf, raised and uneven under my fingers. He squeezed my shoulders. When I lifted my head to meet his eyes, they were shiny with tears.

"It's not pity I feel," I whispered, running my hand over it again. "It's awe." Whatever had happened, the scar meant he'd made it. Survived something traumatic—again.

He leaned down to kiss me, and I bowed up against him, my nipples grazing his chest. He found the hem of my dress and lifted it over my head. He tugged the elastic from my hair, letting it fall softly around my chin. Outside, the hummingbirds and northern flickers began the daybreak chorus.

Lifting me to my feet, he roamed my body with his hands like a moth searching for light. "Ro," he moaned before we locked lips again, finding new and familiar thrills in the feel of each other's bodies. I turned us around, so the back of his knees nudged the bed. With a gentle push to his chest, he sank to the mattress, his eyes, his body, his spirit ready to fuck, his cock stiff and throbbing. I couldn't wait another second.

I climbed in his lap, straddling him, my pussy slick with need. He wrapped his arms around me tightly, my knees brushing his shoulders as I rocked in his lap. We found a perfect rhythm, our breaths growing heavier, our moans louder, until we were balanced on the brink of climax. I tipped over first, pulsing around him in ecstasy until he could no longer hold on and I felt first the throbbing, then the last, deep thrust of his orgasm. Once it was over, we stayed fused together, our chests heaving, our lips touching. August held my gaze as long as I let him.

"I missed you."

I left his statement hanging, just collapsed into the warmth of his chest as he lay back, his body so familiar yet mature, the muscled shape of a swimmer in the place of the lean boy I remembered. Exhilarated and sated, we drifted to sleep.

A beam of sunlight startled me awake sometime later. I sat up straight. *Do not freak out*, I willed inside. *Fuck, the apricots!* I struggled to get my bearings as I took in the faded rose-print wallpaper and the view of the cottage across the orchard through the unshaded window.

I pressed my fingers to my temples. Two things struck me as crucially important: I had to beat Pappy to the chores—and he absolutely could *not* see me slither out of the estate house and creep home.

I slid out from under the unzipped sleeping bag and got quietly to my feet. Tiptoeing so as not to disturb August, I found my dress on the floor in a pile with his jeans. I couldn't bring myself to look at him. Better to slip out unnoticed.

"What are you doing?"

Shit. "Getting dressed." I didn't turn around.

"Can't that wait?"

"No."

"Are you okay?"

I spun back to face him, fiddling with the straps on my dress. He pushed up to his elbows, the muscles in his arms flexing like a Greek god's. Damn, he was beautiful. But that didn't change what this was—who he was. Someone I couldn't trust. A distraction—now that we'd gotten the sex out of our systems. "I'm fine."

"You seem upset."

"I'm fine," I repeated. "Look, thanks for…" I pointed to him, at the bed, between us.

A grin spread across his face. "This—" he echoed my gesture "—was just like I remember. Better than I remember."

"Yah, well, this—" again I pointed back and forth to him and me "—isn't happening again."

He mock-saluted me. "Got it. Listen, do you have time—"

I shook my head, gathered my hair at the nape of my neck, and bent to pick up my elastic from the floor.

"Whatever it is, I don't." Patting my bun in place, I moved for the doorway. At the precipice I paused to drink in one last look at him. Sprawled on the bed, still propped on his elbows, sun streaming through the window, hair mussed from a night of passion, he was gorgeous. But not gorgeous enough to deter me from the work ahead that day—and every day—or from the fact he was leaving in three weeks. Just as he'd done before.

"Gotta go, Quinn. See ya around." I skipped down the stairs and into the blazing sun.

CHAPTER 9

Rose

Did you call it a walk of shame when you left one part of your own property to get to another? I hurried to the cottage to change and get out to the orchard before Pappy was any the wiser.

I almost didn't recognize the woman I saw in the mirror when I brushed my teeth. Gone were the dark circles under my eyes that usually stared back at me every morning. My skin glowed, my cheeks were flushed, and even my hair, which I released from its elastic, fell around my face in easy, pretty waves.

"Guess you needed that," I said aloud. Seeing myself like this, I wondered what my life would've been like if my mom hadn't died, if the Quinns hadn't left, if I'd been able to get through my early twenties without the heaviness of grief. Would August and I have made it—together? Would I still be here on the farm? What would it have been like to have a carefree youth?

Last night was fun—really fun—but today I was back in reality. Pappy and I had a lot to do: harvest the apricots, pollinate the corn, weed the raised beds, figure out which bills I needed to pay and which could wait. Sundays were the one day I could fully dedicate to Big Oak, with no deliveries to make or markets to attend.

After the airiness of the dress I'd been wearing last night, pulling on thick cotton shorts and an old T-shirt felt like a mantle of responsibility. I sighed.

Pappy stirred in the kitchen.

"Sleep okay, Pappy?" I set a pot of coffee to brew in the machine.

"Like a log."

There was nothing suspicious in his tone; I'd escaped having to explain why I'd spent the night in the old estate house. Would August slink off the farm and back to Bayview without saying goodbye? Did they film on Sundays?

Pappy served up two bowls of oatmeal topped with fresh strawberries and dollops of almond butter. I closed my eyes around its gentle nuttiness, letting the breeze that floated through the screen door center me to the present. It carried with it the distinctive warbles of song sparrows and the scent of earth baking in the sun. It was going to be hot out there.

August

I felt different this morning about being here on Orcas Island. That anxious gnawing in the pit of my stomach I'd woken up with the first week had morphed into something like…settled. Since I'd joined the FBI, my life had been a well-oiled machine. Even after the accident, when Noah and Sam had started down this new career path with me, I'd had a semblance of control. But being home on the island, life had been unpredictable—even fun.

Maybe you were always just attuned to the rhythms of life where you were born, and the push and pull of the waves against this wild little island were like a gently rocking cradle for my soul. Or maybe it was waking up on Big Oak Farm, away from the hustle of the Driftwood Inn and the film production.

Who was I kidding? The spectacular night with Rose definitely had something to do with it.

From the veranda of the old house, I could see her in the orchard, cap pulled low on her head to shield her eyes from the sun as she assessed the fruit trees. Pappy's cheerful whistling carried over the property, although I couldn't see where he was.

I wanted to stay, spend the day with them, help out around the farm like I did when I was a kid. I had a day off from *Shore Thing*—everyone did, needing to regroup after the disaster with the narrowboat. I grabbed my boots and sat on the steps to pull them on.

Beyond the orchard and raised beds, the nearest part of a big field was divided in three sections. As I approached it, following a dry, dusty path, I could make out the dark, leathery leaves of broccoli plants planted in rows, each with a large flower head that punctuated the middle like an exclamation mark. To the right, the green vines of runner beans climbed up a series of X frames made with bamboo canes and tied at the top with twine. In the middle third of the field, even rows of corn swayed in the breeze like singers in a gospel choir. Farther out, the rest of the field lay fallow, carpeted with tall grass and the last of spring's wildflowers.

Knowing how much Rose and Felix cared about

the place, I was surprised to see such a big swath of land go unused.

I met Rose in the orchard at the same time Felix did. "Head's up," she called from where she stood atop a ladder. I cradled my hands to catch what she'd thrown. "First harvest of apricots. Test it for me."

I rolled it around in my hand, its velvety skin warm and firm. It was a beautiful yellowy orange, and its scent was strong and sweet. I took a bite of the fleshy fruit and let it melt on my tongue, sucking in to keep the juice from dripping down my chin. Rose waited, one hand on her hip and the other on a rung of the ladder, for my review.

"Sweet and tart," I said after I swallowed. "Like a peach and a plum had a baby."

"Perfect." She turned to where Felix was maneuvering a picking pole on a nearby tree. "Pappy, let August take over. I need you on this side." She pointed to her right.

I was happy to oblige. The three of us began working together, Rose from the ladder, me with the picking pole. After twenty minutes wrangling the thing, I got the hang of it. Felix worked the eye-level branches, gently twisting off ripe apricots and tossing them into metal pails at his feet.

It was almost like old times; the only thing missing was Rose's mom. I could see now why Rose was so dedicated to making things work here. It was an honorable legacy to uphold. When I asked about their plans for the farm, she seemed to light up at the chance to talk about converting to organic.

"The government has this Organic Certification Cost Share program that's helping us with the cost. Otherwise I'm not sure we could do it."

"This is important to you."

"Big Oak is my place. My history. My purpose. Growing food, feeding people—it's a privilege. I want to do it the best way I can. I really believe in the philosophy of organic. And so do my customers." She climbed down from the ladder with a full pail and placed it on the ground next to the others. Felix nodded proudly at what she'd said, then began hauling the buckets to the old estate house.

"It's cool in there," Rose explained when I asked where he was going. On his return trip, he passed us right by and headed for the cottage. "Lunch soon," he called over his shoulder.

I curved my hand over my eyes to block the sun and get a good look at Rose. She was alive like this, as magnificent in her T-shirt and shorts as she'd been last night. A worn canvas apron was slung low on her hips, with pruners, string, and a trowel poking out of the pockets. A vision flashed in my mind of the two of us, working hard beside each other, carrying the legacy of Big Oak Farm into the future. Then I remembered: *She'll never trust me again.* She needed someone strong, capable, dependable. Not someone who'd betrayed her—and who was healing a painful injury.

I shook the fantasy from my head. Working underwater with Sam and Noah was exactly what I should be doing. I had two guys who trusted me, who didn't know me as the boy who'd turned his back on someone who counted on him.

"Take the Driftwood, for instance," Rose was saying when I tuned back into her. "Your Hollywood friend, Domino? She wants the hotel to use only organic ingredients in its menus." She turned her gaze to the west, in the direction of Bayview. "I was skeptical of her at first." She laughed, handing another full pail of apricots down to me. "Make that resentful. I mean, who did she think she was, waltzing into Bayview and buying a stake in the oldest hotel on the island. I assumed—wrongly—it was a vanity project. But she's really helped make it special. Now I just hope we can keep being a grower she can depend on. Especially if she gets more movies made here."

"Hollywood North?" It was a term I'd heard thrown around to describe how film studios were choosing towns and beaches around the Pacific Northwest—as far north as Vancouver—to cut costs on production.

"Hey now, let's not go that far." She laughed again, scanning the trees around us. "How's it going?" She tipped her chin at the picking pole in my hands.

"Pretty good. I think."

"Let's walk," she said, climbing down from the ladder.

We ambled among the apricot trees, slow enough my leg didn't bother me, with Rose assessing the fruit of each one to make sure we hadn't missed any that were ripe. "On to the corn next," she said when we reached the edge of the orchard. "Or have you had enough?" She nudged my shoulder.

"Never."

CHAPTER 10

Rose

It definitely felt like his "never" was about more than picking fruit. But no matter how wonderful—and it was wonderful, if I let myself acknowledge it—it was to have him at the farm, working the land with me and Pappy, it was a fleeting moment in the grand scheme of things. It didn't pay my bills. It wouldn't help me sleep at night to have him here for an afternoon.

Although I was glad to have the chance to reconnect anyway, to forgive him, to learn he was okay after he'd vanished for all those years, it didn't change the irrevocable fact of just that: he'd vanished. And he'd be leaving again when *Shore Thing* wrapped. The last thing I needed, or could afford, was to let him back into my heart or my business. It was me and Pappy against the world. Always had been.

But I'd use him while I had him. It was a boon to have a third set of hands for the day.

We lugged the last pails of apricots to the parlor in the old house, then followed the dusty path to the cottage for a lunch of loaded BLT sandwiches—one of Pappy's favorites. Again August brought up the subject of Chip Thurlow, and again Pappy told him to let it go. "If nothing else, the man lost a boat yesterday," Pappy said. "It doesn't matter anyway, does it? You've got a job to do—that's why you're here. Not to open up old wounds."

August nodded and let the subject drop, but I could tell he hadn't absorbed Pappy's words.

After lunch, he and I headed back outside and toward the big field. "A few years ago we sectioned off a half-acre," I said, pointing to the split-rail fence that framed the boundaries of our growing area. The cedar was silvery gray from years of summer sun. I hated seeing the empty space beyond; it reminded me of what we'd had to give up. It was a delicate balancing act to calculate what we could grow each year with what we had to spend.

"I don't remember this being here," August said of

the fence. He ran a hand along one of the logs, looking beyond at the long grass stirring softly in the breeze. "What happened there?"

I bit my lip. How much did I need to tell him? *As little as possible*, a voice somewhere inside said. I stood up straight, hoping it projected confidence. "We're focusing on the conversion right now, keeping it manageable." I climbed over the fence near the corn plants.

At five feet tall, the jade-green stalks were days away from the silks emerging, their anthers a bright, creamy yellow. "Here. Watch me." I started down the first row of corn.

He followed behind, watching as I gently shook the stalk of one plant, then the next, then the next. "We gonna talk to them, too, or just give them a little dance?"

I turned to face him, hands on my hips. "Well, you can sing to them if you want, wise ass, but we're here to help them pollinate."

"All the more reason to sweet talk them, no?"

I couldn't help but notice the way the skin around his eyes crinkled when he laughed and the scar on his cheek melted away for a moment. I grabbed his shoulders and spun him around, giving him a little shove back to the start of the row. "Start on the next one, will you?"

He moved up the row beside me. We inched along together, carefully shaking stalks side by side. "Ro?"

"Yes?"

"Why are we doing this again?"

"The plants aren't getting much wind right now, so we're bringing the wind to them." I stopped and lifted my hat to wipe the sweat from my forehead. "Giving them a shake helps release the pollen from the tassels. The idea is it floats down to the silks below."

"That works?"

"That's the hope."

"And if it doesn't?"

I couldn't bear to think of losing even a few plants this year. Our margins were that tight. "It will." I was ready to change the subject. "Tell me about diving—and the FBI." We continued to the next rows and found our rhythm again. "All we've done is talk about me."

"The diving part is pretty incredible actually. Noah says it's like snorkeling all day long."

"Oof, not for me." Despite living on an island surrounded by ocean, I much preferred swimming on the surface of it rather than deep down below. "And the FBI part?"

"Like I said last night, we were on the USERT. We did underwater investigations. Sometimes the mission was to find evidence. Other times we looked for bodies." I recoiled. That was dark work. "Once in a while we had to disarm and recover explosives. Remember Wild Bill, the serial killer in Anchorage?"

"The one who was killing homeless men?" We reached the end of another two rows and moved to the next two.

"After he was caught, he volunteered evidence about one of his victims. We were called in and recovered the remains under five feet of ice."

"Yeesh. Pretty creepy."

"It's so much more than that, though. I learned a ton about marine life all over the world, and we got to raise awareness about the importance of our oceans and marine conservation. When I was working… Well, before we started this film thing, I didn't get much of a chance to really *explore* life underwater. Our dives were mission based, usually with a lot at stake. Now, though, I get to see things most people will never see in their lifetimes. And I get to capture it all on film."

I finally asked the one question I'd been dying to know the answer to. "Why did you leave the FBI?"

He was quiet for long enough I knew I wouldn't get a straight answer. "Oh, you know," he finally said. "We were ready to move on, and Sam had this connection in LA—it just seemed like the time was right." I couldn't see his face, obscured by the spiky yellow tassels between us, but the tone of his voice had deepened. He cleared his throat. "Tell me what it takes to get this place certified."

I noted, not for the first time, how skilled he was at steering the conversation away from himself. "Well, crop rotation is one of the basics." I shook the stalk of a plant near the end of the row I was in. "We rotate the crops we grow in these plots each year. The goal is to interrupt insect life cycles, prevent plant diseases, increase biodiversity, prevent soil erosion—all kinds of stuff."

"Corn was somewhere else last year?" We moved to the next two rows.

"No. We mix it up. Follow one plant with another from a different crop family, then wait a few years before replanting the initial crop. Our last crop of corn was..." I stopped for a moment, thinking. "Four years ago."

"Doesn't that make everything more difficult? What about your customers? Don't they expect you to grow the same things?"

"Aha." I waved a finger in the air above the corn. "It's all in how you train them." I resumed stalk-shaking, working quickly down the row. "By now the locals get excited to find out what we're growing every year. Take this year, for example. Everyone loves the chioggia beets. I sell out of them every week."

He considered that thoughtfully. "That's pretty cool."

We continued in harmony, up and down the rows, tussling corn stalks to shake the tassels free of pollen. Pappy kept near the cottage, weeding the shaded raised beds while Fig chased bugs nearby. When I reached the end of my eighth row, I stopped and surveyed our work, admiring August's methodical progress.

"You know, you're not half bad at this."

"Not my first day on the farm, remember?" He stood straight and pulled a long swig from the canteen of water Pappy had sent him outside with after lunch. "You can take the boy off the island, but you can't take the island out of the boy. Or something like that."

I laughed. August definitely wasn't a boy anymore. As I'd witnessed last night, he was all man now. He popped out from the end of his row, stopping to rub his right knee. I admired the biceps bulging against his shirt sleeves, the way the sun caught the hair on his forearms.

"You gonna tell me about that?"

August

Something in me resisted telling her about the accident. She seemed to have accepted my presence here, even just temporarily, and I wanted to sustain this feeling of normalcy while I had it. I wanted to forget the accident, forget the hurt my family caused, pretend it was just like the old days, when we sneaked kisses in the shadows of the estate house and relaxed under the big oak tree on summer afternoons.

"It's nothing."

"If you say so." She didn't press it but eyed me skeptically. "Look, just four rows to go." She pointed to the corn left to be pollinated. "Two each?"

"Last one to finish buys dinner?"

"Oh, I got you beat!" She moved nimbly along a row, shaking stalk after stalk, their yellow anthers bobbing back and forth. I feigned an effort to keep up, but I wanted her to win. Nothing would make me happier than sharing dinner after this perfect afternoon.

As I reached from corn stalk to corn stalk, I thought about just how different I was now. The teenage boy who thought he'd live here forever might be gone, but for a few hours this afternoon, I felt like I fit in here again. Still, the ache in my knee made it obvious I belonged in the water now, wherever that took me. Once *Shore Thing* was over, I'd be off on the next adventure with Sam and Noah.

I sure hoped I could spend more time with Rose until then.

"Done!" She did a little jump of victory when she reached the end of her rows. I lagged behind by half a row.

"Damn," I said, shaking my head. "Guess I gotta take you out to dinner." I rolled my eyes like it was a hardship.

She pumped the air in triumph. "Where're we going?"

"What do you know about Isola?" I named a restaurant I passed on Water Street on the way to Grind House every morning.

"Are you kidding? I love Isola." She clapped her hands with excitement. "You know who owns it, right?"

I shook my head again.

"River Black." I didn't know why I was surprised so many of our old classmates had made a way for themselves here. Ginger Kidd with Grind House. Fern and Forest Russo with the Driftwood. Rocky Black was mayor of Bayview, and now I'd learned River owned one of the town's hottest restaurants.

"Everyone's still here, huh."

"Most of us. Like you said, you can't take the island out of us."

"Not entirely true." I aimed my thumbs in at myself. "I've had a pretty good run out in the real world." *Not by choice*, I didn't add.

Rose eyed me for a minute, taking in my dusty boots, faded jeans, and shirt damp with sweat. "Uh-huh. Not true. You've still got the island in you. I saw how you worked the farm today. Just like riding a bike." She also referenced the pride on my face as I'd looked around the farmers market last week. I didn't have to say it. Orcas Island was imprinted on my soul.

I thought that over. She was right. I felt at ease here. But whether I belonged—and whether anyone wanted me here long-term—was something else. I knew what it was like to be part of a tight-knit community—and the way you looked at outsiders with immediate distrust simply because they were outsiders.

"Even if I could stay, Rose, I..."

"Oh, you think I mean you should stay?" She shook her index finger. "Uh-uh. No, I don't. You're here for a good time. Not a long time." She laughed.

"But what if..."

"Hey, don't get me wrong," she said. "It's nice to see you. To know you're okay. We agreed to be civil while you're here, and last night… Well, it was a damn sight more than civil. Last night was amazing. But last night doesn't change anything." She took a swig from her water bottle. "You don't belong here anymore, August. You and I both know it."

She rendered me speechless. That was it, wasn't it? No amount of forgiveness or attraction could erase the damage my family did a decade ago.

Rose rubbed her palms together, wiping off the dirt. "I think our work here is done. Nice job, Quinn."

"That's it?"

"Pappy and I will do it again in a few days. After we fertilize over there." She pointed where Pappy was hunched over the raised beds, weeding between the strawberry plants and lime-green leaves of butter lettuce.

"Wait, you *fertilize* organic crops?"

"Alfalfa meal. It's not cheap, but it has triacontanol."

My eyebrows knit together. "Tria…what?"

"Triacontanol. It's a natural stimulant that boosts growth." She smiled. "Just add water and wait three months."

"You make it sound easy."

"Ha, well, there's a few more steps in there. I wouldn't say easy. But there's nothing simpler or more natural than growing and caring for food. Here, grab those water bottles. We can drop them at the cottage."

"Guess that's true." I picked up the empty bottles and followed her to the porch. She set them on the table outside, ready for cleaning later. I glanced down at my grubby jeans and T-shirt, streaked with soil where I'd wiped my hands. I bet I smelled like a farm, too.

"Tell you what," she said, looking down at her own dusty shorts and blowing a strand of hair from her eyes. "Go back to the hotel. I'll meet you there. Say six? We can walk to Isola together. I'll text River, see if he can save us a table."

"It's a date." I tucked the loose strand behind her ear, my hand lingering longer than necessary.

CHAPTER 11

August

River hadn't just saved us a table; he'd saved us the best seats in the house. Our spot at the window overlooked Water Street and the bay beyond, gauzy and pink in the golden hour before sunset. We could see down to the marina on the right, where the *Redemption* remained the only boat docked in a slip. People strolled along the worn planks, silver under the low-hanging sun. Kids bent over the water, peering in, hoping to see the seals that hung around at this time when fishermen usually cleaned their catch. Three teens sat at the end of the farthest dock, feet dangling over the edge.

"You look beautiful." I spent more time looking across the table than I did at the view. Rose wore a knee-length slip dress the color of the apricots we'd picked today. Her hair hung loose around her face, grazing her jaw, and a trio of delicate gold necklaces glimmered on her chest. She took my breath away.

"Thanks." A blush of pink crept up her cheeks. "You're not so bad yourself."

I'd traded the dusty jeans for a clean pair of Levi's, paired with a blue cotton henley and desert boots. I buried my face in the menu, uncomfortable with the praise. "What's good here?"

A server appeared at the table. "Can I get you some drinks?"

"What do you think, a cocktail?" Rose asked.

"Your choice."

"In that case, two Sicilians, please."

"Very good." The server disappeared.

I scanned the menu in search of what she'd ordered.

"Grapefruit gin from Orcas Island Distillery, Campari, sugar, lemon, and prosecco," she read for me.

I grinned. "Trying to get me drunk?"

"You wish. Although they do have one of my favorite wines here."

"Oh? Which one?"

"The Bardolino."

"The rosé."

"Of course." She tipped her chin back and laughed. "Would you expect anything different?"

I snapped the menu shut. "You know what? Why don't you order for us? Surprise me. It's your town."

"Challenge accepted." Excitement danced in her brown eyes. I watched her read the menu carefully, appraising each item, sometimes nodding and other times subtly shaking her head. When the server returned with our cocktails, she was ready. "To start, we'll share the kale salad, the burrata, and an order of house-made focaccia." Rose waited for the server to take down the order, but instead he just nodded, committing her selections to memory. "Then I'll have the spaghetti," she said, "and for him, the tagliatelle."

"Excellent. We'll get that started for you. Anything else?"

I sipped the tart but perfectly sweet Sicilian.

"Oh, nearly forgot," Rose said. "A bottle of the Bardolini with dinner, please."

"Very good." The server vanished into the busy hum of the restaurant.

"Okay, August. Time to confess."

"Huh?"

"You gonna tell me what happened—or keep pretending your leg doesn't bother you?"

I stared out the window, trying to decide how much to tell her. I knew I was bound to hear the usual responses: "It'll get better, right?" "You're still healing," or "Just give it time." But the doctors hadn't minced words when they told me I would never recover 100 percent. What was the point in pretending?

I took a deep breath. "Remember I said we sometimes had to recover explosives?" Concern wrinkled her forehead. "For this one mission in Australia, we spent four nights checking for bombs on the underwater structure of a massive stand for spectators at the World Surfing Championships. Someone had called in a bomb threat."

Her eyes went wide like dinner plates. "I never heard anything about that."

"They keep this stuff quiet. That way the perpetrators don't know how much the FBI knows. Anyway, the first three nights went smoothly. We didn't find anything and were pretty much resigned to the idea it was an empty threat." I picked up the napkin in front of me and twisted it in my hands. "The fourth night was a nightmare. Noah was the one who found it first." I scrubbed a hand over my face. "Procedure says the most important thing is to detach a bomb if it's hooked to a boat or some other structure. That went fine. We managed to cut the zip-ties that were holding it to the stands. After that, we were supposed to take it out farther, so if we didn't disarm it in time, we'd minimize the damage nearby."

"And that's where things went wrong." She said it matter of factly.

"I don't remember much after that point, to be honest. What I do know is we managed to get the bomb far enough out that the explosion didn't damage the stands." Rose crossed her arms on the table and grabbed the bottoms of her elbows. "All I remember after that is waking up in the hospital in Sydney three days later with a concussion and a fractured tibia and fibula."

She clapped a hand to her mouth. "Oh my god. That sounds awful." Her words were muffled by her fingers.

"It didn't end there. I developed something called compartment syndrome. Basically the swelling put too much pressure on the nerves and muscles in my leg. I'll spare you the details. But to treat it, they had to make an incision to relieve the pressure. I ended up with a skin graft the full length of my calf. And some permanent loss of function."

"Oh, Auggie. I'm so sorry. Will it get—"

"Maybe." I shrugged. "I should be grateful I didn't lose my leg. I *am* grateful. But it's been a hard year, full of appointments and exercises and…" I gulped back my cocktail. "Everyone says I'll keep getting better. I just don't know how many more physiotherapists' offices I can visit or acupuncture needles I can stand to be jabbed with." I twisted the napkin again in my lap. "Anyway. I don't need anyone feeling sorry for me. I do that plenty enough for everyone." I didn't tell her I'd given up on treatment a month before the *Shore Thing* shoot.

"Sam and Noah, they've stuck with you through all this?"

"Yah. Some days I don't know how—or why—they're hanging around. But then we get in the water, and everything feels normal. Working on these movies saved me, gave me something to do. I'm so glad to be working, still doing something I love—spending time in the water."

Rose sat back in her chair, her forearms on the table. "Your scar—does it hurt?"

"No. Not physically at least. Not anymore." I straightened my leg under the table, resting its weight on my heel. "I can't believe you weren't turned off by it last night."

A smile spread across her face, her eyes gleaming. "Guess you had me pretty well distracted."

The server arrived, his arms laden with plates. "Kale and crispy pancetta salad with grand padano, potatoes, and lemon dressing," he said as he set down the first dish. "Burrata with charred tomato and olive salsa." Down came the second plate. "And house-made focaccia." He dropped the basket of bread with a flourish.

Another server appeared at the table, Bardolino in hand. "We'll pour, thanks," Rose said.

"Thank you. Looks great," I said. The servers retreated back to the kitchen.

"Mmm, heaven." Rose bit into a slice of still-warm Italian bread topped with fresh rosemary, olive oil, and flaky sea salt.

I portioned some salad and burrata onto my plate, grateful for the chance to change the subject. "You're still tight with Bluebell, then?"

"She's my rock. I'd never make it without her," she said between bites.

"What's she been up to? Working at the Driftwood this whole time?"

"Oh, you have no idea. Bluebell works so hard. In her spare time—which there isn't much of between double shifts at the inn and helping me and Pappy with Big Oak—she's been developing a skincare line. With seaweed."

I nearly choked on a mouthful of burrata. "Like, as in rubbing kelp all over your face?"

She laughed. "Well, you could, I guess. Actually she's done a ton of research and testing. Something about the way seaweed absorbs minerals from the ocean makes it a good source of vitamins and amino acids—and really good for the skin. See?" She put down her fork and turned her face toward the window, the evening sun's reflection off the water casting it in a golden glow.

"Aha, that's your secret." I took in her smooth skin, brown from the sun, her hair in loose, flaxen waves. My breath hitched. "God, you're incredible."

She smiled, looking down at her lap, pink tinting her cheeks. "Thank you." When her eyes met mine again, it felt like being bathed in sunshine.

Moments later River Black arrived at the table with our entrées. "Spaghetti aglio olio peperoncino," he said to Rose, setting down a dish of spaghetti noodles artfully twirled around a fork and sprinkled with fresh parsley and crushed red pepper flakes. "Tagliatelle with meat sauce for you, August." With his left hand, he laid my plate in front of me, then clapped me gently on the back. "Great to see you again, man. Glad to be home?"

"Thanks, River. Yah, good to be back. I'm here for only a few more weeks, though. Hey, this place is fantastic. Congratulations."

"Cheers, buddy. Maybe I'll see you again before you go." Turning to Rose, he asked, "Got more nugget potatoes for me? We sold out tonight."

"More this week, promise!" she said, but I detected a flicker of doubt in her voice.

"Enjoy your dinner. Bardolino's on me." River tucked his fingers to his forehead in salute and turned away.

Though Rose had tried to sound confident, it was obvious his question had unnerved her. Even after all these years, I knew her enough to tell when she was worried. I let it lie.

"This looks amazing." The wide egg noodles on my plate were coated in rich-looking meat sauce and sprinkled with shaved parmesan.

"Someone knows what they're doing back there," she said, but she still seemed distracted.

"Things okay at the farm? We talked about the organic conversion this afternoon but not much else. How will you handle the growth that's surely coming?" It wasn't my place to pry about the business of Big Oak, but maybe talking about it would help.

"We got it," she said. "Pappy's the best partner there is. And when we need an extra hand, Bluebell's right there." But her tone didn't match the confidence of her words.

"Ro, you know Felix is going to slow down one day soon."

She was quiet for a moment, then dropped her shoulders and rested her fork on her plate. "You say that, and I know you're right, but I just can't face the thought of it. It's been us—me and him—against the world. For a decade. Forever, it feels like."

I nodded, giving her space to continue, sensing it wasn't easy for her to talk about.

"He still tries to beat me to chores every morning, but I've noticed him moving more slowly lately. I have no idea what to do about it." She swallowed back tears. "Ah, we'll figure it out," she said, waving a hand to dissipate the stress of it.

If I thought I could be what she needed—what the farm needed—this would have been the perfect time to swoop in with an offer of help. A long-term offer. I sat back, assessing. We were still so good together. As good as we'd ever been. Last night was incredible. And spending the day with her was the balm I didn't know I'd been yearning for since arriving here two weeks ago. It was everything I'd craved and feared all at once. But with my leg the way it was, and my family's history here, I would be more trouble than help.

She picked up her fork again, and as we ate, I let the talk turn to *Shore Thing*, Domino West, what it was like to work with Damon Mann. I savored the Bardolino in my glass, not wanting the night to end. Outside the sun had dropped below the horizon, painting the sky with pink and purple before giving way to nightfall, but the breeze flowing through the restaurant's open windows was warm.

"I have an idea," I told her after I paid the bill. "Toss me your keys?"

She eyed me questioningly. "I don't think—"

"Trust me."

She fumbled around in her bag and tossed me a ring of keys as we headed for the door. I grabbed her hand and led her to where I could see her delivery van parked a block down the street. Once I was buckled in behind the wheel, she said, "Where to, Captain?"

I smiled as the engine roared to life.

Rose

August turned on Elison Road and followed its winding curves until we reached the three-way stop where I normally turned right to Winslow. Instead, he went left on the gravel path that cut apart big green meadows like the halves of an apple. It wasn't really a road, just a route locals used to get to Moonstone Beach, a pebble-and-sand cove on the other side of the peninsula from Bayview.

"I can't remember the last time I was here." On his side of the van, a fence lined the Blacks' property, where Rocky and River grew up. On the right I could see only darkness. We continued on for ten minutes, the van bumping over dips and mounds in the gravel.

When we came to a stop where the fence met the shore, I mumbled, "Wow," at the same time he did.

The moon hung big and round in the sky like a glowing orb of light. "Supermoon," he said.

"Strawberry moon. First full moon of the summer."

"C'mon, let's go." He opened the driver's side door and jumped out. I slipped out of my sandals and left them on my seat. When we came to the front of the van, he grabbed my hand and started forward.

"Here, let me lead." I laughed as he got tangled in the long grass alongside the path, its soft spikes swishing around our feet. "I bet I remember better than you." He let me pass him, hand grazing my low back. I led the way past a big boulder that marked the start of the beach trail. When we came up to the concrete ledge, I stepped down a set of log stairs.

The cool stones on the beach shifted beneath my feet. At the edge of a log, pale and enormous in the moonlight, I stopped, breathing in the salty air, my hand still wrapped in August's. Waves broke softly, pushing and pulling the rocks on the shore in a rhythmic lull, the moon a huge gray sun that lit up the rocky outcroppings in the bay.

"I'm glad I'm here." August's voice beside me in the dark sparked fireflies to life in my chest.

So am I. I let his hand drop and stepped up on the log, picking my way along it, loving its rugged strength under my feet. I felt light as a feather, like I'd been carrying a heavy weight and suddenly came free of it. I was more open, more hopeful, more...*me*. It was like I'd finally found part of myself again.

August kicked off his boots and socks. "Here, this way." He traced a finger down my arm and took off ahead of me toward a shadow at the end of the beach. I followed him, the briny ocean air cool and soft on my bare shoulders. As we got closer to it, the shadow took shape as a rowboat. In the moonlight, we could see two oars resting inside.

"Did you know this was here?"

"Just lucky, I guess." He moved to the rear, then bent to roll up the cuffs of his jeans. "You make me lucky. Here, let's pick it up and take it in. I don't think we should drag it over the rocks." He grabbed the back end and hoisted it waist high.

"You sure you can do this?"

"Don't worry about me. Grab the bow."

It was surprisingly light. In ten steps we had it in the water, the back end out deeper. August held the sides of the bow while I climbed in and found my balance on the back seat. In one long, smooth shove, he pushed the boat offshore, knee deep in water before he climbed aboard as well.

"Steady, steady!" I laughed as we rocked back and forth, August holding his stance like a surfer on a wave. When he was in position in the middle of the boat, I handed him the oars one at a time, watching as he placed them on the crutches. He dipped them in the water to propel us, breaking the stillness of the bay. It took him a few goes to find a steady rhythm. "Been a while, huh?"

"Ha. It's like riding a bike," he said. "Almost." The water was smooth and flat in the protected cove, moonlight bouncing off it like a mirror.

I peered around us into the great black night. Out here, away from the shore, the only sounds were the gentle lapping of waves against the sides of the boat and the steady creak of the oars turning in their crutches. Seeing August in the front, a dark silhouette against the stars, peace settled over me. He'd always had that effect on me, hadn't he?

He dipped the oars again and again, moving us forward. The stars twinkled brightly above, and I felt like I was at the center of the universe, my worries dwarfed in the significance of it all. After the excitement of getting the boat out to sea, we were quiet now, comfortable in the silence of each other's company.

He stopped rowing, and the boat drifted lazily. "Remember that day we skipped school and took the ferry?" I asked. It was as clear in my mind as the moon in the sky at that moment.

"And saw the orcas? Yah. I do. Thought of it the other day actually."

"It's funny, I'd forgotten it until now."

"I'll never forget."

"Remembering it now, I can't believe I almost did." I thought for a moment. "I guess my mom dying and you leaving—those were pretty traumatic events. I rarely let myself think about those days. It's just too painful."

August rested the oars in their crutches and leaned back, staring up at the night sky.

"But it was special, wasn't it? The way they swam beside the boat, floating in and out of the water? They looked weightless. I long to feel that way. Free to explore, free of responsibility, free of grief." I fought the urge to feel sorry for myself. I'd done enough of that.

"We have right now," he said. I looked at him, his face blue in the moonlight. "Only two things matter here. The moon, the stars, and the deep black sky— and us. The farm and the island… Leave your worries about them here. Drop them in the water and let the waves carry them away. It's just you and me."

I tilted my head back, too, and studied the sky. How did August know just what to say—just what I needed to hear? I closed my eyes and imagined each worry was a pebble in my hand. One by one, I pictured them dropping through my fingers and disappearing into the Pacific. *Sail on*, I willed them. *Let me be free.*

Zoe's words echoed in my mind. "*You need to put the past behind you and part ways with it.*" I'd dismissed her when she said it, but it rang true to me now.

"Better?" August sat forward again, resting his elbows on his knees. He reached for my hands and wrapped them in his, warm like a fire on a winter night.

"Better," I said, and I meant it. The weightless feeling I'd felt on the log was still with me. I wanted it to last forever.

He let go to grab the oars, dipping them in, out, and in again to row us to shore. The waves lapped along the sides, the oars creaking out a rhythm in their crutches. When we reached the beach, the boat thudded softly against the bottom. August climbed out first and pulled it farther in. I hopped out, too, holding the skirt of my dress to keep it from trailing in the water. He stepped to the stern and waited for me to take my spot at the bow so we could lift it back where we found it.

I linked arms with him as we trundled along the beach in our bare feet, toes wet with seawater. It was easier to see in the dark now, easier to spot August's boots by the side of the log where he'd left them. I waited while he brushed off his feet and stepped into them. We found our way back to the log stairs, where he stopped and clasped my hands in his.

"Listen, Ro. I don't know where things are going here. What kind of future there is. But I don't want it to end when I finish *Shore Thing*."

I wasn't sure what to say—or even what to think. It went against everything I'd thought about the guy for the ten long years to imagine a life with him. I closed my eyes, trying to listen to my instinct.

"I closed my heart to you ten years ago, August. I don't know if I can ever open it again."

CHAPTER 12
Rose

The week was a rush of harvesting and delivering orders, fertilizing crops, and reviewing our organic conversion plans and records before the certification agent came on Thursday. Maybe August was right: it was time to think about finding some help. But unless something changed—fast—paying a salary for outside help was impossible.

The restaurants in town counted on our produce, and with the attention Domino West was bringing to the island, I'd begun to dream about how Orcas could set an example for sustainable communities around the Pacific Northwest. Today, though, the farm was stuck in a place where there was too much work for two people, even when Bluebell pitched in, but not enough money to hire someone. I bit my lip, worrying about the growth we'd outlined in our plan. If we could barely afford to make ends meet today, how was anything going to change tomorrow?

I folded the corner of a page in my notebook where I'd jotted down ideas about how restaurant owners and suppliers on the island could join together to help address food insecurity and sustainability. My grand ideas would have to wait.

I tipped back my mug, sipping the last of a tea made with mint from our garden. *Mint*, I wrote at the end of my list of things to bring to the farmers market. For me, tea made with dried leaves didn't compare with the flavor of fresh herbs. And in weather like we were having, it was just as good steeped cold in a big jug with lemon and a few spoonfuls of honey.

Rosehips, I added to my page, imagining a future where I could specialize in artisanal teas.

Rosehip tea held a special place in my heart. Like most of the women my age on the island, I was named for a native plant. Mine was the Nootka rose, a bubblegum-pink bloom derived from Nootka Sound on the coast of Vancouver Island. My mom and I used to love collecting the reddish-orange seeds the plants produced after the roses faded, which we'd dry and make tea from. Every spring I was buoyed by the sweet, subtle scent of the wild rose shrubs that were scattered across shorelines, thickets, and roadsides on the island. But in fall and winter, when the leaves fell and the flowers turned to hips, the branches bare and prickly, all I could think was how much I missed my mom.

I rubbed my eyes and looked at the clock. Nearly midnight. Pappy had gone to bed an hour ago, Fig trotting lazily behind him. Lately this was what evenings looked like: me hunched over the kitchen table, papers and notepad spread out in front of me next to a laptop. The computer was great for accounting, and inventory, and all the records we needed for certification, but nothing beat a to-do list on paper.

Pushing up from the table, I rustled the papers into a pile and took my mug to the sink. I was exhausted. As I shuffled to hit the light switch on the way out of the kitchen, I thought of August for the hundredth time this week. *Am I lovable?* The question he'd asked Zoe held more significance now I knew about his injury and the guilt he carried about his father's mistakes. As much as I'd resented him all these years, he still lit a flame in my heart that warmed me like the old woodstove in the estate house. It felt like delicious relief to imagine a world where he came to live on Big Oak, and together we worked the land and helped build a sustainable community to be proud of. But could I ever really trust him? Or would I be forever waiting for the other shoe to drop, for him to disappear again without a trace? I was beginning to find an answer to that question. Hope flickered in my chest. Despite what I'd told him last Sunday, maybe we did have a future after all.

He'd trekked out to the farm several times this week, driving one of the movie crew's rented vans. The old connection between us was reforming like the branches of two trees joining—a process called inosculation. Latin for "to kiss into," it was a word I loved to think about. In inosculation, the branches first grew separately in proximity until they touched. The bark where they met gradually abraded away as the trees moved in the wind, and the tissues of the two trees self-grafted and grew together.

As I drifted off to sleep, an image of two big oaks, limbs intertwined, fed my dreams.

August

Filming *Shore Thing* was anything but straightforward. We were down a camera after the debacle with Chip's narrowboat and had to wait for a replacement.

Sailboats kept drifting into the background of every important scene. And even though Damon Mann had trained to be a diver, it became apparent he'd done so in a lake or somewhere without the rolling waves of the Pacific. Being out on the ocean made him seasick. Some days it was all we could do to get four hours of actual filmmaking in a twelve-hour day.

It was hard not to feel discouraged, especially since I couldn't shake the feeling I had something to prove being home. Sam and Noah kept me grounded, Sam with his exacting habit of doing precisely what was needed and when, and Noah with his relaxed, carefree demeanor. Everything seemed to come easy to them. They seemed to know just who they were and what their roles were in the world—something I was still figuring out about myself. In the anticipation of coming here, I'd wondered if being on Orcas Island, confronting my past, would provide closure, but instead it had opened another wound I was desperate to heal.

"Would you just ask her out already?" Noah told Sam over dinner in the dining room at the Driftwood. All week we'd watched him flirt with Fern.

"That obvious, huh."

"You could power a city with the energy that passes between you two." I wiped my fingers on the napkin in my lap.

Sam gazed at where Fern worked behind the bar but shook his head. "Nah. She's gorgeous, but you know the type. Works in a bar, flirts with all the customers, maybe even dates some of them. Not what I'm looking for. I know my match is out there. It's just a matter of time." Just saying the word *time* had him looking at his watch. "All right, boys. T minus seven hours. Big scene tomorrow." He lined up his knife and fork in exactly the middle of his plate.

"Still not on island time, hey?" I laughed.

"Island time?"

"Yah, you know. The time–space continuum that happens when you live on an island at the edge of the world. Haven't you noticed everyone here moves nice and slow?"

Sam shuddered. "Ugh. No thanks. How do people stand that? I need structure, discipline. That's how you get it done."

"Tell us something we don't know, buddy." Noah clapped Sam's shoulder. Turning to me, he said, "Hey speaking of islanders, what's the deal with Rose?" He lifted an eyebrow in suggestion.

I supposed it would be good to get their perspective. Maybe I was too in my head about her to know what was real. Besides, I wanted to watch Sam squirm by delaying awhile longer. It was good for the guy to live off the rails a little.

"We're just catching up is all." Noah and Sam exchanged nods. I guessed they'd presumed as much.

"The one who got away?" Noah said.

"Something like that." I rubbed my eyes with the backs of my hands. I needed to tell them what happened ten years ago. I couldn't put it off any longer. "You know I grew up here, but what you don't know is why—or how—I left. The circumstances were…less than ideal." I told them about my dad, about his scheme to swindle money out of people who trusted us, about our disappearing act—and about how I'd lost my connection to everything I knew in one fell swoop.

"You didn't even say goodbye?" Sam probably couldn't imagine not going through his list of friends and acquaintances and making sure they all had his new address.

Shame burned my cheeks, and I covered my face with my hands. "I wanted to," I said quietly, "but I just…couldn't. You don't understand."

"Try us," Sam said.

"It was so humiliating. I was so ashamed." I looked down to see my knuckles turning white. "And it was impossible to fit into this new world in Seattle. It was enough just to keep my head above water until I could join up."

"You do know it wasn't your fault, right?" Noah

sat back in the booth. "From my perspective, I gotta say it looks like she forgives you. Or wants to, at least." He tapped his fingers on the red leather upholstery. "That's about all you can ask for."

"But what if…" Why was it so hard to say it out loud? "What if I want more?" There. I'd said it out loud. No one laughed. No one told me it was impossible. They simply listened and nodded. "But she's got a farm to run, a business to save, a grandfather who needs her. And with this leg, and the Quinn reputation…" I trailed off.

"Hey, if it's meant to happen, it'll happen." Noah's arms were spread wide on the back of the booth, an eagle spanning the wind.

"Hah! That's not a thing." Sam unfolded his napkin on the table and folded it again. "When you want something, you've got to work at it. This is no different. You need to show her she can't live without you. That you're the right man for the job. The right man for the farm. The right man for her."

They were both right in their own way. I needed to show Rose I cared not just about her but also the farm and its future—and Pappy. But I knew I couldn't force her hand. I wanted her to want it as much as I did.

"Seriously, can we go now?" Sam's patience finally broke, and he stood up from the table. "If we don't get a good night's sleep, tomorrow is ruined."

Noah pushed himself up, too. "Wondered how long you'd last," he said, laughing.

I pulled the phone from my pocket and checked the time as I got up. "A whole twenty minutes! Just wait. We'll get you on island time yet," I told Sam. I waited for the blood to flow through my leg. "Let's do it."

With a long look at Fern behind the bar, Sam led us up the three steps to the lobby. "She's pretty, all right," he said as we waited for the elevator under the lifeless eyes of a taxidermy deer hanging above the door. "But how could you take things seriously if you work at a bar? Life isn't all cocktails and late nights. Sooner or later you have to get serious."

"Oh, right. Tick tock." Noah referenced the schedule Sam had in his mind for how—and when—things were supposed to happen in his life. According to his calculations, he had only a year before he reached the age he planned to marry.

The elevator door slid open. "All I know is this movie better wrap on time so I can get off this island and find the woman of my dreams." He boarded the elevator in front of us. Noah and I eyed rolled eyes at each other as we stepped in behind him.

The next morning, on my way to Grind House, I thought about *Shore Thing*. It might have big-name stars, but as Domino's first producing project, she'd taken it on with a smaller budget and fewer resources so she could get the hang of things. It was why she'd agreed to hire three underwater cameramen who weren't that experienced in film. And it was why I hadn't raised any questions about the "accident" that had claimed Chip Thurlow's narrowboat.

Sam, Noah, and I were united in our commitment to the project. We showed up on time and prepared, happy to take direction and willing to offer opinions when asked. I was also conscious of making the shoot a positive experience for Orcas Island. Even though I no longer lived here, the last thing I wanted was to give anyone from my past more reason not to trust me.

Today we were filming an underwater sequence—the most important sequence of the movie. I mentally scrolled through the shot list as I walked past the now-familiar shops and restaurants on Water Street. I'd grown fond of seeing Ginger every day. In high school she'd been the smartest kid in our class. Everyone had expected her to leave Orcas Island and never come back. She'd excelled at science and math and even won an award for her grades. Since I'd been here, I'd learned she did go away to school—to Stanford, to study geophysics. But after a few years at a tech start-up in Silicon Valley, she'd left sunny California with an ache in her heart to return to her old community.

She wanted to do something at home, she realized, where she could make a difference to people's lives every day.

It'd seemed like an odd choice when she first told me, but now I'd been here a few weeks and seen how she lit up with every customer she served, I had a sense Ginger was right. I admired that about her; she'd found out what she *didn't* want to do, taken the time to explore it, and decided on a career that aligned with her personal values. I couldn't find fault in that. She infected everyone around her with joy and positivity, always with a friendly smile and a skip in her step. Today she and Julian Cooper, a kid of about eighteen who worked with her most mornings, were talking about where they could find fans for the café.

"Hardware store?" I named what I thought was the obvious answer.

"Sold out," Julian said as he slid a coffee across the counter to me.

I shrugged. "I'm sure you'll find one somewhere. See you tomorrow," I told Ginger, picking up my espresso and doughnut. On my way to the door, Angela Fletcher waved from her stool by the window.

"Hello, August?" A bicycle helmet rested on the counter beside a small black notebook, a pen clipped along its spine. When I was a kid, Angela Fletcher was known for riding her bike all across the island, in all kinds of weather. It looked like that hadn't changed.

"Hi, Ms. Fletcher." I stopped at the door and nodded, hands full with the pastry and my cup.

"Please, it's Angela now." Her short red hair had faded to auburn, and her face was creased with lines, but her round green eyes were just as lively as I remembered them. "So you're here for the movie, are you?"

"Yes, ma'am— I mean, Angela."

She slid the pen out of the notebook and flipped it open. Pages and pages were filled with neat handwriting. "Tell me, what happened with Chip Thurlow?"

I squirmed under her inquisitive gaze. She held the pen above the page, ready to take notes on whatever I told her. I cleared my throat, stalling while I figured out what to say. Was she hoping I'd incriminate him somehow? Or was she implying I was in cahoots with him? A bead of sweat trickled between my shoulder blades. "I'm afraid I can't say, Ms. Fletch—I mean, Angela. Why, what have you heard?"

Angela's lip twitched to one side, and she tsked with disappointment as she flipped the notebook closed. "Oh, you know. Everyone's got a different story. Just thought since you were there, you might have—"

"Well, I don't. Sorry." I looked at my wrist where there would be a watch if I wore one, clasping my doughnut in its wax-paper bag. "Anyway, Angela. Nice to see you again. I have to be going."

Before she could even say goodbye, I elbowed the door open and stepped outside. A seagull squawked on the wind above, and the sun glimmered off the water in the bay. Leo Wolffe lifted a wave as we passed on the sidewalk. It was a normal morning on Water Street. So why was my heart racing in my chest?

Calm down. She didn't mean anything by it, I repeated in my mind on the way to the production office. But the acceptance I'd gradually convinced myself I felt here turned shaky with fear the community still didn't trust me.

I stopped just inside the doors of the production space, letting my eyes adjust to the dim light. Sam was bent over a table on the left side, checking the equipment we needed today. Noah hadn't arrived yet.

"Hey, you're from here," Sam said as I set my coffee on the table. "What do you know about this heat dome that's coming?" He seemed even more fidgety than usual this morning, checking and rechecking the cameras and their underwater housing.

"Heat dome?" Being on a team with someone as prepared as Sam over the years had meant learning about every new meteorological term—which seemed to be increasing in number. We'd worked through a polar vortex, thundersnow, even a weather bomb. But heat dome was a new one.

He slid the phone out of his pocket and called up a weather app. When he turned the screen to face me, I was shocked by the blocks of bold text I saw. I moved closer, squinting to see what it said. "Extreme heat warning," I read aloud. A map of Washington State was overlaid with varying shades of red, from bright orange to angry-looking burgundy, indicating predicted temperatures over the next three days.

"Jesus. What does that say, a hundred and four degrees?" I shook my head. "Not around here, it won't be."

"It's all over the news. You haven't heard?"

"Nah, man. Although that'll be why they were talking about fans at the coffee shop."

The big barn doors opened, and light flooded the space. Once inside, Noah shut them again, sending us back into darkness.

"Hey, you hear about the weather?" He set a large stainless-steel water bottle on the table. "Think we ought to change out any gear?"

"I was just thinking that," Sam said. "I mean, while we're under, everything will be fine. It's keeping the equipment cool on the boat we need to worry about."

I held up a hand. "Listen, guys. I know I haven't

lived here in a while, but I can tell you one thing. I know the Pacific Northwest. And heat bombs, or heat domes, or whatever you want to call it—they just don't happen here. Hell, we barely get anything close to a heat *wave*." I gestured to the rolling shelf that held all our camera equipment. "It's fine. It'll all be fine. Trust me."

"But—" Sam started.

"Don't worry about it. I mean, beyond your usual level of concern." I chuckled as I tore open the bag that held my doughnut and took a seat at the table. "All right, should we go over today's scenes one last time?" I bit into the soft, fluffy pastry, glazed in sugar syrup that looked like a layer of ice. "Guys?" I prompted when they didn't join me.

Noah was glued to his phone, uncharacteristic worry wrinkling his forehead. "Okay, yeah," he said, glancing up at me. "But it says here to expect the hottest temperature in history on Monday. Listen to what the *Washington Post* says: 'An exceptional weather pattern and climate change have cooked up a heat wave unmatched in regional intensity.' I dunno, August. I'm with Sam on this one. I think we oughtta be careful."

Sam finally stopped fidgeting with the equipment and pulled out a seat at the table. "Take it from me. I know heat—I'm from San Diego, remember?"

"Hmph." I wasn't convinced there was anything to panic about.

"Except in San Diego we're used to it," he added. "Everyone has air conditioning."

I shrugged. "Well, either way, we need to be ready to shoot. If it gets that hot, we can worry about things then."

CHAPTER 13

Rose

I dried the sweat on my forehead with my shirt sleeve as I packed up my table at the close of the market. It was a hot afternoon, the brown grass beyond the rows of stalls alive with cricket chirps and the warbling songs of the purple finch. All anyone had talked about today was the weather. "Thousand-year record event" and "unprecedented heat" were phrases I'd heard repeated all afternoon.

Even without the heat wave, I had enough to worry about, not the least of which was the certification agent's visit on Thursday.

Next to me, Ida's husband, Bob, began dismantling

the Pies & Otherwise tent while Ida collected her few remaining jam jars and paper-wrapped bundles of chocolate-chip cookies. "Think it'll get as hot as they say?" Bob said when he saw me watching him.

"Sure hope not. But keep an eye on this one, will you?" I pointed at Ida. "We've already had one scare. Let's not have another."

"Oh, stop your fussing," Ida said. "Here, take one of these." She tucked a bundle of cookies into one of my baskets.

"Normally I'd say no, since you know I can't eat just one. But I need to stress eat."

She laughed, squeezing my hand.

"If only I were kidding." I took a cookie from the package, holding it between my teeth while I wrapped the rest back up. "The certification agent is coming this week. Even my usually unflappable pappy is…well, flapped." I bit into the buttery chocolate-chip cookie and closed my eyes in bliss. It was perfect: crispy on the outside, soft and dense inside, with creamy chocolate chips and a hint of crunch from toasted pecans. I opened my eyes to find Ida smiling at me. "The chocolate is just soft enough it's like it's warm from the oven. Delicious. Thank you."

"I'm a phone call away if you want more," she said. "If it's chocolate-chip cookies you and Felix need to power you through this week, I'm ready."

I brushed a loose strand of hair from my eyes and pulled Ida in for a sweaty hug. Bob waited patiently, munching on a cookie of his own.

Ida held my shoulders at arm's length. "You got this." She gave me a gentle shake. "Go on. Tell that sweet grandfather of yours we say hello." She backed away to where Bob waited.

Bob tipped an imaginary hat in my direction. "Until next week."

Minutes later they drove off, their tires crunching as the car hit the gravelly road that led out of the grounds. I sat cross-legged in the dry grass by the van and ate another cookie. It *was* getting warmer, but things would cool down the way they always did at night by the ocean. I peered over my table at the remaining vendors. Everyone seemed to be moving more slowly than usual as they closed down their stalls.

"Cold brew?"

I jumped in my spot, nearly tossing the cookie I was holding. From where I was sitting, I couldn't see anyone passing by. I pushed the ground behind me and stood, peeling the damp shirt from my back.

"Ooh, yes please. Wait—let me get my cup." I bent down to fumble around in my baskets for the thermal tumbler I'd emptied of water. I held it out to Ginger.

My red-headed friend filled it from a large carafe,

the sides of which were dripping with moisture from all the ice it held. I took a sip, turning to Ginger in surprise. "Wow, that's different!" It was slightly sweet, with an added jolt that made it especially refreshing.

"Glad you like it. You *do* like it, don't you?"

"I've never had anything that tastes even remotely like this does." I took another sip of coffee, trying to identify the flavor on my tongue. "So great. What's in it?"

"I'm trying something new. It's called *kopi jahe*. It's Indonesian coffee with ginger. I've only seen it served hot before, so I wanted to get people's opinions before I put it on the menu at Grind House."

"Coffee with ginger? What a great idea." I reached for the package Ida had given me. "Here, you have to have one." I handed a cookie to Ginger.

She rested her carafe on my table and bit into it, closing her eyes like I did when it melted in her mouth. "When I make chocolate-chip cookies, they never taste like this." She chewed another bite and swallowed, then tapped the cookie against the cup of cold brew in my hand. "So what do you think? Too on the nose with the ginger?"

"No, no. Just the opposite. I say go for it." I tasted it again. "What else is in there?"

"The coffee and ginger, plus crushed cardamom

pods, coconut milk, a little brown sugar." She smiled. "I love TikTok. I always learn the coolest things."

I barely managed to have Instagram and Facebook profiles for Big Oak, which my customers were always begging me to update. It never failed to drop to the bottom of my to-dos. "You're amazing, Ginger. Seriously. I'm so proud of Grind House—and how you somehow knew just what you wanted to do. Just what the community needed."

Pink colored her cheeks like sun-blushed apples. "Are you kidding? *You* inspire *me*. Big Oak Farm has the best produce on the island. And you manage it all by yourself, with your grandfather? All the farms around here have teams of men doing all the hard work. It's kinda unbelievable, really. It's the best way to honor your mom."

Now it was my turn to blush. "Well, will you look at us—a real mutual-admiration society, aren't we?" I slung an arm around her shoulder. "Now, about your plans for this coffee. Need ginger root on the regular? 'Cause I happen to know someone who grew a bunch last year."

She clasped her hands together. "That'd be a dream! Aren't I the lucky one. But isn't ginger a fall plant?"

"It is, but last year was our first time growing it, and we didn't plant enough to sell. So I peeled it, chopped it into knobs, and threw it in the freezer. I'll bring some by this week, and you can make sure it works for you. On the house."

Ginger, too, was one of the girls on the island named for a native plant. When she was born with a shock of red hair, Ginger had been the obvious choice. The wild ginger native to the Pacific Northwest was different from the Asian kind most people used for cooking, though. Local ginger was an evergreen plant with thick roots, trailing stems, and heart-shaped leaves that smelled like spicy lemon when you crushed them between your fingers. It was important to me to plant and nurture native plants wherever I could on the farm; some of Ginger's namesake grew in the shady, wooded area at the western edge of the property.

"In that case, you can help me name it. Any ideas? Something memorable. The Summer Kick, maybe?"

I thought about it. "Got it." I snapped my fingers. "The Big Chill."

"The Big Chill. I love it!"

We stood side by side for a few minutes watching the folks around us pack up and leave. I sipped my Big Chill while Ginger took tiny nibbles of cookie, trying to make it last as long as she could. A trail of cars and trucks lined the gravel drive out of Grange Hall. In no time at all it was just me, Ginger, and Zoe, the tarot card reader, dawdling under the shade of our tents. I inadvertently caught Zoe's eye, then quickly averted my gaze, but she sent me a friendly wave anyway.

I waved back reluctantly. The last thing I wanted was another forecast of bad luck, but it was too late. She came barreling toward us, a flurry of long skirts and scarves. Her bracelets jangled as she approached. "Incoming," I muttered under my breath to Ginger.

"Hello there, ladies!" Zoe said. I had to give her props for one thing: she didn't shy away from talking to people.

"Hi, Zoe," Ginger said. I smiled politely.

"Listen, I've been thinking about that reading I gave you, Rose." Up close like this, it was clear Zoe's long-sleeve black shirt and ankle-length skirt weren't ideal for the heat. Droplets of sweat dotted her forehead, and her hair was damp and limp.

"Let's not, okay? I have an important week coming up, and I don't need some kind of curse hanging over it."

"Curse? I would *never* issue a curse." She shook her head wildly, her drop earrings swinging. "I know, the Death card is shocking. I could see on your face I didn't explain it very well. What it means is—"

I interrupted her. "Really, Zoe. It's nice of you to come over here, but as I explained that day, I don't believe in this stuff anyway." I tossed my empty tumbler in one of my baskets on the ground. "You know, it's almost worse when someone tells you about a superstition or something, because it almost seems like bad luck *not* to follow it." Zoe looked crestfallen. I'd been a little blunt. I backpedaled. "It's okay. I know you mean no harm. It's just not for me."

She shrugged, but I still sensed I'd hurt her. "Suit yourself," she said. "You know where to find me if you change your mind."

Looking from me to Zoe, Ginger picked up her carafe and linked arms with the tarot card reader. "I'll take a reading, Zoe. And you can be another taste-tester for me." She led Zoe in the direction of the table and chairs still set up outside her stall. "Thanks for the cookie, Rose. Good luck this week!"

Ginger glanced back over her shoulder at me, and I held my hands together in a prayer position at my chest. "Thank you," I mouthed before I folded my table, packed up the van, and got on the road.

Dinner tonight? I texted August when I'd pulled to a stop in front of the cottage. I grabbed the brown-paper bag from beside me and hopped down from the driver's seat. I'd picked up feta, olives, and a few other things I needed for Greek salad from Mimo's General Store in Winslow on the way home from Grange Hall. Pappy could barbecue the chicken breasts I'd thawed this morning so we could avoid turning on the oven.

It was stiflingly hot. I headed for the porch, my shirt stuck to my back with sweat. Maybe there was something to the weather warnings, after all. Usually by late afternoon on Orcas Island, the temperature began to drop, even in midsummer, as cool air came in off the Pacific. Today, though, the heat was holding steady. I climbed the two steps to the porch and squinted to read the outdoor thermometer that'd been fixed to the side of the cottage for as long as I could remember. Seventy-seven degrees. I frowned. That was definitely high. I waved to Pappy, who was watering the raised beds now the sun was off them. Fig lay in the grass nearby, chewing on a bone.

My phone buzzed on the kitchen counter as I put away the groceries and a rustic white loaf I'd bought from Ida first thing this morning. **Already on my way,** August's text read. **What can I bring?**

Just handcuffs and a blindfold, I tapped back, giggling. I'd forgotten how fun it was to flirt. **And maybe a six pack.**

Three dots appeared on the screen, indicating he was typing back. They disappeared, then appeared again. **Can't stop thinking about the last time I came for dinner,** he texted, followed by the blushing-face emoji.

I got that giddy feeling in my chest, the one where it felt like your heart might burst out of your skin. I'd felt it a few times since the night I spent with August, remembering the feel of his skin against mine, being cocooned in his arms, safe from everything in the world. But whenever I felt it rise, I tried to tamp it down, each time a little less successfully. I smiled again despite myself. The idea that I was hanging out at the farm, waiting for my high-school sweetheart to show up for dinner, had been unimaginable a month ago.

I rushed to shower before he arrived, setting the temperature to low, letting the water soothe my nerves. After a few minutes under the cold stream, I zeroed in on a singular thought: *Don't let your head talk you out of what your heart wants.*

Toweling dry afterward, I felt confident I'd landed on a breakthrough moment. That was exactly what I'd been doing all these years: letting my mind deny what was obvious in my heart. Maybe it was time to let the past go. *Really* let it go. Free myself of the heartache I'd held for a decade and let rule my life. It had influenced how I interacted with people, how I responded to things, whom I depended on. For ten years, I'd been incapable of real trust—which meant denying myself the joy and pleasure that came from meeting new people and being a true part of the community. For ten years, Pappy and Bluebell had been the only people I counted on.

It was time to break those chains and start *living*

again. I felt it in my bones.

I had August to thank for that. Even if his presence here was temporary, he'd broken through my defenses enough I could see him for who he really was: a friend.

My wet hair dripped down my shoulders as I stood in front of my closet, struggling to pick something to wear. In the end I chose a black-and-white-striped boatneck tee and black linen shorts that were light-weight and showed off my tanned legs. I was pleased at what I saw in the mirror. Fresh, clean, and just the right amount of sexy for dinner with my ex-boyfriend and grandfather.

I heard the crush of gravel and a squeak of brakes as a vehicle pulled to a stop outside the cottage. Tucking my wet hair behind my ears, I went to the porch, where Pappy was already greeting August, a big grin on his face. Fig's little body wagged from side to side as she waited to be petted.

I stood in the doorway, admiring the man August had become. I could finally see him for who he was now, not the boy I'd held in my memory all those years. His skin was golden from hours on the water. A white T-shirt clung to his muscles in all the right places, his bicep flexing when he shook Pappy's hand. And he was back in those perfectly faded Levi's he'd worn last week. He'd always worn Levi's. I loved the way they hinted at his ass without hugging it, like a Bruce Springsteen album cover.

When he noticed me by the door, I let the warmth of his gaze wash over me, erasing any lasting effects from the cold shower. I took in the genuine happiness in his expression, the sexy lines that framed his green eyes when he smiled, his teeth white against his tanned skin. Pappy stood there, watching the two of us look at each other, a satisfied glimmer in his eyes at the connection sparking between us.

"Hi, Ro." August came to my side and wrapped an arm over my shoulder, giving me a gentle hug. "Should I put these in the fridge?" He held up a six-pack. Summer Haze Wheat Ale. The man had a good memory.

"Oh, yes!" I suddenly found my manners. "Sorry, I don't know where my mind went."

Pappy chuckled, and I could have sworn I heard him say, "I do," under his breath.

"Come on in." I opened the screen door and motioned August inside, Pappy and Fig behind him. "Let me grab some glasses."

"No need. I'm happy with a bottle. Unless you want one?"

I shook my head. "Fine by me." I took the cold beer he handed me and held it against my neck, letting its condensation drip down my shirt and between my breasts.

"What can I do to help?"

"Nothing at all. Everything's ready—just waiting for you before we put the chicken on the barbecue. Pappy, you good?"

When Pappy nodded, I pulled a plate of seasoned chicken breasts from the fridge, removed the plastic wrap, and handed it to him. Beer in one hand and plate of meat in the other, he kicked open the screen door, whistling Jack Johnson's "I Got You" as he went.

August laughed. "Pretty hip for an old guy."

I rolled my eyes. "That's my fault, I think. I like playing mellow music when we garden. It makes the plants happy."

"This from a woman who balks at tarot cards?" He looked at me questioningly. "You don't seriously buy that, do you?"

I took a long sip of beer, then set the bottle on the counter and began slicing thick rounds of Ida's bread. I shrugged. "Look it up. Plenty of studies on it. Best theory is the vibration of sound waves helps transport nutrients." I grabbed a fistful of fresh oregano from the kitchen counter and held it up. "Reserve judgment, why don't you, until *after* you eat dinner?"

"I'll keep an open mind, promise." He held up a hand like he was swearing on a bible.

With the bread in a basket and covered with cloth,

I put my hands to my hips and surveyed the room. "I know I set the table in here, but I think we should eat outside. Feels like we had the oven on even though we didn't."

August collected the three plates I'd set on the table along with the cutlery and napkins. "Gotta say, I'm surprised it hasn't cooled down yet."

I admired the way his muscles moved under his shirt. When I glanced up to his face, it was spread with a big grin. He'd caught me. I wasn't embarrassed by it, though. I was allowed to admire beauty, wasn't I? I smiled back cheekily as he nudged open the screen door, arms full.

"Ready now?" Pappy was happily cooking chicken breasts, almost dancing in place as he moved them around the grill with a set of tongs.

"One more minute," he said. I ducked back into the kitchen to fetch the Greek salad from the fridge and the basket of bread.

We sat at the little table on the front porch, passing around the big bowl of chopped cucumber, tomatoes, olives, green peppers, onions, and feta—and fresh oregano from the garden. The combination of hot, humid air, the flavor of fresh food, and the company of my beloved pappy and—well, my good friend, I supposed—filled my heart with gratitude. Finally, after all these years, I felt at peace.

August

What a difference a week had made, I thought as I crunched on Greek salad and watched Rose sip beer from the bottle. Last Saturday under the old oak tree it had felt impossible to break down the walls she'd built around herself. Yet here we were, seven days later, and she seemed open, tender, willing to let me into her heart. I couldn't take my eyes off her as twilight descended, coloring the sky around the cottage in strokes of gold and pink. I'd been all over the world with USERT, but nothing compared to sunsets on Orcas Island.

"Tell me, August, how's the motion picture going?" Felix asked as he laid his knife and fork on his plate.

"They're just called movies these days, Pappy," Rose teased.

"Aha! Movie, then. What's it like, being part of that?"

For a man like Felix, who'd spent his whole life working the soil with his hands, movie-making was probably all mystery and magic. "It's really cool," I said. "I bet you'd love it. Like farming, you get to see the fruits of your labor pretty quick."

"Oh?" Felix leaned on his elbows, resting his chin in his hands. He looked tired. We all did; heat did that to you.

"You know right away if you're doing a good job. We watch the footage the day we shoot it. Which is good and bad. Bad in that if you're not doing a good job, everyone else knows it, too. But that can work in reverse as well." I scratched my chin in thought. "I've only worked on two movies before, but this one is kinda…different."

"How so?" Rose asked.

"I dunno. A lot of problems."

"You mean like Chip's rotten old boat?" Felix chuckled.

Just the mention of Chip's name quickened my pulse. "Like that, yah, and just… This stays here, right?"

"Mm-hmm." Rose leaned back in her chair, folding her leg up and resting her heel on the edge of the seat.

"Well, for one, Damon Mann keeps getting seasick."

Felix's eyebrows shot up. "Damon who?"

"That's the lead actor, Pappy," Rose said. "Remember in *Badlands*, the guy who played the sheriff?"

Felix nodded. "That's him."

"Anyway, he insisted on doing his own stunts, which in *Shore Thing* means a lot of dives. Turns out he's no natural."

"Uh oh," Rose said.

"Other stuff, too. The director—you've met him, Rose. He's... I'll just say *exacting*. When things don't go perfectly, all hell breaks loose on set. So it's been hard."

"What about that actress, the one who married Forest Russo?" Felix asked.

"Domino? She's great. A real pro and a pleasure to be around. Between her and being here on the island, it's a toss-up which one's keeping me motivated at this point."

I explained some of the challenges of underwater filming and how important it was to get things right the first time. In the water, you didn't have the advantage of endless takes, the way you did on land. I spoke, too, about working with Noah and Sam and how much their friendship meant to me.

Seeing Felix's eyelids growing heavy, Rose touched him lightly on the shoulder. "You don't have to stay up with us, Pappy." She indicated the empty plates and bowls in front of us. "We got this."

"Thanks, sweetheart," he said, getting to his feet. Fig stretched her legs out in front of her. "One beer does it to me every time." He leaned over to kiss Rose's cheek. "Good night, kids. This was a treat."

I stood to shake his hand. "Night, Felix. Sleep well."

Once he disappeared into the cottage, Fig trotting behind him, Rose stood, too, and began clearing the table. She reached for the salad bowl just as I did, our fingers touching, the bowl caught between us like some kind of lightning rod. I held her gaze. "I got it."

She looked down, as if hoping I wouldn't notice the blush that colored her cheeks. "Okay," she said, letting go of the bowl. "C'mon, let's get this stuff inside."

While she loaded the dishwasher, I rinsed the empty beer bottles and wiped the counters. Once we were done, we stood staring at each other, the sounds of crickets and katydids outside punctuating the air.

"I have an idea," I said, reaching out a hand. "Trust me?"

CHAPTER 14
Rose

"Trust me." It was the second time he'd asked for my trust. My rib cage tightened, my heart suddenly thudding in my chest as my nervous system prepared for battle. But instead of heeding my involuntary response to August's words, I steadied my breath and connected with the earnestness in his clear green eyes. *Follow him*, I instructed my body. I grabbed on before I could stop myself, his fingers steady and strong in mine.

He led me out into the dusky twilight, down the steps, and to the van he'd borrowed from the crew. "What's with the two of us and vans?" I laughed as I climbed up into the passenger seat and hefted the creaky old door closed.

August slapped a hand against the dashboard. "I dunno, but let's go with it. Hasn't led us astray yet." We wound down the windows to let out the trapped heat.

Dust kicked under the tires as he reversed, then headed down the driveway to the main road. Tom Petty sang "American Girl" on the radio.

I hummed along. I couldn't help myself. It felt like the perfect song, on the perfect night, with the perfect man. I felt myself falling deeper into the good feelings that'd begun to form around August again.

The chorus came on, and we sang at the tops of our lungs. I looked at August next to me, grinning ear to ear as he navigated the familiar roads. Outside, the trees were black against a purple sky as the last of the day made way for the stars. Wind whipped my hair around my head like blades of wheat in a storm. I felt gloriously free in a way I hadn't in years.

"Where are we going?" We were heading south, toward the tip of the island.

He glanced at me, surprise in his features. "You don't remember?"

"What?" I filed through my memories of the places we'd frequented in our youth. "No. Are you kidding me? But we don't have any bathing suits..."

August nodded enthusiastically, his eyes back on the road. "Don't need 'em. Feel how hot it still is?" He stuck his arm out the window and let his hand float on the air.

"But what about—" I threw my head back and laughed. "Okay. I'm in. What the hell."

He reached for my thigh and wrapped his fingers around it, and I couldn't stop smiling. Butterflies whooshed through my stomach as he slowed to turn down a road lit only by the moon. "Hasn't changed much," he said, squeezing my knee. "Guess it's still a secret."

He stopped at the end of the road, lifting his hand from my leg to put the van in Park and shut off the engine. He leaned across the console and kissed my cheek, his lips soft.

"What was that for?"

"Just... You make me happy is all."

I let his words sink in, willing away the instinct to protect myself from the fear I would lose him again. I opened the passenger door and slipped out before he could pull the keys from the ignition. "What're you waiting for, chicken? Let's go!" I took off running down the beach, tugging off my shirt as I went, tossing it to the sand behind me.

August

I chased behind Rose, kicking off my boots and yanking my shirt over my head, any pain in my knee tranquilized by excitement. A white lace bra glowed in the sand where she'd thrown it, and desire bolted through me like lightning. When my toes hit the sand, I stopped to shuck off my jeans and boxer briefs. I felt light in my body, limbs tingling with energy, being with Rose after all these years.

She was just ahead of me, her figure silhouetted in the glow of a half-moon. The water was flat, a mirror of the stars above. She turned back to find me, her breasts like pale white orbs, tipped with nipples the shape of rosebuds. The smooth curves of her stomach trailed down to a delicate V. My cock, hard in the warm night air, throbbed with need.

"Race you to the rock." Without waiting for a response, she started into the water, taking two large leaps, then diving under. She surfaced a moment later, her wet hair shiny as she swam toward the rock I knew from memory was a hundred yards out in the bay. I leaped in after her, the saltwater like silk on my skin.

A minute later I was passing her, my strokes long and even. Sheltered from currents and heated by the long day of sun, the Pacific was a few degrees warmer than its usual frigid temperature.

I slowed when I neared the dark outline of the rock rising from the ocean like the smooth head of a giant. Grasping at a fracture in its surface, I pulled myself from the water and sat down. As solid and cool as it was beneath me, it was no match for the flames of passion burning in my veins.

"No fair," Rose called from the water, her strokes graceful. "The rock" in East Sound was a secret only locals knew. On summer nights it had always filled up with teens, thrilled to have a few hours to themselves, newly exploring their bodies and the power of hormones. I wondered if they'd been here earlier.

I was spellbound with longing for the woman I watched rise from the water in one long, fluid glide. I admired her confidence, her awareness of her body and what it was capable of. Her hair slicked back, her skin glistening wet in the moonlight, she was breath-taking. Her chest heaved with the effort of swimming. I reached for her hand, and when she took hold, I tugged her down beside me.

I held her gaze, her brown eyes soft, her eyelashes wet and long. I ran a hand down her back, watching her chest rise and fall. Knees bent, her leg brushed the scar on my calf. I flinched at first, by instinct, then relaxed. She'd seen it before. When she reached for my cock, I let my legs fall straight and leaned back on my palms.

She stroked it gently at first, then squeezed tighter as pressure built within me. I was hard as the rock we were on, and she knew just how to touch me. I moaned. Everything was different between us now, but not this. This connection we shared—the ability to understand each other with just one touch—was as strong today as it was a decade ago.

I moaned once more, and she let out a groan as well. I wrapped my hand around hers and lifted it, grasping it between us, my belly on fire.

"Let me." I shifted to face her, the round silver moon reflecting in her eyes like two pools of ice. My gaze went to her lips, then back to her eyes, then back once more before I leaned in and kissed her. I couldn't hide how she made me feel. I never wanted to stop touching her, feeling her skin next to mine, inhaling the delicate scent of roses that followed wherever she went. Now I was near her, the past ten years felt like a diver swimming for the light, lungs bursting with the need for air. I could breathe now. I'd made it to the surface.

I laid her back on a flat part of the rock. She let me look at her, my eyes traveling her body, taking in every curve, igniting my senses from the inside out. I loved her like this: vulnerable, ripe with desire, naked. I stared at her for as long as she let me, trying to commit what I saw to memory, before I bent my head to kiss her breasts, round and lovely under the stars.

CHAPTER 15

Rose

My senses spiked curveballs at me that blurred the lines between the rock, the sea, the air around us, and me. It all felt superheated, and I didn't know if it was the heat dome or the fervor August had whipped in my loins. He kissed the curve of my stomach, then positioned himself above me, and my heart beat like a hummingbird trapped in a net. When we made love last week it was beautiful, but this…this was lightning in a bottle. He stretched me open, his tongue light and feathery, and my pussy clamped around his fingers as I began to lose control.

We heard the echo of my moans across the water.

My pussy throbbing, I tangled my fingers in his hair, urging him on, to keep holding me open, keep lifting me toward ecstasy. Swells of pleasure floated through me like a rising wave, until a surge of euphoria rushed to my core, the stars in the sky spinning like fireworks behind my eyes.

Afterward, August lay beside me, an enormous smile on his face. He traced a finger from my collarbone to my belly button. "You're incredible," he said.

"You just shattered my world, August Quinn." Floating back to earth, I began to notice the sights and sounds around me again. Water gently rippled against the rock. A heron croaked in the distance. I slowly pushed to sit, pulling my knees to my chest. August sat up beside me, droplets of sweat trickling down the lines of his chest. "Lie back again," I said.

His eyes locked to mine, and he rolled back against the rock, clasping his hands behind his head. Sprawled out like this, his cock pointed straight up to the moon, thick and proud. It was my turn to take him to the heavens.

I curled over his body, my breasts grazing his thighs as I ran my tongue up the length of him and down again. He squirmed with pleasure. I took him in my mouth, wrapping him in heat that sent the salty taste of him down my throat. I sucked in and out, in and out, his cock growing impossibly harder. His balls tightened in my hand, and I sensed him slip out of this world and into another as he let out a guttural moan. I felt his hands around my ears, his groans coming louder now, until— "Rose, I'm gonna…" But before he could voice it, electricity pulsed through him, and he pumped into me from deep inside.

I lay back next to him, splayed naked on the rock again, and grasped his arm. In all the years he was gone, no one had made me feel the way August did.

He knew my greatest hopes, my worst fears, my wildest dreams. And I knew his. That much remained.

But this was nothing like old times. My mind flooded with unwanted thoughts: about the way he'd left, about the farm—and about how his time here was temporary. Yes, we were back in each other's lives— for now. But I couldn't depend on him, the way I depended on the sun rising in the morning and setting at night.

"Rose, I think we should…"

The sound of his voice called me to the present, back to this rock at the end of the world. I sat up. "Get back before our clothes are washed away by the tide?" I finished for him.

He sat, too. "We should talk, I meant. About this. About us." He gestured to the space between our naked bodies.

Whatever he was about to say, I bristled at the

thought of ending this magical moment with words we might not be sure we meant. I brushed off his suggestion. "We will." I bent my knees and leaned forward to stand. "But I'm not kidding about our clothes. I don't know about you, but I don't fancy a pantsless ride in that old van." With that I stepped to the edge of the rock, a spot I knew from memory was safe to dive from.

August

Rose extended her arms in line with her ears, one foot in front of the other, and pushed off in a dive that yielded so little splash I barely heard it.

I ran my fingers through my hair and laughed. She wasn't wrong. The thought of my bare ass on the ripped upholstery in the driver's seat was motivation enough to save our conversation for later. I dove off the rock and caught up with her, and together we swam to shore. The water was even more refreshing now, a salve for the intensity of what we'd just shared.

On a normal summer night, the temperature on Orcas Island dipped low enough the water felt warmer than the air. Tonight was the opposite. Maybe there was something to this heat dome, I thought as we strode out of the water and onto the beach.

Rose's striped shirt was easy to spot in the moonlight. "Here's your jeans!" she said as she grabbed them. She kicked around in the sand until she found the shorts she'd flung to the ground earlier.

I was overcome with modesty now we'd sated our desires. Figuring I could stuff my boxers in my back pocket when I found them, I slid into my jeans. The soft old denim was just as comfortable as underwear. Rose shimmied into her shorts. "Find everything?"

She bent to pick something up. "Got the other." She waved her hands in the air, each holding a sandal. "How about you?"

I stumbled upon my boots, impressed I'd taken the time to stuff my socks inside them in our race to the shore. I sat on a log to pull them on.

"Were you always this beautiful? Maybe it's the moonlight," Rose said. She leaned down to grab something else from the sand. "Your shirt." She handed it to me. "That's it, then? Do we have everything?" She tucked wet her hair behind her ears.

I scratched my chin and chuckled as I stood. "Not quite."

She looked me up and down; everything seemed to be in place. "Oh?"

"Guess I'm going commando."

She giggled and moved to stand behind me, where she wrapped her arms around my waist and gave my cock a squeeze. "So you are." I hardened again. "Oh well, maybe it'll help keep you cool," she teased. She let go and started down the beach, leaving me aching for more. "C'mon, Quinn. The sun'll be up if we stay here much longer."

At least then I might find my underwear. But Rose was right. I had to be on set at sunrise.

On the way to the van, I thought again about what I wanted to tell her. I was more certain than ever that I wanted to make things work between us. We just…fit. And in more ways than the one we'd just practiced on the rock. My first weeks on the island had been shaky, but now things felt more like they used to. We understood each other on a cellular level. I believed she saw me for everything I was now.

I'd begun to feel lovable.

My hopes for the future centered around a fresh start on Orcas Island, one that included Rose and Felix and Big Oak Farm. I hadn't told Sam and Noah yet. I wanted to wait until I had things figured out—until I was sure Rose would have me. But could she trust me? Or would she be forever waiting for me to disappear again?

I waited until we were on the road to Big Oak, the

van rattling over the old pavement as the sky lightened from black to cobalt blue. "So, Rose..."

"All right, lay it on me," she said when I hesitated. "What's going on up there?" She reached over the console and touched a finger to my temple.

I stole a glimpse at her, still figuring out what I to say. "I guess there's only one way to do this," I settled on. "Just bite the bullet and let it out."

"Uh oh. You better not be about to tell me you have an STI." She wiggled her index finger.

"What?" I laughed. "No, of course not. It's... It's just..."

"Come on, out with it, Quinn. I don't bite."

"I love you." There. I'd said it.

"O—kay?" Her inflection rose at the end like a question. "I mean, thank you. But I'm not sure what to do with that."

"I want to be together. You and me. Like before."

She sighed. "Forget before, August. There's just right now. And right now I've got a failing farm and an aging pappy to take care of, and the organic certification, and a business to save. Besides, you're leaving in—what, a month? How do you imagine this could work? How do I know you won't just disappear again? No. Uh-uh. Not gonna happen."

The road came at me in the windshield as I struggled to find the right words. "I don't know. But I'm going to figure it out."

"You'll find someone else, August."

I scratched my chin, stealing another look at her. Her arms were crossed over her chest now.

But Rose was it for me; it was no use pretending otherwise. No other woman stood a chance. When you felt so strongly about someone, how did you block out those feelings? "It's only you," I blurted, emotion tight in my throat. "It's always been you. Whatever it takes, I'll be here. You need help with the farm? I'm there. Need someone to drive vegetables around the island? I'm your guy. Need the best orgasm of your life?" I looked at her again. She smiled at that one, at least. It gave me a glimmer of hope. "August Quinn at your service."

"But what about your leg? I thought a career diving was the only thing you wanted to do now. Wouldn't working on a farm only make things worse?"

"I'll get better. I *know* I will. Promise. Whatever it takes." I pulled over and stopped the van on the side of the road, dust and gravel flying up behind us. I swiveled to face her, my chest open, pleading. "Trust me, Rose. You can trust me."

CHAPTER 16
Rose

There was that word again, but this time, instead of my pulse kicking up and shoulders tensing, I felt a sense of ease. August's green gaze in the blue hour before sunrise was so sincere I thought I might burst into tears.

My mantra from last night played across my brain like a news channel chyron. *Don't let your head talk you out of what your heart wants.* I thought, too, about what Zoe had said about the Death card. *Let in the new. Purge the baggage in your way.*

Wasn't August worth purging my baggage for? Yes, my heart screamed. Excitement lit up every cell in my body.

I unclipped my seat belt and climbed over the console, laughing as my leg caught in the strap. He pulled me into his lap, hands steady at my waist, eyes wide. I was exhilarated with possibility, intoxicated by the freedom that opened in my chest.

Cradling my cheeks, he tilted his head up to kiss me. His lips were gentle this time, without the urgency of earlier, tender and sweet. Time seemed to stop and the world around us disappeared—the old borrowed van on the side of the road, the buckle digging into my knee, and the kiss of dawn brightening the sky all ceased to exist.

"Yes," I whispered against his cheek when we finally pulled apart. We stayed locked in each other's arms, hearts pressed together, breathing in tandem, until the buzzing of August's phone broke the spell.

He reached for it in the pocket of the driver's side door, holding it over my left shoulder to shut off the alarm. "Shit," he said, laughing. "I gotta go."

As we drove among graceful evergreens, the sun casting its first long shadows, we bubbled over with ideas, cutting off each other's sentences with plans for the coming months. August would finish out the film, then join me full time on the farm. I'd work with Pappy to see the organic certification through. We'd harvest this year's crops and find new customers for the next. By the time the van rolled up the driveway, I was overcome with relief.

The farm was drenched in pink morning light, the orchard scenting the air with fruity perfume. Tiny brown wrens flitted among the trees, their sweet, trilling song welcoming the day. Everything was going to work out.

I watched until August reached the end of the drive again and disappeared down Elison Road. Kicking off my sandals, I treaded through the grass to the cottage, the ground warm under my feet. Even at this hour, my clothes were sticky against my skin. I stopped to read the old thermometer by the back door. Eighty-five degrees. I rubbed my eyes and checked again. How could it have gotten *hotter* overnight? Inside the cottage was even warmer. Too tired to do anything about it, I headed for my bedroom and collapsed on the bed, asleep before my head hit the pillow.

The sound of water hitting the roof woke me a few hours later. *It's raining now? What's next, frogs falling from the sky?* Dragging myself from the bed, I peeled off my shorts and shirt, damp with sweat, and changed into work clothes. I went to the window and drew back the curtain to peer out. Sun shone bright as a glowing flame, despite the sound of raindrops on the roof.

"Pappy?" I called into the kitchen. No response.

The door to his bedroom stood open, his bed neatly made, just as it was every morning. I pushed through the screen door to the porch, shielding my eyes from the sun.

Pappy stood a few yards from the cottage, hose pointed directly at the roof. Fig was sprawled in the dry grass next to him, tongue lolling from her mouth like a long pink ribbon. Pappy's eyes alighted when he saw me, and he waved me over.

"Morning, sunshine. Thought I'd get a jump on this heat." With his free hand, he adjusted his hat for maximum shade on his face.

"By watering the roof?" I'd seen him do a few odd things, but this took the cake.

He winked. "Don't worry. Your old pappy hasn't lost the plot. When the roof is wet, some of that water evaporates into the air, taking heat with it. Every bit of solar energy that evaporates the water is a solar energy that isn't heating the cottage."

"Huh."

"Too early for a science lesson?" He chuckled. "I'm more than just a pretty face, you know." He looked behind him to see how much hose he had to work with before moving on to the section of roof that covered the kitchen and living room. "You'd better have something to eat. I figured this wasn't the morning for a hot breakfast, but there's leftover bread, a bit of peanut butter, and coffee in the pot.”

What would I do without him? I planted a smooch on his cheek, knocking his hat sideways. “Love you, Pappy.”

“Love you too, sweetheart. Now stop wasting time. We have a lot to do today.”

Climbing the two steps up to the porch, I was almost afraid to check the thermometer. Ninety-seven. And it was barely 9:00 a.m. If I’d thought all the talk at the market yesterday was overkill, now I worried it wasn’t alarmist enough. I grabbed the phone from my room to find a local news station to listen to over breakfast.

When I tapped the screen to life, I smiled at the text message waiting for me. **Last night was incredible. I can’t get you out of my mind.**

Same. See you tonight?

August would be at work by now; I doubted he’d get the message until later. I tuned in to a live radio broadcast from Seattle and grabbed the peanut butter from the cupboard.

“We’ve already broken a record this morning, folks,” said a rich, resonant voice.

“That’s right, Joe,” a woman’s voice agreed. “Last time it was this hot was 2017. And we’re not done yet. Today will be hot, but tomorrow will be the real scorcher.”

"Better crank up those fans and drag your mattress down to the basement, Cindy," Joe told his co-host.

"Barring that, I'll hit the beach. It might be the one time in my life I run headlong into the freezing waters of Puget Sound," she said. "Okay, time for sports. The Mariners are tied two–two with the Padres—"

I tapped the screen and hit the stop button as I drank my coffee to the sound of Pappy dousing the roof with water. A familiar knot of stress took hold in my gut that had me instinctually reaching for pen and paper. It was what I always did when I was over-whelmed: I made a list. I knew from heat waves in the past the first crops to suffer were fruit—especially at this time of year, when the cherries were coming into season.

Netting, I wrote at the top of the page. When I was studying for certification, I'd read about how orchard netting was sometimes used in organic farming. The modest shade it yielded could help lower the sun's intensity on the trees it covered. Our cherries were only days away from harvest; I worried about them the most. We were counting on a bumper crop this year to fill all our orders. It was money we needed—badly.

Sprinklers, I wrote next. A bead of sweat dripped from my forehead onto the page in front of me. How were we going to make it through the day if it was already this hot? Pappy's roof-cooling technique would have to work on the fruit trees as well. We normally watered early in the morning or late at night, but today I planned to keep the sprinklers on all day if I had to.

Next on the list: *Water.* Seemed obvious, but I wasn't taking any chances. The scare with Ida was cemented in my brain. When the mercury rose, you needed to be careful. I decided I would fill as many jugs as I could and leave them in locations across the farm, so we'd never be far from a drink. I made a mental note of various trees on the property where I could set up makeshift cooling stations in the shade. Better to go overboard than not do enough when it came to keeping Pappy safe.

My phone buzzed. **You guys ok?** Bluebell's text read.

So far. You know Pappy. He's out there watering the roof. You?

What?! Ok, Pappy. :) Three dots hung on the screen as she typed another message. **Nothing like rolling brownouts at a hotel at the busiest time of year.**

I glanced up at the clock on the microwave to see it glowing steady with the correct time. **Still have power here.**

I'll come by after my shift, around 2? You'll be ready for the inspector, don't worry.

Oh god, the inspection! My focus on getting through what would likely be my hardest day ever on the farm, on the heels of the magical night with August, had pushed the organic inspection right out of my mind. But the inspector was coming this Thursday, heat dome or not. I flipped through my notebook to find the most recent list of things I needed to do before then.

My phone buzzed with another text from Bluebell. **You fall off a cliff or something? Jk. I know you're busy. See you later.**

Scanning my list helped me realize I really didn't need to panic about the inspection. All our records were organized in a binder, and on a thumb drive, to share with the inspector. I'd checked our qualifications and checked them again. Included were records of our last three years of cultivation and tillage practices, crop rotations, cover crops. I had proof we used only biological controls for pests, weeds, and diseases. And I'd kept records of the organic seeds and planting stock we'd grown for four years now. We were ready.

Provided this heat didn't destroy everything we'd worked so hard on.

I stepped out to the porch to check on Pappy, who was now watering the roof at the other end of the cottage, Fig at his feet. I flashed him a thumbs-up and went back inside. In the pantry I gathered nine one-gallon jugs to fill with ice cubes and water, then refilled the empty ice cube trays and slid them in the freezer. We would need them later.

Grabbing my Mariners cap, I went back outside with the first armful of water jugs, then trekked across the property to drop them off in the shady spots I'd plotted in my mind. On the third trip I delivered the last one—under the branches of the big Garry oak. It was already scorching, the air thick with heat. The tree's branches felt heavy around me, its leaves weighed down with humidity.

I couldn't help but think of my late-night chat here with August. Had that really been only a week ago?

I lifted my cap to wipe my forehead. How quickly I'd gone from keeping him at arm's length to agreeing to... What? Spend my life with him?

Zoe and her tarot cards were right, after all. I'd visualized a new possibility, and the change it brought was astounding. Was it really that easy? My heart leaped with hope. I started down the rise to the cottage. Suddenly I couldn't wait to share the news with Pappy.

But when I found him, he was sitting under the shade of the porch. He looked exhausted already. My stomach churned with worry.

I squeezed his shoulder and went inside to fetch a glass of water. "You know, you're right? I think it *is* cooler inside," I said, elbowing through the screen door.

"Told you so." He tipped back the glass and drank it all in one go.

"Why don't you stay here in the shade while I run to the hardware store." I fished around in the pockets of my apron to find the keys for the van.

He nodded. "Think I'll do that. Fig needs it. Look at her." He pointed to the dog splayed out under his chair. "What do you need from the store?"

"Netting. Lots of it."

"Clever girl." I knew he'd read the same information about using netting for shade. "I'll turn the sprinklers on in a minute."

"Back in a jiff."

August

Someone was banging on the door to my room at the Driftwood. "August!" I bolted upright. *Shit*. I'd meant to put my head down for ten minutes. Was that Sam? The voice shouted my name again. Definitely Sam. I rolled from the bed and grabbed a sheet to cover me.

I opened the door. Sam looked me up and down, then eyed his watch, a frown wrinkling his forehead.

"You're not ready?"

"I, uh—"

The crease in his forehead deepened. "It doesn't matter. You need to be down in the lobby in—" he twisted his wrist to look at his watch again "—fourteen minutes."

"I'll be there in ten."

"With all your stuff."

"My camera equipment?"

Sam shook his head. "Uh-uh. Pack your bag, Quinn. We're leaving Orcas. Arthur's orders." What the hell was he talking about? Before I could ask, Sam started down the hall, bypassing the elevator for the door to the stairs.

I turned back into my room and threw open the shade. It looked like half the town was on the docks or wading into the water in the bay. Two transport buses were parked out front of the hotel. The building itself was eerily quiet—no noise from the air-conditioner or showers running in other rooms. On the bedside table, the screen on the digital clock was black. *Power must be out.* I looked at my phone. Six fifteen.

I raced around gathering my belongings, hating the idea everyone was waiting for me. I'd have to text Rose when we got to...wherever we were going. I rushed to the bathroom to brush my teeth and splash water on my face.

Noah and Sam were waiting in the lobby with the rest of the crew, their luggage propped up next to them, sipping coffee and awaiting instructions. Damon Mann was especially bleary eyed at this hour. By the time I'd helped myself to a cup from the coffee station set up in the dining room, Arthur and Domino had joined the group.

"You, pull yourself together," he spat at one of his assistants, who was slumped in a chair next to me, scrolling through her phone. She jumped to her feet, gushing apologies, her cheeks dark pink.

The front door to the hotel swung open, and a grubby-looking Chip Thurlow stepped into the lobby.

What the fuck is he doing here? His eyes searched the room, and when they landed on me, he pushed through the crowd in my direction. His jeans were filthy, his hair slick with grease. "We need to talk," he leaned toward me and sneered. His breath reeked of alcohol.

I took a sideways step away from him. "No, we don't."

"Listen up," Arthur's gravelly voice shouted to get everyone's attention. The lobby area quieted. "We'll be in Pasadena by noon. The sooner we're there, the sooner we can get this fucking film finished." He stuck his pointer finger in the air. "Follow me!" He stalked to the front door, his assistants scampering behind. Domino hung back a bit, nodding assurances as the crew fell in step behind Arthur, a herd of sheep being shuffled out to pasture.

I stepped forward, too, but Chip clawed his fingers around my arm. "I mean it, man. We need to talk."

I shook his hand free, but something in his eyes stopped me. It was…sinister.

I left my suitcase where it was and looked around. "In here." I led Chip out of the lobby and into the dining room, stopping at the bottom of the stairs. It was deserted at this hour. "What do you want?" I dug my hands in my pockets, impatient to get rid of the guy.

"Do your friends know?" His beady eyes darted around the room, sweat dripping down his temples. He rocked back and forth on his feet, as if unable to stay still.

"Do my friends know what?" I peered past him to see the last of the movie crew filing out the front door.

"You know. What you did."

"Look, I don't have time for this, Chip. Goodbye." I stepped forward, but he moved sideways, blocking my path.

The smell of alcohol wafted over me again. "You'd better make time, movie boy." He smiled menacingly, his teeth yellow.

"Or what?" I moved closer to him, hands on my hips, chest forward. "My friends know everything, you little weasel. Get out of my way."

This time I used my arm to push past him. "But I bet that pretty actress doesn't know, does she? Or Mr. Big Shot out there?" He cackled behind me as I climbed the stairs to the lobby. I wanted like hell to turn back and punch the sneer right off his ugly face. Instead I clenched my jaw and kept walking.

Fern stood openmouthed behind the long front desk, but with rage choking my throat, I ducked my head, grabbed my suitcase, pushed open the front door, and stepped outside.

Arthur waited next to the buses, arms crossed in front of him, scowling impatiently while the cast and crew loaded their bags into the cargo holds. I was the last one. I lurched forward to toss in my suitcase, but my knee wobbled painfully as I stepped off the curb, knocking me off balance. My case dropped to the ground.

"Damnit, Quinn!" Arthur hissed, his face purple. "Can't you do anything right? Always with the goddamn leg. What's a loser like you doing on this crew, anyway!" Before I could respond, he spun around and climbed aboard one of the other buses, leaving me reeling.

I heard a sharp intake of breath behind me. I

hadn't seen Domino standing in the open door of my bus. *Fuck.* My ears burned with shame as I picked my suitcase off the ground and loaded it into the cargo hold. I put my foot on the stairs to climb aboard, but she laid a hand on my arm, her angelic face radiating concern. "I'm sure he didn't mean that. He's just stressed." She put a palm to her chest. "Please, let me apologize on his behalf."

I nodded, unsure how to respond exactly—or whether I even could.

"You're wonderful. Really, August. The work you and your guys are doing is fundamental to this movie. I couldn't do it without you." Her sapphire-blue eyes held so much compassion I nearly found myself apologizing to her, too. "Now, let's go to California and get this thing in the can."

I smiled, trying fiercely to act like Arthur's rebuke hadn't pierced a hole in my confidence the size of a football. As I took a seat alone at the front of the bus, fury and humiliation fought with alarm inside me about Chip's threat. He'd looked desperate.

And desperate men did desperate things.

CHAPTER 17
Rose

Pappy and I spent the rest of the morning on the netting. Based on what I'd read, we had two options for hanging it. The first involved making frames to hold it away from the branches. That wasn't an option. As each minute ticked by, the sun grew hotter—and the threat to our crops grew more dangerous. So we went with the second method: draping. We worked out a system where I stood on one side of the end of a row of trees, netting in hand, with Pappy on the other. The netting was light. I could toss it high in the air, holding on to the end, and when it fell over the first tree, Pappy could reach up and grab it. Once we'd got the first tree in a row covered, it was a matter of working our way down it, pulling the netting in long swaths on each side.

When we finished the first row, we turned back to assess what we'd done. Shrouded in white mesh, the cherry trees looked like a line of conjoined brides on their way to the altar, veils over their faces. The shamrock-green leaves of the cherry trees turned a muted pistachio under the fabric.

At the end of each row, we stopped to cool off and drink from the jugs of water I'd set there earlier. The ice had long since melted, but it kept us hydrated.

"Sort of pretty, isn't it?" I asked, gazing across the orchard.

"I s'pose." Pappy stood thinking. "Something's changed," he said. "In all our years here, we've never had to do this. The world... We made a mess, my generation. I'm so glad I listened to you about going organic. It has to be the way of the future." He patted my arm. "And I've been thinking, Rose. What do you think about hiring someone? Once we get the certification, demand for our goods is only going to grow. We have to think about the future. I'm not gonna be around forever, you know."

My shoulders slumped, the truth of his words hitting me like a sledgehammer. "But you have to be. What would I do without you?"

"Oh, you'll be all right."

I shook my head, frowning. "I don't want to think about that." I took another swig from the jug. "But I do think it's a good idea for you to start slowing down. You can't keep beating me out of bed in the mornings. And I can't keep trying to beat you out of bed either! Some days I'm so tired I can't think straight." I laughed, seeing a grin spread across Pappy's face. "I do have some good news on that front, though." Happiness bloomed in my heart at the thought of August becoming a permanent fixture on the farm.

"Oh?"

"August wants to stay."

"On the island?"

"Here. On Big Oak. With us. For good."

Pappy clapped his hands together, the joy on his face smoothing away the wrinkles. "Wow. Wow! Well, ain't that the best news. I remember you two running around here as kids, two peas in a pod. I was so sad when he left. I'm real happy he's back."

I did a little hop, then hugged my grandfather tight. "Me, too, Pappy. Me, too." I pulled my sweaty top away from my skin, my eyes drawn back to the rows of ghostly trees. The air felt like molasses. "Cherry trees are done. Just the apricots to go. Come on. Another hour of effort, then lunch."

Together we worked on the apricot trees, shrouding them in clouds of white netting, keeping our pace slow and stopping for water at the end of each row. It was two o'clock by the time we finished. Pappy headed back to the cottage while I made a loop, collecting the empty water jugs from around the property.

At the door to the cottage, I checked the thermometer. One hundred and two degrees. "Oh my god," I muttered on the way inside, arms full of jugs.

Pappy sat at the kitchen table, a wet towel around head and his shoulders, leaning over Jean-Martin Fortier's *The Market Gardener*. Two fans were pointed at him from opposite sides of the room.

"Good idea." At the sink I filled up the jugs, storing as many as I could fit in the refrigerator to keep them cold before we needed them again. I leaned down to open a drawer and grab a dish towel for myself. "Ah, that's nice." I leaned back in a chair across from Pappy once I'd soaked the towel in cold water and draped it over my neck and shoulders. "Hungry?"

He scratched his forehead. "Starved."

"Tell you what. I'll make salad. I think there's tuna in the pantry."

When we finished eating, the wet towels had warmed to the point we shrugged them off. I cleared the plates from the table, then pulled my phone from the pocket of my apron. No news from August. *He must be busy on set.*

The crunch of tires sounded on the gravel outside. Peeking through the screen door, I saw Bluebell's little red hatchback come to a stop beside the van, the windows all rolled down, her curls askew from the wind.

"My kingdom for a car with air-conditioning." She peeled herself off the seat, crawled over the middle console, and squeaked open the passenger-side door. The heat made her curls even more tightly wound than normal. The door creaked again as she kicked it shut.

She took in the rows of fruit trees veiled in netting. "Whoa. What's with the ghost trees?"

"Kinda funny, isn't it? It's netting to help keep them cool. Ish." I beckoned her into the cottage.

"Hi, Felix! Ooh, cold towels. What a great idea," she said as Pappy ran his under the tap, squeezed the water out, and draped it over his head.

"It might not be newfangled, but it works," he said.

Bluebell stuck her hands on her hips. "What's the plan for the rest of the day?"

"I want to harvest as much as I can. Pappy, why don't you go down to the estate house. We'll pick and load into crates and deliver them to you to soak in water. That way nothing sits out in the heat."

"Just show me where to start." Bluebell said.

We worked hard for the next three hours, harvesting lettuce and strawberries and potatoes and even wild roses from the raised beds and vegetable plots around the farm. I made sure we stopped for water breaks and that Pappy was keeping cool in the shade. The heat squeezed us for everything we had, but I wasn't going to stop until we'd salvaged every last leaf and vegetable we could before the sun destroyed them.

When we were finished, the three of us were soaked to the bone with sweat. Our foreheads and cheeks were smudged with dirt, and our clothes stuck to us like glue. In the parlor of the estate house, we teased one another about who looked the most ridiculous.

"Tell you what. Let's put the sprinklers on the trees, then wash up and go into town for dinner. My treat," Pappy said. "We could all use a few hours of air-conditioning."

"Meet you back at the cottage," I told him. "We'll walk the orchard, see how the cherries look."

He picked up his hat and bounded down the steps and along the path.

Bluebell and I grabbed the empty water jugs and plodded over to inspect the cherry trees. I lifted up the netting to duck underneath. "Hey, you know I think it *is* a bit cooler under here!"

I heard Bluebell shriek before I felt water from the sprinklers drizzle over me. It was like manna from heaven, as refreshing as a plunge in the Pacific. I freed myself from the netting and joined Bluebell, spinning in circles as the drops fell like rain all around us.

"Man, I needed this," Bluebell said, her curly hair now soaked and slicked back.

I blinked, looking up at the sky, twirling around in relief. "Pappy's missing out."

"That's where you're wrong." She pointed to the edge of the orchard by the cottage, where Pappy stood between a few trees, letting the sprinklers cool him off, too. Spotting us, he raised two fists in celebration.

"Whoo-hoo!" Bluebell yelled. I threw my wet hat in the air, giddy with relief.

We strolled among the trees, soaking up the cool mist. By the time we reached the cottage, I felt almost...normal. "Use the shower in my room," I told Bluebell. Pappy had already disappeared inside. "I'm just going to check a few things."

Once she skipped up the steps to the door, I skirted under the netting of the closest cherry tree, needing to confirm what I thought I'd seen. My stomach dropped like a lead weight. The leaves were almost brown, like someone had taken a blowtorch to them. I plucked a couple of cherries. They were soft and hot to the touch. Blood thrummed in my ears. I feared even more for the fruit I couldn't see—the cherries closest to the tops of the trees.

We had only one option if we were going to save this crop: harvest it all before it was too late.

I headed inside, panic gnawing my insides about what to do. I knew what I didn't want: to worry Pappy. We were going into town for dinner. I could meet up with August and figure something out while we were there.

In my room Bluebell was out of the shower, wrapped in a towel, wet ringlets framing her face. "Pick anything you like," I said, gesturing to my meager closet.

I looked at my phone before I jumped in the shower. Still nothing from August. *They must be scrambling like we are to get things done before it gets even hotter tomorrow.* Still, I typed out a message to him, letting him know we would be at the hotel for dinner, and not the farm, if he wanted to join.

In under half an hour, Pappy, Bluebell, and I were dressed and ready to head out to Bayview, Fig in tow. "Wait—let's take some vegetables," I told them. "Might as well empty some of what we picked today before it wilts to nothing. And I'll drop some nugget potatoes at Isola." I drove the path around the perimeter of the orchard to the estate house. Pappy swung open the back doors while Bluebell and I bustled in and out, carrying crates of lettuce and kale, strawberries, herbs, rhubarb, and potatoes. When we'd loaded as much as we could fit, I started the engine and steered us onto Elison Road.

The streets in town were eerily quiet. "People must be keeping their activity to a minimum," Pappy said as we turned off Water Street into the parking lot at the Driftwood Inn. Even the marina was empty of tourists. It was a bizarre sight this time of year.

"You go on ahead, Pappy. Let Fern know we're filling the cooler." On his way inside with Fig, he propped open the back door to the hotel with a rock, and Bluebell and I set to work unloading all the produce.

When we'd stored everything in the walk-in cooler, I surveyed the kitchen. "Not very busy tonight, huh?" I asked Tommy. He looked up from the fish he was fileting and shrugged.

"That's weird." Bluebell stood next to me, fiddling with a curl. "Come on, let's find Fern."

I pushed through the swinging door first, expecting to find the dining room bustling with activity, the way it had been since production started on *Shore Thing*. Instead a few locals were seated at the bar, the rest of the tables empty. The ceiling fans whirred overhead, circulating air-conditioning to the handful of guests.

Fern stood behind the bar, chatting with Pappy. Fig had found a cool spot on the floor next to him.

"What the hell?" I asked as I caught Fern's eye. "Where is everyone?"

"Gone."

"What do you mean, gone? What about all the movie people?"

"That's who I mean. They're gone. They filed out of here this morning, heads down, all in a hurry."

"Wait—who filed out of here?"

"Everyone. Domino, Damon Mann, that horrible director—even August and his two sidekicks."

My mouth dropped open. August had left? Why hadn't he told me? I shook my head. "That can't be. They're probably just out on a shoot." I checked the time on my phone. "It's only six thirty. There's still plenty of daylight."

"Don't think so. They had all their luggage with them."

I dropped onto a stool at the end of the bar, looking at my phone again. No texts or missed calls. I typed out a message.

Hey. At the Driftwood. Where are you?

I stared at the screen for a few minutes, willing a reply, some rational explanation for where August was—and why. But no response arrived.

Bluebell plopped down next to me and slung an

arm over my shoulders. "I'm sure he'll check in soon. You're probably right. They're probably doing a crucial scene, and he can't check his phone without getting hell from that asshole Arthur."

I nodded, but my shoulders drooped, and I couldn't ignore the pit of despair that began to knot my belly.

Pappy sprang to his feet. "Well, I'm starved. Let's eat, girls." He held out an arm to showcase a booth by the window like a game show host displaying a prize. "Tell you the truth, it's a lot nicer in here without all those Hollywood types. And would you feel that air-conditioning?"

I assessed him. He seemed to have regained some spirit and vigor since we'd arrived. The longer we sat in the cool air, the more like himself he seemed.

"You know, I think you're right," Bluebell said. "I'm gonna enjoy life on the other side of the table for once." She shepherded me over to the booth. Fig curled around Pappy's feet under the table. "Fern, what's on special?"

Fern tucked a pen behind her ear, grabbed a notepad, and sidled up to the booth. "We've got Two Rivers beef tenderloin with local blue cheese and kale salad—your kale, of course."

"I'll have that," Pappy said, a surprise to no one.

"You got it." She pulled out the pen and made a

note. "Next is Sunset Farm lamb—"

"Sold." Bluebell raised her hand. "I love Salt Spring Island lamb." Sunset Farm was on a nearby island known for its vibrant arts and crafts scene—and its plentiful sheep farms.

Fern turned her attention to me.

"I'll take the fish."

"Want to hear about it first?"

I shook my head, eyes glued to my phone again, willing a reply. "I'm sure it's good."

Bluebell and Pappy kept each other company while we waited for our food, trying to distract me with talk of the heat dome and climate change and how the seaweed Bluebell used in her skincare line might be affected.

"Like humans, the ocean is a resilient place," Pappy was saying as Fern and Tommy delivered steaming plates of beef tenderloin, succulent lamb, and crab cake with poached prawns and fennel slaw. "It's used to being thrown hardballs by the environment. No matter how bad things get this week, it'll recover."

His eternal optimism buoyed my spirit a little. I forced myself to put aside my worry over August and enjoy dinner with my pappy and my best friend. Pride ballooned in my heart, looking at the plates of food in front of us. The results of all our hard work and sacrifice at the farm were right here, being enjoyed by all who came through the Driftwood Inn.

I relished the last bite of panko-crusted crab cake drizzled with remoulade sauce, then sat back in the booth. For the first time since I'd opened my eyes this morning, I felt several degrees cooler than melting hot. It was divine.

Tommy came bursting through the swinging door from the kitchen, shaking his head. "One hundred and sixteen degrees, they're saying for tomorrow. How is that even possible?"

Silence fell on the tiny group of us gathered to bask in the cold air at the inn. A flicker of worry crossed Pappy's face that told me everything I needed to know. Biting my lip with worry, I excused myself from the table to use the restroom. On my return, I beckoned Fern to the end of the bar for a discreet chat.

Bluebell watched from the booth with interest. At my proposal, Fern nodded vigorously before striding out to the lobby.

I took my seat again, feeling pleased and determined. Pappy was gazing out the window, where the marina was still bizarrely empty, the docks baking like bread in the evening sun. "Put a fork in me, ladies. I'm done. Shall we head out?"

"Not you, Pappy. You get to stay here tonight. You and Fig both." Pappy being Pappy, he started to protest, but I waved a finger at him. "Nope, don't even try. You heard Tommy. It's not getting any cooler, and I need you in tip-top form when the inspector comes. Fern has you all set up with a room."

"Lucky duck." Bluebell clinked her water glass with his. "That's an offer you can't refuse, Felix. In fact, if you do, I'll take that room myself. And you don't want to fight me for it." She lifted her arm and flexed a bicep.

Pappy feigned intimidation at her muscles, his eyes darting from them to me and back again. It was written all over my face this was an argument he couldn't win. "Oh, all right. I suppose I could use a little R&R."

Tommy cleared our plates, and Fern appeared at the table with a key card. "One good thing about the hotel emptying out. The best room goes to the most deserving guest." She bent down to kiss Pappy's wrinkled cheek. A spark lit in his eyes at the attention from the pretty blonde.

I agreed with all my heart, although the pit of despair in my stomach deepened at the reminder of August's departure. I flipped my phone over on the table to check it again. Still nothing. "Well, I for one want to see this room Fern's bragging about. Let's get you settled, Pappy."

We followed Fern to the elevator in the lobby, Fig barking at our excitement. When we all climbed in,

Fern hit the button labeled PH, and my mouth dropped open in surprise again. I would have been happy with a regular room for Pappy and Fig, but the penthouse? What a treat.

The elevator door opened into a massive suite with wraparound windows and sweeping views of the Pacific. A two-way fireplace inlaid with ocean rocks separated the living room from the bedroom. Sprawling sectional couches faced the fireplace, where a big-screen TV hung above the mantel. The decor was all muted greens and grays, echoing the tones found in nature all over the island. In the bedroom was a king-size four-poster bed and a ceiling of paneled wood. One feature wall was papered with a textured pattern that mimicked moss growing on rocks.

Hearing Pappy exclaim from the bathroom, I followed him in to see a walk-in shower tiled in stone, and right there, in front of the windows, was a freestanding tub that looked like a cocoon. A bathtub was one of the only things I really missed living in the little cottage on the farm—a place to soak all my worries away. I was as pleased as Pappy that he'd be able to enjoy one tonight. And if soaking in a bath overlooking the bay wasn't enough, another flat-screen TV was mounted to the wall opposite, so he could watch TV if Mother Nature proved too boring.

We met back up with Fern and Bluebell on the

balcony, where the sun hung low in a sky tufted with cotton-candy clouds. When it was hot like this, it was hard to tell where the ocean met the sky on the horizon, the waves of heat somehow blurring the atmosphere.

"What do you think, Felix? Will you be comfortable here?" Fern asked.

He cleared his throat, almost giddy. "Er—I'm not sure comfortable's the right word. More like indulged." His glee was contagious, and I, too, started grinning ear to ear. Pappy bent to scruff Fig's fur. "What do you think, Figgy? You like it here?"

I swear Fig smiled.

"We'll leave you to it, then." I pecked him on the cheek and gave his shoulders a squeeze. "Try not to have too much fun, hey? Don't forget, we have a big week ahead of us."

"I'll be thinking of you every second. When I'm not in that tub, sprawled across that bed, or drinking whiskey on that deck, that is." He winked at Bluebell. "Pick me up tomorrow?"

"Tomorrow," I agreed, although I wondered if it would cool down enough in the next twenty-four hours that I'd feel confident about bringing him back to the sweltering cottage.

Fern went to the elevator and pressed the button to call it up. The door slid closed on a vision of Pappy kicking off his shoes and falling backward on the bed, dwarfed by its size and its fluffy white comforter, Fig's tail wagging beside him.

"Thanks for doing this," I said on the way down. "I've been worried sick about how to get him through the next few days."

"It's the least I can do for my favorite farmer." Fern's ponytail swished as she reached out for a hug. "Besides, I hate to see that suite go empty in Damon Mann's absence."

"*That's* where Damon Mann slept?" Bluebell's voice went up an octave. "Now you tell me. If I'd known, I would've flung backward on that bed myself." Her palm went to her heart. "What a babe."

"Ack, I've seen better." I shrugged and waved at the air. "Anyway, ever since I heard he gets seasick, I can't look at him that way."

"I'll nurse him back to health." Bluebell clasped her hands together as we reached the lobby.

Once we were back on the main floor, reality set in, and I thought of the hot, bruised cherries I'd held in my fingers earlier. We'd been enveloped in cold air for so long it'd been easy to forget about the searing heat.

We had to harvest the cherries tonight. With or without help from August.

"What is it?" Bluebell asked, sensing my anxiety.

"I need your help. If I don't get those cherries off the trees—tonight—we're going to lose them. Can you pull an all-nighter with me?"

She nodded immediately. "Of course. Anything you need."

"I'm in," Tommy said as he passed with a big bag of ice.

"Are you serious?" I was surprised he'd even heard our discussion.

"You bet."

"Me, too," said Fern.

"But I can't ask you to—"

"Nonsense. Forest'll be here to man the fort. That's what living on Orcas is all about, isn't it? A community of friends you can count on?"

Oof. That hit me like a blow to the stomach. If there was ever a time I needed to count on August, it was now. And it would've been good to have Sam and Noah pitch in as well. I checked my phone again. Nothing. Worry, frustration, and disappointment roiled through me.

"Ginger's coming, too," Bluebell announced, looking at her phone. "And she's asking around at Grind House for more help."

My spirit lifted a little. *This is what matters,* I thought. *People I can count on being there when I need them.*

I didn't have time to wallow in disappointment. "Let's go," I told Bluebell.

"I'll drive Tommy and me after we close the bar," Fern called after us as we headed through the kitchen to the back door. With a quick stop at Isola to deliver potatoes, we were on the road to Winslow and a long, hot night of hard work.

It was dusk by the time we reached the farm. As we turned up the driveway, I was heartened to see several other vehicles already parked around the property. A small cluster of people was gathered in front of the cottage. Ginger was there, her red hair fiery against the hazy evening sky. So was Ash Vincent, another high school acquaintance who'd returned to the island after studying ornithology in Connecticut. Poppy Willoughby, a local writer turned assistant to Domino West, was there, too, along with her mom, Georgia.

"How did you all...?" My question trailed off when Ginger raised a hand.

She laughed. "Sometimes coffeehouse gossip is a good thing. When I announced I was closing early— and why—everyone in the place volunteered to help."

The sound of tires on the gravel had us all squinting to see who else had arrived. "Must be Tommy and Fern," Bluebell said.

"Not in a Tesla, it's not." I recognized the distinct

shape of an electric SUV. "Rocky Black. Who would've thought?"

"Figures. He'll do anything for votes," Georgia muttered.

"Mom! Rose needs all the help she can get."

While the others laughed awkwardly, Bluebell leaned in and spoke quietly in my ear. "Hey, weren't the sprinklers on when we left?"

Had she really forgotten dancing under them just a few hours ago? "Um, yah, remember we…" My thought trailed off, and I marched past the group to where the rows of apricot and cherry trees began.

Fuck. When we'd left there was a wheeled sprinkler cart at the end of every third row. Now there was nothing but bare hose cut into strips like black rubber snakes in the grass. Rage squeezed my rib cage, and I fought the urge to scream like a banshee. I balled my trembling hands into fists at my sides, forcing myself to inhale through my nose, exhale through my mouth. Inhale, exhale. Inhale, exhale. Gradually my heartbeat seemed to slow.

"Rose?"

I hadn't heard Bluebell come up behind me. I nearly jumped out of my skin.

"Oh, fuck," she repeated as she surveyed the strips of hose that lined the edge of the orchard. "But…why?"

I rested a hand on the top of my head, gobsmacked about what had happened. "The aluminum and copper—they steal it."

"Who steals it?"

"Petty thieves? People looking for quick, easy cash? I've heard of it happening on the mainland. Not here."

Bluebell kicked the grass with her sneaker. "So what are we gonna do?"

I turned to look at the group gathered behind us. These were people who loved the farm like it was their own, had looked out for me when my mom died, when the Quinns disappeared.

Fern and Tommy were here now, too. I counted them all. With nine pairs of hands pitching in, we just might make it.

"I'll tell you what we're going to do. We're going to save these cherries." I marched back through the grass to where they stood by the cottage.

I divided the group into teams of three and assigned each a section of the orchard to work.

"Be right back," I called as they split into their teams. "No one starts until I say go!"

I disappeared into the roasting heat of the cottage, instantly glad of the decision to park Pappy at the hotel for the night. The image of the Death card still loomed in my mind, despite what Zoe had said about its true meaning.

I rustled around in the pantry and kitchen drawers, sifting through elastic bands, bread clips, and batteries until I found what I was looking for. Grabbing my work apron from a hook on the back of the door, I filled its pockets with what I'd come in for.

Before I went back out, I called the sheriff's office. The sooner I reported the theft, the more chance they had of catching whoever did it. Ford McNamara, the sergeant on call, promised to get a couple of deputies on the case. After I hung up, I paused at the kitchen table, staring at the phone in my hand. If I brought it outside, I'd be checking it all night. I laid it facedown on the table. If August hadn't called by now, he wasn't going to. I had to set aside the hurt swirling in my stomach like a cyclone. I had a farm to save.

CHAPTER 18
August

Arthur was pulling an all-nighter.

I rubbed my eyes, staring blankly around me at a swimming pool in Pasadena. Noah and Sam were red-eyed and grim-faced next to me.

Way over budget, Arthur had come up with a cockamamie scheme of shooting the underwater night scenes in a backyard pool. At some point late yesterday, to make the clear, chlorinated water match the murky haze of the ocean, he'd had his assistants dump a gallon of powdered milk in the water. The air reeked like wet cardboard and beef tallow.

Domino and Damon were equally frustrated with

the vitriolic director. More than once Domino had pulled him aside to try to reason with him—or at least let everyone have a few hours' sleep, but he was a man possessed.

"August, phone." Sam nudged me with his elbow.

"What?"

"Answer your phone."

I looked to my right to see my phone on the bench beside me, screen lit up with an incoming call. Who could be calling at two in the morning? I turned away slightly. I did not need Arthur Dagon breathing down my neck. "Hello?" I murmured.

"August Quinn?"

"Yes?"

"This is Sergeant Ford McNamara. I'm with the Bayview sheriff's department." The voice on the other end of the phone was polite but blunt.

What the hell? "How can I help you?" I whispered.

"Can you give me your whereabouts, please?"

I glanced around. *Somewhere between Burbank and hell* was the first thing that came to mind. I cupped my hand around the phone to muffle my voice. "California, sir. May I ask what this is about?"

"I see. How long have you been in California?"

"Since noon yesterday. Sorry, Sergeant, did something happen? Is this about Rose Hardy? Is she okay?"

"Did you say Rose Hardy?"

My heart skipped a beat. "Is she okay?" *Goddamnit. Why won't he answer my questions?*

"Chip Thurlow. He's an associate of yours. Is that correct?"

"An associate? No. Fuck no." I stood, catching Arthur's attention. I no longer cared, though. If something had happened to Rose, I needed to know—now. I didn't care what Arthur or anyone else thought.

"You spoke with him yesterday. Isn't that true?"

I thought of Chip's shady threat in the dining room of the Driftwood Inn, and my stomach clenched in anger. "Yes, that's true." There was no point in denying it. Besides, I hadn't done anything wrong.

"And you have extensive knowledge about Big Oak Farm. Is that correct?"

Anxiety prickled my spine. Something *must* have happened. "Is she okay, sir? Is Rose okay?"

"There's been a theft, Mr. Quinn. Someone took all the sprinkler carts and piping from Big Oak Farm. And we think you had something to do with it."

"What?" I was practically yelling now. Arthur stormed toward me, but Noah stood, blocking his path. "That's fucking ludicrous, sir. Pardon my language, but I would never, ever do anything to hurt Rose. Ever." I scrubbed a hand over my face, trying to calm myself. "Look, Sergeant…McNamara, did you say? I'll be back on Orcas by morning. I'll tell you everything I know."

"You do that," the sergeant said. "If you're not here by noon, I'll send a deputy to find you."

"I'll be there." I ended the call and stared at my phone, fury coursing through my veins. *Fuck Chip Thurlow.* If he had hurt Rose or her grandfather, I would strangle him.

"Do it again!" Arthur spat at the crew. "You!" he growled at me, Noah, and Sam. Even in the backlighting set up for the scene, the man's face was so red I half expected steam to shoot from his ears. "Back in the water."

Sam and Noah turned to me. "We can handle it from here."

I was already packing my belongings. "I know you will."

My mind raced with fear in the cab to the airport. Why hadn't I called Rose? Why had I let Arthur and Chip get to me? By the time we'd boarded the ferry to the mainland yesterday, I'd been riddled with doubt about who I was and whether I deserved her. She was better off without me, I'd decided. But I hadn't been able to bring myself to tell her that by text. I figured I owed her a full explanation, at least. In person.

No matter what else happened, I was determined

not to repeat history.

I'm on my way home, I texted her. **We need to talk.**

Rose

The thermometer on the porch read one hundred and six. I shook my head in disbelief. A hundred and six degrees? At night?

I stumbled down the steps and rejoined the group. Pinching my lips around my fingers, I whistled to get their attention and beckoned Bluebell to stand next to me. "Listen up, folks! Bluebell's handing out head-lamps." From my apron pockets I tugged three of the headlamps I'd found in the kitchen and gave them to her, keeping one for me. "There's one per team. We'll be bringing out ladders, too, once we get started. First things first, though—safety. It may be dark out, but it's hot—a hundred and six degrees hot." A murmur of astonishment passed through the group. "So make sure you drink plenty of water. I'll keep jugs filled at the bottom of each row of trees. If you start to feel light-headed or sick, stop what you're doing. Noth-ing's more important than your health—not these cherries, or how many you pick, or my bottom line."

Poppy exchanged a meaningful look with her mom. Georgia looked fit, but this kind of heat could easily take a toll.

"The Tesla has a full battery," Rocky volunteered. "So if anyone needs to chill out, they can sit in the air-conditioning."

"That's helpful, thank you. Now, the cherries. The darker red they are, the riper the fruit. You'll be able to tell with your headlamps on. I suspect we'll find most of the cherries are ready after today's heat, but if you see any orange ones, leave them on the tree. Save your energy for the red ones. I'd like to keep all the netting in place if we can, which will add another layer of challenge.

"Use these secateurs—" I beckoned Bluebell back to my side and pulled five pairs of secateurs from my apron pockets, one by one, then nodded to her in instruction to pass them out "—and cut the stem of each cherry near the top of the stalk."

"You mean one at a time?" Tommy said, eyebrows raised.

I nodded. "That's right."

"That's gonna take—"

Fern whispered something in Tommy's ear.

"A while," he finished, laughing.

"I know it's painstaking," I said. "But pulling

them risks damaging the branches for next year." *If they survive until next year.* "Any questions?"

"Not a question, but I brought goodies," Ginger called from where she stood. "Whatever was in my display cases when I left Grind House, I tossed in a box and brought. And I've got cold brew if anyone wants caffeine later."

A cheer went up. "Awesome!" Tommy shouted above the group, raising a fist in the air.

I assessed the little teams of three, watching them point to their areas of the orchard and discuss how to get started. *This is what love is. It's this group of people, right here, together for a singular purpose: a love of community.* I could live without the other kind of love, I realized—the romantic kind—as long as I had this. Nothing was better than knowing you had people to depend on and who could depend on you. I swiped an arm across my forehead to dry the sweat, ready to get started.

I had assigned Poppy and her mom to my team, figuring Bluebell's and to a lesser extent Fern's familiarity with the farm was best split between the other two groups. And I hoped I might get a chance to grill Poppy about why the *Shore Thing* crew had left so unexpectedly. Surely she was in touch with Domino.

"Okay, let's huddle!" I waved everyone close and

held a fist forward. They each piled a hand on top, and we all gave one big shake. "Don't mess with the West!" I shouted. It was the school cheer we'd chanted at games at Orcas Island High. That drew laughs from everyone.

"Because we're the best!" a few shouted in response. We split apart buoyed with laughter and hope.

"Georgia, Poppy, you come with me." I sent the others to get started in the orchard. Bluebell led one team with Ginger and Ash, and Fern took charge of Rocky and Tommy.

I led Poppy and her mom into the cottage kitchen and got them filling water jugs while I went around the side of the house. Several ladders were laid flat on the ground. I carried one out to Fern's team on the west side of the orchard, stopping twice to wipe the sweat from my eyes. *It's gonna be a long night.* I shuddered to think of the alternative: losing our crops to the heat dome—and potentially the farm, too, if we couldn't make our quotas this year.

I wanted more than anything for Pappy to retire knowing Big Oak would continue to feed the folks on the island for generations to come.

I trudged back out with a ladder for the second team, retracing my steps once more to set the last one in place for my group. When I returned, Poppy and Georgia had carried nine jugs of water to the porch and were looking in askance for where they should go.

"Well done, ladies. That's a nice even three per team. Just drop them at the bottom of each group's area of the orchard, would you? I'll meet you at the east end." I pointed to that side of the property, where the silhouette of the big Garry oak was black against the night sky.

I blew out a breath, willing away the memories of my midnight stroll to the tree with August. It seemed like forever ago. In that time I'd gone from resentful and angry to open and in love and all the way back again.

My team started on the first row of the trees I'd assigned us. I reached the highest fruit using the ladder, while Poppy and her mom worked the lower branches. As I tossed handfuls of dark-red cherries into a pail, my mind went to Zoe and her tarot cards. *This* was the Death she'd predicted, I was sure. And the thing I needed to let go of was so obvious now: waiting for August to swoop home and fix what he'd broken. Fix me.

I'd learned I was ready to love again. I'd just picked the wrong person.

Zoe had gotten something else right. It'd taken me ten years to let go of the past, but I realized now how much that hindered me. I rested my secateurs on the top of the ladder and scanned the scene around me. I had friends and neighbors who supported me, their cheerful voices carrying through the orchard, their headlamps bobbing in the dark like twinkling stars. Something stirred deep in my soul: the promise of renewal.

We moved systematically among the trees, plucking warm fruit by the light of our headlamps, shrouded in netting and sticky from the heat. I had no idea how much time had passed, but we were ready for a break. From my perch on the ladder, I put my thumb and pointer finger, sweet with cherry juice, to my lips and wolf-whistled. "Let's regroup," I called. "Meet under the oak tree."

Headlamps bounced in the darkness as the group trekked to the far side of the farm. At the top of the rise, I removed my lamp and sat it on the ground, pointing the light up at the branches. The others with headlamps did the same. Peals of laughter broke out as we got a glimpse of one another. After hours of swiping at sweat with cherry-stained fingers, we looked like something out of a horror movie. People bent to sit in the dirt under the tree, loosening their shoelaces and stretching out after a few long hours on their feet.

"Great work so far, everyone. I reckon we're more than halfway now. Anyone have questions or needs I can answer?"

"Rocky needs a bandage," Fern said.

"Nah, I'm fine. It's just cherry juice."

"Unless you're squeezing a cherry right now, I'm pretty sure you nicked your finger." Fern reached for his hand, folding all his fingers over except his middle one, which she held up in the air.

"I'll get it," Bluebell said. She trod down the slope toward the cottage before I could thank her.

"No need to play the tough guy around here, Mr. Mayor. I'd rather keep you picking cherries than watch you slowly bleed out. Now, who's hungry?"

At the chorus of "mes" and "I ams" that went up, I had my answer. "Tommy, can you help Ginger grab the food she brought?"

He scrambled to his feet. You didn't need to ask Tommy twice when food was involved.

Bluebell returned, a box of bandages in one hand and a bottle of hydrogen peroxide in the other. "Let's get you fixed up," she told Rocky. Georgia picked up one of the headlamps to direct light at Rocky's finger while Bluebell cleaned and bandaged the cut. By the time that was done, Tommy and Ginger had returned with a cooler and a large Rubbermaid tub.

Ginger handed out sausage rolls and doughnuts and even some of Ida's famous chocolate-chip cookies, along with cups of her new signature drink, the Big Chill, to wash it all down.

"Oh my god, Ginger, this coffee is to die for," Fern said. "I don't know if it's the heat or that it's four in the morning and I'm starting to get delirious, but I don't think I've ever tasted anything this good."

Even the usually quiet Ash spoke up in agreement. Ginger seemed bashful at the praise—especially, I noticed, from Ash.

"So, Ash, tell us what you're studying right now," I said, hoping to encourage him to speak a bit more.

"Oh, I, uh—" He cleared his throat. "I'm working with the Audubon team to predict how climate change will affect birds' range."

"You mean range as in their songs?" Georgia asked.

He shook his head. "Not in this case, no. Although that's an interesting thesis. Where birds live is known as their range. Several species are at risk here in the Pacific Northwest. American goldfinch, American robin, yellow warbler, red-breasted nuthatch... The sky as we know it will look different in five years."

The group went quiet, contemplating his words.

"That's awful," Ginger said.

"What can we do?" Georgia asked.

"Whatever we can to reduce carbon emissions," Ash said. "And appreciate what we have."

I noticed Rocky in particular paying close attention. *Hopefully he'll make this part of his political agenda*, I thought.

Just then, as if on cue, an owl hooted some distance off, a mourning call with long notes at the end. Poppy giggled, but Ash held up a finger. "Shh. Listen again."

We heard a second hoot, this time a series of eight notes.

"That's a different one. Sometimes they call to each other," Ash said. "'Who cooks for you? Who cooks for you all?'"

"Well, I did the cooking tonight—" Ginger started.

"No, listen. It's how we describe the call of the barred owl."

The group went quiet again, waiting to hear another call. Sure enough, moments later we did.

"Oh my god, you're right!" Bluebell said. "That's so cool."

I thought about how much August would've loved learning that little fact about the owls of Orcas Island. But rather than feeling sad he wasn't here, I was again struck by the wonderful people around me under the sturdy old oak. I closed my eyes and inhaled deeply, taking in the smell of dry earth mixed with sweet cherries.

Fern rallied the gang to regroup.

"Thanks, Ginger, for fortifying us," I said as folks began to trudge down the rise and back into the orchard, the light from their headlamps bouncing off the trees.

"Anytime!" I heard in reply. I could just make out Ginger waving. The sky was beginning to lighten. As I started down the hill, I noticed Poppy and Georgia just behind me, still seated in the dirt.

"You okay?"

"I am," Poppy said. "But I wonder if just you and me could finish our rows. I think my mom's about ready to crash."

I didn't hesitate to agree. "Why don't we take up Rocky on his offer? Hell, it's not often you get to sleep in a Tesla," I teased. I reached out a hand to each of the women and helped them to their feet. "I'll find Rocky and see you over there."

Five minutes later Rocky had the gull-wing doors open on his car and was ushering Georgia into the passenger seat. He stepped into the driver's side and switched on the air-conditioning. The relief on Georgia's face was instantaneous. Once she was comfortable, Rocky stepped out and closed his door.

"You know, no one would blame you if you lay back and embrace it," Poppy told her mom. But Georgia didn't need convincing. She reached for the seat adjustments and began positioning herself. "We'll be right over there if you need anything."

"And I'll be right here," Georgia said, smiling. "I'll be fine."

I linked my arm through Poppy's, and we traipsed

back to the orchard to finish what we'd started—saving this year's cherry crop and potentially the whole farm in the making. First, though, I needed to ask about August.

"You're still working with Domino West, right?"

"Yep." Poppy reached up to tighten the end of her ponytail.

"What's with the disappearing act?" There was no point beating around the bush.

Poppy tsked. "That asshole Arthur. He sprang it on everyone this morning that they had to get to California to shoot a few scenes. Domino tried to reason with him, but there was no budging him. Seems like a colossal waste of money to move an entire cast and crew when they were already set up here."

"Huh."

"Yeah. Kinda weird, right? August didn't tell you?"

I shook my head, my headlamp pinging left and right.

"Well, don't feel bad. Domino barely had time to tell me—she had to send Forest to the coffee shop to let me know. With the rolling power outages, it was a mess trying to get a hold of anyone."

"Huh." That should have made me feel better, but it didn't.

Sensing my unease, Poppy let the topic rest. When

we got to the spot in the orchard where we'd left off, she gently squeezed my hand.

Robins serenaded the daybreak as we worked. I wasn't sure if it was Ash's lesson or just the fact of being fully awake at this hour, but I reveled in every second of chickadee trills and swallows chittering. How lucky was I to own this piece of paradise? Nothing could convince me there was a better place on earth.

From the top of the ladder, holding the netting aloft from my head, I gazed across the orchard as the sky took on the spectacular colors of sunrise: blue, purple, red, and everything in between. Each team, I could see, had reached the last few trees in their sections. At the end of each row, pails and pails of freshly picked cherries were lined up, ready for me to move to the estate house. Based on what I'd seen while I picked, I guessed we might lose about 15 percent of the crop. Had this group not banded together, the damage would have been much, much worse.

My chest puffed with pride as I descended the ladder for the last time, my T-shirt glued to my skin, my wet hair slicked back. I walked out from under the netting to high-five Poppy as she set down the last pail of cherries. Two red-stained hands came together in the air, both of us laughing in relief.

"I don't care how bad we smell, I need to do this."

I wrapped her in a hot, sweaty hug. We giggled as we separated, peeling our shirts where they'd stuck to our chests. "Thank you so, so much. I don't know how I can ever repay you."

"No repayment required," she said. "Honestly, I had a great time."

"So did I," Rocky said, his boots squeaking as he came toward us.

I peered down at his feet. "Those look pretty new."

He chuckled. "Yeah, well, I don't do a lot of real work these days. Mostly sitting in offices or shaking hands at events. Nice to put them to the test."

"I think you're gonna have a few blisters," Poppy said. "Don't take them off until you get home or you'll never get them on again."

"I already know you're right. But it was worth it." The three of us watched the sun kiss the horizon, bathing the swaths of white netting in an otherworldly orange. Bluebell, Fern, and Tommy were making their way to join us, Ash and Ginger following behind.

"Hmm. I never would have paired those two, but there's definitely a spark, isn't there?"

"To tell you the truth I barely see him talk to anyone," Rocky said. "Always seemed afraid of his own shadow, even in school."

Rocky had been one of the most popular kids in

high school, the star of the basketball team. I struggled to remember whether Ash had even been in any of my classes. He'd always just sort of blended into the background.

As they got closer, it was plain to see he had eyes for Ginger. "No wonder he's always at Grind House." Poppy put two and two together. "I'm there a lot to write," she explained, "especially when it feels like the walls of my apartment are closing in."

A pang of jealousy pierced my chest at the thought of Ash and Ginger together. How easy it would be to fall in love with someone who was always where you expected them to be.

I'd proved one thing to myself, though. I could handle Big Oak on my own if I had to. I had all the help I needed with this ragtag group of people and all the others who made the island such a special place, from Mary and Louis at Cottle's to Ida and Bob and even Zoe.

"Good night, y'all. Or good morning. Whatever time it is," Bluebell said and started off in the direction of her red hatchback, tucked along the side of the estate house.

"Oh no, you don't." Fern grabbed the end of Bluebell's shirt. "It's way too hot to sleep in your car. You're coming with me." When she protested, Fern said, "The hotel's empty, remember? It's no big deal."

As much as I knew Bluebell hated the idea she might be a burden, the relief was plain to see in her eyes.

I sent everyone home with a pint of cherries and a sticky hug as the long shadows in the orchard shortened with the rising sun. It was hotter than ever this morning, but in place of the anxiety that had knotted my gut yesterday was a sense of calm I hadn't felt in weeks. No matter what, I realized, everything would be okay. Even the thought of the upcoming inspection didn't rattle me. We had this, Pappy and me. I was sure.

Fatigue settling into my bones, I pulled down as much netting from the fruit trees as I needed to cover the vegetables, herbs, and flowers.

I trudged across the farm, towing it behind me, to where rows of kale leaves were scorched black by the blazing heat. But the plants were at the end of their season now, so I convinced myself not to panic. The netting would block out at least some of the sunlight—enough, I hoped. Tomatoes and corn were pretty resilient, but I worried whether the broccoli would survive.

Finally, I dragged my tired body to the cottage, checking the thermometer on my way in. One hundred and eight degrees. I'd been so hot for so long I wondered if things would ever return to normal.

Inside, I laid a hand on my phone on the kitchen

table, closing my eyes and inhaling a long breath before I flipped it over.

I'm on my way home, August had texted. **We need to talk.**

Too little, too late, Quinn.

I didn't reply, just powered down the phone and left it where it was. In the shower, the temperature set to cold, reality took hold: August hadn't changed. When I'd needed him most, he'd disappeared. Just like he had ten years ago. Cool water washed over me, the pool at my feet fading from blood-red to clear as cherry juice and dust swirled down the drain. Afterward, numb with exhaustion, I collected all the fans in the cottage and pointed them at my bed. I crashed in a heap, unconscious in a blink.

CHAPTER 19

August

The sergeant's warning about sending out a deputy rang in my ears, but noon was several hours off yet. I went straight for the Driftwood Inn as the twilight of dawn hit the horizon, hoping desperately someone would be up.

The lobby was dark when I tugged open the front door, but as I stepped forward, I felt a glimmer of hope. By the doorway to the dining room, a strip of light crossed the floor.

Forest sat at the bar, steam from a mug in front of him disappearing into the pendant lights above. He was bent over a book, chin in his hand. "Hey, man," I said, descending the three stairs from the lobby. Forest startled, his book falling shut.

"What the fuck, August?" He slapped the counter. "What are you doing here?"

"I need your help."

"Tough."

"Excuse me?" I stood at the bar, the heels of my palms sweaty against the counter.

Forest spun on his stool to face me, folding his arms over his chest. "Do you know where my sister was all night?"

"Listen, I really need—"

"At Big Oak Farm," he interrupted. "With Blue-bell. And Ginger. And a half dozen others. Where were you?"

I dropped my hands to my sides and slumped forward, staring at my feet. A familiar tinge of shame spread through me like pins and needles, my heart thudding in my ears.

What you send into the universe comes back to you. Zoe's words suddenly echoed in my mind. *The magic of fate is behind you.* I stood up straight again. Whether it was fate, or frustration, or the powerful idea of a second chance, I was done feeling guilty for my father's mistakes. Clenching fists at my sides, I felt ready. To take control of my life. To go after what I wanted. Right now.

"I'm here now. And I'm never leaving." Forest sank back slightly on his stool at the conviction in my words. "Will you help me? I need to get to the farm—now."

He stroked his chin, his blue eyes thoughtful. "What can I do for you?" he said after what felt like forever.

"For starters, I need to call Morning Glory Farm. And pray like hell someone is up."

He turned to the windows that overlooked the marina. The sky had lightened, flooding the docks with warm, diffused blue. "It's a working farm. Some'll be up. What else?" He stood and walked around the back of the bar, where he grabbed a laptop, flipped it open, and called up the hotel's contact list.

"I need wheels. A van, a golf cart—whatever you've got."

He reached into his pocket and tossed me a key fob. "A golf cart? What do you take me for, man?" He laughed and pointed to the swinging door that led to the kitchen. "Jeep's parked out back. Go. I'll call Morning Glory, tell them you're on the way."

I raced to where he pointed. "Thanks, Forest. I owe you one!" I called over my shoulder as I pushed into the kitchen and out to the parking lot behind the hotel.

Rose

It was past noon and suffocatingly hot when I woke up. Strands of hair were glued to my face. The whirring of fans and steady *ch-ch-ch* of sprinklers outside filled my ears. The smell of baking earth wafted through the window, the only breeze created by the sprinklers whipping water back and forth.

I bolted upright. *How can there be sprinklers going when all our equipment was stolen?*

I leaped out of bed, slipped into the strawberry-print nightie at the top of my laundry pile, and raced for the door, which let in a whoosh of air that felt like opening an oven. I hopped across the porch as fast as I could, its wooden slats like hot coals under my feet. Blinking against the blinding sun, I couldn't believe what I was seeing. Sprinklers were dousing every part of the farm, from the orchard to the vegetable field and raised beds, with beautiful, sparkling water.

"How the hell?" I muttered, treading across the grass to the vegetable plots. Sizzling hot air enveloped me. Even my light cotton dress felt as heavy as a wool coat.

I lifted a corner of the netting and ducked under it, grateful for the drizzle of cold water that misted across whenever the sprinkler swished by. Most of the plant leaves were ringed in brown edges, scorched by the sun. The runner beans hung limply, the heart-shaped foliage drooping in the intense heat, and our beautiful wild roses were fried like crispy cornflakes. On the small thicket of raspberries, the berries were white and dry. Only the fruit that hung within the thorny branches had the beautiful pinkish-red hue of healthy berries. The leaves on the corn plants we'd so carefully pollinated were flipped upside down, the lighter-colored bottoms facing upward to reflect the light. I'd heard it could happen, but we'd never seen it here.

I pushed back out of the netting, my dress damp and stuck to me, the sun bearing down with the intensity of a flame. Our water bill was going to be huge, but the idea paled in comparison to losing everything in this unprecedented heat. I needed to find who had fixed the sprinklers and pledge my gratitude, but that could wait.

I climbed in the van, played hot potato with the scalding belt buckle, rolled down the windows, and got on the road to Pappy—and the air-conditioning—at the Driftwood Inn. The Pacific Ocean flew by in glimpses of cerulean as mirages appeared and disappeared on the road in front of me.

In the dining room at the hotel, Pappy was holding court at a booth with a group of locals, a cheeky grin on his face. His eyes alighted when he saw me. "Make room for my granddaughter, boys," he told the men at the table, shoving one of them over with his arm. "Come on, Rose, sit."

I dropped into the booth beside him. Nothing soothed the soul like the kind, comforting presence of my grandfather. When he wrapped an arm around my shoulders and gave me a hug, a tear trickled down my cheek, the enormity of the night before reverberating my bones.

"What's this now?" he said. "We're all right here, aren't we? There now. That's right. Everything's okay." He rubbed his wrinkled hand up and down my arm the way he did when I was a girl.

"Word is you were up all night," said Louis Larsen.

His son, Freddy, added, "Heard your sprinklers were stolen, too."

I nodded, my eyes welling again.

"You sure you want to carry on with the farm? I'm exhausted just looking at you," said George the chef.

I nodded again, wiping away my salty tears.

Fern stepped down from the lobby, her ponytail shiny and neat. How did she look so polished on so little sleep? "You should be proud of your girl, here. I know I am. You're looking at the woman who saved Big Oak."

I blushed. "Not true. I counted eighteen hands covered in cherry juice in the middle of the night." At that moment, though, I felt more sure than ever about the future of Big Oak. I sat up straighter, my shoulders back. "But I'll say this. I know today something I never thought possible."

The men at the table sat quietly, waiting to hear what it was. Fern hovered next to us, her arm along the back of the booth.

"I don't have to do it on my own—*we* don't have to do it on our own, Pappy. As long as we have the support of the people on Orcas Island, we'll be okay."

"Guess that means you can retire, hey, Felix?" Louis said.

Pappy laughed. "Nah. I'm like you, Louis. A lifer. What would I do with myself?" He stroked his chin, thinking. "Now you say it, though, I wouldn't mind relaxing a little more. I have more energy today than I've had in years. A good night's sleep—and a long soak in a bathtub with a magnificent view—well, turns out it's good for the soul."

That got me thinking, too. Why were we still depriving ourselves of the comforts of the estate house? "That's it." I slapped a palm on the table. "I'm fixing up the old house, Pappy. You shall have your soaker tub. Just wait."

"Are you sure, sweetheart?" Surprise mixed with concern on his face. He knew more than anyone how much I'd needed to escape the place we'd called home my whole life—until my mom had gotten sick. Something about being within the four walls that'd witnessed Sunny Hardy's long, slow deterioration had felt suffocating once she was gone. But my years in the cottage with Pappy had helped us heal from the pain, and I was ready to throw open the doors on the big house and fill it with life again.

"Positive. Once we've got our organic certification, that's my next big project—restoring the old beauty to its former glory."

"Inspection this Thursday, Felix tells me. You nervous?" Louis asked.

I looked down at my hands, steady and calm in my lap. I wasn't nervous, I realized. "Not one bit. We're ready."

"That's my girl." Pappy beamed with pride and gave my shoulders another squeeze. "Now should we stop lollygagging and get back to the farm?"

I shook my head. "Not a chance. You and me are gonna stay right here and let the air-conditioning swoosh over us all day long."

Pappy looked around at his friends. "Who am I to argue?" He laughed, eyes twinkling.

CHAPTER 20

August

Sergeant Ford McNamara looked just like Kevin Bacon in *Mystic River*, only in a standard issue green uniform in place of the gray suit and tie. His hair was short and brown, his face clean shaven. In the patch on his sleeve, the San Juan County Sheriff's Office logo was sandwiched between the American and Washington State flags. I stared at it while he opened the file folder on the table.

"Thank you for coming on such short notice, Mr. Quinn."

"Mr. Quinn is my father. Call me August." An air-conditioner wedged in the window blew icy cold air through the room.

"As you wish." He tapped a finger on the page of notes in front of him. "Tell me again what happened yesterday morning."

I rubbed my sweaty palms on my thighs. "I was in the lobby at the Driftwood Inn with the production team. Chip barged in the front door and came right for me, like he knew I was there."

"Did he?"

I shrugged. "Beats me."

"What did he want?"

"To threaten me."

"With what?"

"How long have you lived here?"

"Just answer the question, Mr. Quinn."

"August."

"August. Answer the question, please." He tapped his pen on the edge of the table.

"I ask because if you've been here awhile, you might have heard about my dad."

"Mr. Quinn."

Now we were getting somewhere. "Yes, Mr. Quinn."

"No, I don't know about him."

I took a deep breath. "Ten years ago my dad scammed several farmers on Orcas Island out of a large sum of money."

"I see." The sergeant leaned forward in this chair and began taking notes. "What kind of scam?"

"He offered them a deal on farm machinery, tractors, that kind of thing, and took cash payments. Then he took the money—and me and my mom—and left in the middle of the night."

"And you knew about this?"

"No. Yes." I looked down at my lap, shame filling me anew. Dirt still edged my fingernails from setting up the Morning Glory sprinklers at Big Oak this morning. "Eventually, yes. But I was a kid. Eighteen. I didn't know anything until we moved to Seattle."

"Were the police involved?"

"From what I was told, there was no trace of the money—and no signed agreements between him and the farmers." The air-conditioner whirred louder in my ears. "Without evidence of a crime, they had no grounds for arrest."

Sergeant McNamara stopped writing, his pen poised above his notes while he eyed me suspiciously. "What does this have to do with Chip Thurlow?"

"People here on the island know what happened. By my employers… Arthur Dagon, you heard of him?" The sergeant nodded. "And Domino West, and her production company—they don't know anything about it. By design."

"Go on."

"And Chip… He threatened to tell them."

"Or?"

I shrugged. Truthfully, I didn't know. "I didn't stop to ask."

"Then what?"

"Then I left the hotel and got on the bus with the crew. We flew out of SeaTac three hours later." Sergeant McNamara resumed taking notes. "Will you tell me now if Rose is okay? Felix?" Rose hadn't responded to my text. My pulse kicked up. I wiped my palms on my thighs again.

He dropped his pen and sat back in his chair. "She's fine, Mr.— August. Felix is fine. But four thousand dollars of irrigation equipment was stolen."

"Are you serious? I'll kill that bastard." I pounded the table.

"Excuse me?" He leaned forward again.

Shit. "Bad choice of words. It's just... Chip Thurlow is behind this. I'm sure of it."

"Because you helped him plan it? Was that why he came to see you at the Driftwood?"

I shook my head vehemently. "No. Absolutely not." I remembered Fern's wide eyes behind the long desk when I stormed through the lobby yesterday morning. "Ask Fern Russo. She was there."

"We know. We spoke to her."

"And she didn't corroborate my story?"

Ford McNamara shook his head. "I'm afraid not. Said she didn't hear anything. Just that you were angry and left in a hurry."

Elbows on the table, I put my head in my hands.

"But we arrested Mr. Thurlow. Caught him trying to board the ferry with a truck full of sprinklers and piping. Thing is, we wonder how he knew what to take—and when." The sergeant locked eyes with mine.

"I swear I had nothing to do with it. There must be some way..." I sat up, clenching and unclenching my jaw. "That asshole is always up to something," I muttered.

"What do you mean?"

I stood, the metal legs of the chair scraping the floor behind me. "You know about the narrowboat sinking, right?" He nodded. "You're going to want to look into that. And if there were a way to turn back the clock, I'd bet money Chip had a hand in what my dad did. He was always hanging around back then. It finally makes sense why." I walked to the door, then turned back, hand on the doorknob. "Does Rose think I did this?"

The sergeant steepled his fingers in front of him. "I can't say," he said, but I thought I saw an imperceptible shake of his head.

I left the sheriff's office and drove straight to Big Oak in the scorching heat. The sprinkler equipment I'd borrowed from Cal and Harlow at Morning Glory still pumped water across the orchard and netting-covered field, but the cottage was locked, and the delivery van was nowhere in sight.

I wiped the sweat from my forehead and pulled the phone from my pocket.

The call rang and rang, but Rose didn't answer. **I'm here,** I texted. **Where are you? We need to talk.**

Three dots appeared on the screen. My heart skipped a beat, then dropped to my toes when I read her reply. **There's nothing to say. Goodbye, August.**

I swallowed back the panic rising in my throat. **There's always something to say. I'm not making that mistake again.**

The sun beat down like a blow torch as the seconds ticked by. Fifteen minutes later, clothes stuck to me with sweat, I climbed back into the vehicle Forest had loaned me, an ocean-blue Jeep with the Driftwood Inn logo painted across the doors. I let the air-conditioning wash over me while I figured out what to do next.

Rose

I left Pappy asleep on the bed in the penthouse suite after lunch, Fig curled up next to him in a little brown ball. Down in the dining room, Fern was behind the espresso machine at the bar. Forest was screwing a lightbulb into one of the pendant lamps, a pencil between his teeth.

"Coffee?" Fern said as I descended from the lobby.

"Please." I pulled out a stool and sat. "Where is everyone?" The dining room was empty again.

"Movie crew still have their rooms booked." She filled the metal coffee filter with grounds and screwed it into place on the machine.

"So we're getting paid to do nothing." Forest turned the pendant lamp around, examining it from all angles. "Good work if you can get it." He let the lamp drop and steadied it with his hands.

"Bluebell still asleep?"

"I'd say so," Fern said. She bent to open the half-size fridge below the counter and grab a bottle of milk. But before she could set it down, it slipped from her fingers and crashed against the side of the bar. Shards of glass shot out in every direction, and the milk spread like paint across the floor.

"Don't move—I got it." I leaped into action, racing to the kitchen to find a broom and a dustpan. When I returned Fern was frozen in place as Forest bent to pick up glass with his hands. "No, don't touch it. You'll—"

"Shit." Forest stood straight, examining his finger

under the pendant light. Blood oozed from a cut and dripped down his arm in bright red streaks.

"You okay? Let me get—"

"No, stay where you are," I told Fern just as she stepped back, a piece of glass crunching under her shoe. I laughed; I couldn't help myself. 'You—" I pointed at Forest "—go rinse that off and get a bandage. And you—" I pointed at Fern "—stay right there while I sweep up the glass."

Fern raised her hands in the air as if to say, "I give up." Forest wrapped a bar towel over his finger, stepped carefully around the broken glass, and filed out to the lobby.

"You're back," I heard him say as the front door in the lobby door clicked shut.

"What happened to your hand?" August. I'd know his voice anywhere.

"Oh, it's nothing. I'm just going to go and..." Forest's sentence trailed off.

"Sure, man. Hey, have you seen Rose?"

Don't say it, don't say it, don't say it, I willed silently. "Go into the dining room. Fern will help you." *Thank you, thank you*, I repeated in my mind until I realized what was about to happen.

"Oh, fuck," I whispered to Fern and dropped to a crouch behind the bar.

"What are you—" Fern started, but she quickly

shut up when I put a finger to my lips, desperate.

"I'm not here," I mouthed, shaking my head as footsteps approached the bar.

"August, what can I do for you?" I watched her spread her hands wide on the counter to try to shield him from seeing what was going on behind it.

"Hey, Fern. Is Rose here?"

Fern shook her head. "Mm-mm."

"What was that?"

"Mm-mm." I put my head in my hands. She'd said it louder this time, but it was obvious she was hiding something. I held my breath, waiting to hear him bust her.

Instead, chair legs scraped across the floor. "Okay if I sit over here?" It sounded like he'd chosen a table out on the floor, not a stool at the bar.

"Mm-hmm!" I tugged on Fern's pant leg. Seeing the panic in my eyes, she managed to get a normal sentence out. "Can I bring you a coffee or something?"

My pulse slowed just enough I could let out a breath. My knees were killing me. After working all night at the farm, maintaining a deep squat was the last thing my body wanted to do, but I couldn't sit. Shards of glass still covered the floor, and milk pooled around my feet.

"Please," I heard him say.

"Black okay? We're out of milk."

"Fine."

Fern looked down, careful to step around the glass as she turned to face the espresso machine. The shot she'd started for me was still twisted in place. I watched her press a button to start the brew, hands on her hips. Her cheeks were red. *Yah, I feel silly, too.*

She topped it with hot water from the machine and tiptoed out from behind the bar. When she disappeared from sight, I let my butt fall to the floor, my face scrunching up as the cold, wet milk soaked into my dress. My knees couldn't hold me a minute longer.

"Sit with me?" August said.

Again, table legs scraped over the floor.

"So you're back." Fern sounded nervous, her voice oddly pitched.

"I'm back. For good."

"Is that right?"

"Listen, I know you told the sheriff you saw me talking to Chip Thurlow yesterday."

"Well, you were."

"Do you think I did it?" *Did what?* I held my breath again. What was he talking about?

A beat of silence followed. "No. I don't."

"Oh, thank god. Because they already arrested Chip. Caught him at the ferry, his truck full of sprinkler equipment. I would never do anything to hurt Rose. You know that, right?"

"But you already did. You left."

Another long silence. Then he cleared his throat. "I deserved that."

"Yep."

"I mean it, Fern. I'm here for good. I know she's furious with me. And she has every right to be. That's not going to stop me from proving to her how much she means to me. How crazy I am about her. How badly I want to spend the rest of my life with her."

Butterflies leaped to life in my chest.

"Why should she believe you?"

Chair legs scraped against the floor again, and again I held my breath.

"Where are you going?" Fern asked.

"Nowhere. I'm just so pent up, I don't know what to do with myself. I need to tell her how I feel."

"Tell me." She coughed. It wasn't a normal cough; she was trying to make sure I would listen.

"Where do I start? Being without her for a day was pure torture. I love her. I've always loved her. I love her crooked tooth. The way she cares about the farm, about Pappy. I love her smell. It's like someone rubbed her all over with roses. She's loyal and honest, and she never says a bad thing. About anyone. That's character."

Sprawled on the floor behind the bar, bum soaked

with milk, my eyes brimmed with tears.

"And she's beautiful. God, she's beautiful. I don't deserve her. No one does. If she gives me a second chance, I'll grab on and never let her go."

I'd spent ten years waiting to hear his words. My body tingled from the top of my head to the soles of my feet. I could feel the space between my ribs, the thumping of my heart in my chest.

"What are you going to do?" Fern's voice was thick with emotion.

"Can you tell her—"

I couldn't sit a second longer. Not when the man I'd spent a decade mourning the loss of loved me. I pressed the heels of my hands against the bar shelves behind me and stood. "Tell me yourself." Tears streamed down my face. My dress was stuck to my skin where it was wet, and I smelled like warm milk. But I didn't care.

August's eyes went wide, and his mouth dropped open. "You were there? The whole time?"

I nodded, wiping a bubble of snot from my nose.

"Well, don't just stand there, you idiot. Go get her!" Fern laughed.

I stepped out from around the bar as he came to meet me. His green eyes were shiny. He smoothed my hair back from my face, cupping my chin in his hands as he wiped my tears with his thumbs. Oh, how I'd missed him. I fell into him, his body against mine like water after a drought.

"I love you," he whispered against my ear.

"I love you," I muffled into his chest.

He rocked me side to side, his chin on my head. "Rose?"

"Mm-hmm?" Now I was the one mm-hmm-ing.

"Is that milk on the floor?"

"Mm-hmm," I said, like it was the most normal thing in the world.

"And you were…sitting in it?" His hands traveled down my back until they reached where my dress was wet.

"That's right." I squeezed my arms tighter around him. He let out a laugh that shook his whole body, and I broke out in giggles, too.

He cupped my shoulders and held me out at arm's length. "You're a mess," he said, his eyes going from the wet skirt of my dress to my wet eyelashes and finally to my lips, which quirked up with another giggle. "But I wouldn't change a thing. I love you, Ro."

When he leaned down to kiss me, I thought my heart would explode. His lips were soft against mine, his hands strong on my shoulders. I was completely and madly in love.

The sound of clapping pulled us apart.

"Bravo, August Quinn. Bravo." Fern was still at the table, face streaked with tears as she clapped. Pappy stood at the bottom of the stairs, Fig in his arms, his eyes sparkling, his smile wide. Forest was behind him, tapping a bandaged finger against his thigh.

"What's going on here?" Bluebell appeared behind Forest, peeking around his broad shoulders to see what the fuss was about. She shoved him aside and leaped down into the dining room, her curls bouncing. "Ohmygod, *yes*!" she squealed, coming toward us. She wrapped her arms around the two of us and squeezed.

"Rose?" she said into my shoulder.

"It's milk," August and I said in unison, and we fell apart laughing.

"Oh, thank god you didn't pee your pants at a moment like this."

August trailed his fingers down my arm and grabbed my hands in his. "I wouldn't care if she did," he said as our eyes locked together. "Nothing's gonna make me leave her this time."

My eyes welled with fresh tears.

"All right, you lovebirds," Pappy said. "Let's go home."

CHAPTER 21

August

Rose and I were up with the sun on Thursday morning, tending to the plants and tidying the property before the certification agent arrived at ten. Just when I thought the rumbling in my stomach couldn't get any louder, Pappy whistled from the porch of the cottage, ushering us in to eat. The kitchen table was laid with fried eggs, crispy bacon, baked tomatoes, and thick slices of Ida Pease's heritage grain bread. What more could a man want? I wondered, taking it all in. The love of a beautiful woman, homegrown food, and a little corner of paradise in the Pacific Northwest.

"Thanks, Pappy. That was just what I needed,"

Rose told him when she'd finished. She laid her knife and fork on her empty plate.

"Still feeling ready for this morning?" Felix held a rasher of bacon aloft while he waited for her answer. Fig whimpered at his side, drool dripping from her tongue.

Rose nodded resolutely. "We got this."

His blue eyes sparkled. "That's right, isn't it? Just goes to show—you can do anything you set your mind to."

"Doesn't hurt to have the best partner a gal could ask for." She patted his shoulder and leaned forward to collect our plates.

Felix held up a finger. "Hear that?" Through the open door, the sound of a car engine grew louder as it approached. Rose dropped the plates in the sink, wiped her hands on her canvas apron, then grasped one hand in mine, one hand in Felix's. Together we went out to the porch.

An older woman climbed out from behind the wheel of a tan sedan. With short, graying hair, stern eyes, and a clipboard clasped in her arm, she looked like she meant business. She shielded her eyes from the sun with the clipboard and strode confidently toward us. "Good morning. My name is Margo Graham from the US Department of Agriculture. I'll be doing your inspection today." She held out a hand to Felix, but he cocked his chin at Rose.

"Good morning, Margo. My granddaughter Rose, here, is in charge."

"Morning. Welcome to Big Oak Farm," Rose said. Margo shook Rose's hand, then Felix's, and finally mine as Rose introduced us. Her grip was firm and businesslike.

The woman nodded perfunctorily. "I received your package." Margo pointed to the clipboard, which was affixed with documents labeled Big Oak Farm. "Everything looks to be in order, but as you know I'm here to see if your production is in accordance with Title 7, Part 205 of the Code of Federal Regulations. Shall we get started?"

Felix looked slightly taken aback, but I appreciated the woman's efficient, no-nonsense style.

"Of course," Rose said. "Why don't we start in the vegetable field. Follow me."

She led Margo on a tour of the farm, describing the systems approach she and Felix had implemented as part of the transition to organic production. Once she launched into how they considered the way soil, water, plants, insects, fungi, and other parts of the system could interact to cause problems or prevent them, the inspector's face changed from doubtful to thoughtful.

I sensed she was impressed by Rose's passion—as I

was. Rose articulated clearly their methods on crop rotation and seed stock and their crop plans for the coming years. She spoke about how over the course of the four years since they began, as they'd added organic matter, populations of soil microbes had naturally increased, resulting in rich, productive soil.

As we walked through the orchard, Margo began asking about their approach to insect control, one of the biggest challenges to organic farming, I'd learned.

"Like everything else we do, we start with a systems-based approach," Rose said. "A well-designed, healthy organic system naturally has fewer pest problems. So crop rotation plays into that, as well as cover drops, using disease-resistant varieties, intercropping." Margo nodded again, encouraging Rose to continue. "Here in the orchard we remove branches infected with fire blight, then burn them on the far side of the property." She pointed in the direction she meant. "Fortunately, that's been only a handful of times in the past three years."

"And if that fails to work in the future?" Margo stopped in the midst of the cherry trees and looked down her nose at Rose.

"Well, we'd introduce insect predators and parasites, use canopy management, soil solarization..." Rose's gaze went from the inspector to Felix and back again. "We are committed here, Margo. Whatever it takes, we will do what's best for the health of our farm and our customers, now and forever."

Margo didn't respond, just eyed the three of us, as if evaluating every move and facial expression. After a long silence, she looked around at the parched fruit trees and the bone-dry grass beneath our feet.

Rose could explain all she wanted about the careful planning and dedication she and Pappy had put into the farm, but nothing could cover the effects of the heat dome that'd hit Orcas Island this week.

"I think I have everything I need here," Margo said and once again began her purposeful strides.

For the first time since she arrived, I felt a flutter of panic in my chest. I quickly caught up with the inspector, Rose and Felix loping behind me. "What you see here... We can explain—"

"It's the process itself I'm here to inspect," she interrupted my nervous justification. "Not the products that result from it." She kept walking as she added, "Let me tell you, I've seen a lot worse this week. You've fared very well."

My chest swelled with pride for Rose and her grandfather. When we reached Margo's car, the woman turned and held out a hand. "You should hear from the USDA next week." Margo shook Rose's hand—two firm pumps. And then she was in the driver's seat and starting the engine. With a brisk wave, she was off down the drive, dust billowing up behind her.

The three of us watched until she turned onto the main road.

"Congratulations, sweetheart. I think you won her over," Felix said.

Rose kicked her boot in the gravel. "I'm not counting those chickens yet, Pappy. But I'm proud of us." She wrapped her arms around his birdlike frame.

He returned the hug, patting her back. "Me, too, sweetheart. Me, too."

CHAPTER 22

Rose

"Coming to the wrap party?" Bluebell asked over cod dogs two weeks later at our Friday Cottle's lunch. Another of Freddy's ideas, they involved tempura-battered pieces of cod on a hot dog roll with dill dijonnaise, tartar, lemon-pickled onions, cucumbers, and pea shoots. She took an enormous bite, oblivious to the sauce on her chin, her curls bouncing as she chewed.

"Nah. Not really my scene." I sipped on a Corona, the perfect drink for Freddy's delicious dogs.

"Not your scene? It's everyone's scene," she said. "I know for a fact Domino's going above and beyond to make it special for islanders."

I shrugged.

"Aw, come on, Rose," she pleaded. "You have to come. Please?" She put down her dog and held her palms together in a prayer gesture. "For me?"

I grabbed her hands to end her entreaty. "Begging won't work," I teased. "But you deserve to have a great time—with or without me."

"Because August isn't home yet?" He'd had to leave for California after the inspection to rejoin the film shoot and wasn't expected home again until Sunday.

"What? No. Pappy and I have things to do. You know, we've started getting orders from as far south as Portland. River's friend just opened a restaurant down there, and he wants Big Oak produce."

"That's great. But we're not changing the subject. You're not getting off that easy." She wiggled a finger at me.

"I'm not trying to—"

"Then come," she interrupted. "You and Felix were a big part of making everyone feel welcome here—Domino told me so herself."

"She did?"

"Yep. She said more than one crew member told her how special it was to eat locally grown food while they were here. And several others mentioned the farmers market. She said they all think Orcas Island is the best place they've ever stayed on location for a shoot."

"Well, look around. It's paradise." I waved to my right, where a fishing boat bobbed in front of the pier, a giant Sitka spruce stood tall against the sky to the east, and the outline of Mt. Baker, the third highest peak in the state, towered in the distance.

"It's the people, though, she said. Hey, Domino moved here, remember? And her attention is bringing in more tourists, which means more money in the economy, making it easier for year-round folks like you and me to thrive. I, for one, am super grateful. I just want you and Felix to be there. It wouldn't be the same without you."

I took another bite of cod dog and contemplated. Around us, seagulls cried and crows squawked amid the familiar sounds of Mary and Louis greeting customers and taking orders.

"Don't forget—Felix deserves a celebration, too," Bluebell continued her case. "You worked really hard doing this organic thing. You know he loves a good party."

Swallowing the last bite, I clapped my hands together. "I can't believe I forgot to tell you!"

"What?" Bluebell watched as I dug furiously in my bag until I found my phone. "Whaaaat?" she said again when I didn't answer, just called up my email and scrolled to find what I was looking for. Finally I turned the screen to face her.

Bluebell squinted against the sun to read, "United States Department of Agriculture National Organic Program. Big Oak Farm, 106 Winslow Road, Orcas Island, Washington, meets all the requirements prescribed in the…" Her voice trailed off, and she leaped to her feet, napkin dropping from her lap. "Ohmygod ohmygod. Rose! That is *huge*!" She ran around to my side of the table. "Congratulations, friend," she said, pulling me to my feet and wrapping me in a hug. "You did it!"

She held me at arm's length, a hand on each shoulder. "I'm so proud of you," she said, then turned and told everyone within listening distance, "Everyone, say hello to the best organic farmer on Orcas Island!"

A whoop went up at the take-out window, and I looked across to see Mary leaning forward, two thumbs up in the air. "That's our girl!" she called and started clapping. Soon the customers around us joined in, several of who wolf-whistled in celebration.

Bluebell grabbed my hand and hoisted it in the air. "Hip-hip hooray!" she said.

"Hip-hip hooray!" came a chorus of replies.

I was embarrassed at the attention but thrilled to be celebrating the hard work and dedication Pappy and I had devoted four years of our lives to. I did a little curtsy to show my appreciation, heat tingling my cheeks, but my smile felt like it stretched from ear to ear. Louis came to our table with another round of Coronas.

"On the house," he said as he set them down. He, too, took me in a heartfelt hug. "Congratulations, my dear. You did us all proud. Will we see you and Felix at the party Sunday?"

"You're going?" I was surprised. It would mean closing up shop on what was normally the busiest day of the week at Cottle's.

"Wouldn't miss it." He winked before he retreated through the double doors to the kitchen.

"See? Everyone will be there," Bluebell said. "Including you and Felix. Right?" She nudged my arm. "Right?" she repeated when I hesitated.

Finally I lifted my shoulders in a shrug. It seemed futile to resist. "Oh, all right."

"Yay! Another reason to celebrate." She reached for the Coronas, passed one to me, and clinked her bottle against mine. "Come on, let's look across the sound while we drink these." She led me to the side of the pier, where we could take in the vast stretch of ocean before us. Buoys wobbled in the bay, waves gently lapped the pillars below, and the July sun kissed our cheeks as we soaked up the sounds and smells of this wonderful place we called home.

CHAPTER 23

August

My knuckles were gripped around the armrests as the ferry docked in Bayview on Saturday. I wasn't anxious about work, though. I wanted everything to be perfect for Rose. I'd thought carefully about what I wanted to say to her and how I wanted to say it. But before that, I needed to talk to Felix.

It was market day. I'd flown back a day ahead of the crew to speak with him before Rose arrived home from Grange Hall. Felix didn't have a cell phone, so I was at Bluebell's mercy to both delay Rose's departure from the market and keep me posted when she headed out for home.

Command to Bluebell, I texted. **What's your status?**

I was relieved when she texted back right away. I crossed my fingers for good news.

The subject is in sight. Bluebell followed it with a detective emoji. It was cute and all, but I needed the hard facts.

And?

And we're at Grange Hall. Ginger's in on the ruse. Ever had whiskey with ginger coffee?!

Sounds revolting. But keep it up. Docking now and going straight to the farm.

Roger that, she replied. I dropped my phone in my duffel bag, picked up my belongings, and headed to the stern of the boat, where I waited with the other passengers to disembark.

I sprinted up the ramp to the terminal as fast as my knee would let me and hot-footed down the hill to the Driftwood Inn, where, just as she'd promised, Fern was waiting out back with the keys to the hotel's blue jeep. With the ocean breeze blowing through my hair, on my way to see Felix Hardy about my girl, I was on top of the world.

My phone buzzed in my pocket as I neared the turn for Big Oak. I pulled into the driveway and stopped, fearing Bluebell had bad news.

Don't know how much longer I can hold her. Out of whiskey.

I chuckled. **At the farm. I'll text as soon as I talk to Felix.**

Better hurry.

I took her instruction to heart and floored it to the cottage, dust and gravel flying in my wake. The screen door pushed open, and Felix appeared on the porch, his hand shading his eyes to see who it was. Fig rushed to the top of the steps and barked, her tail wagging. I parked the jeep and hopped out.

"August! You back from your trip? Rose isn't home—"

"I know," I interrupted him. My palms were suddenly sweaty, and my heart was thudding against my rib cage. "I don't have much time."

"Did something happen?" His forehead creased with worry.

"No, no. It's nothing like that. Walk with me?" In my mind when I'd played this out, Felix and I were under the old oak tree.

His brows unfurrowed, but he still looked befuddled. "Well, all right, son. Let me just get my—"

I hated to interrupt him again. I touched his arm. "You know, let's just stay here. Time's running out." I joined him on the porch.

"Time for who? What's the hurry?"

I felt my phone buzz in my pocket, sending my nerves jangling all over again. I tried to remember what I'd planned to say to him, but my mind was blank. *"If you're kind and loving to others, they'll be kind and loving to you.*" I heard Zoe's words in my head. I was better off speaking from the heart anyway.

"I love Rose," I said.

Felix chuckled. "Tell me something I don't know, kid. You've always loved her."

Of course he knew. No one had spent more time around Rose and me than him. He'd watched us grow together, fall in love the first time, watched us stumble and find ourselves again. I nodded. "You're right. I love this place, too. What you two have done here..." I looked out over the property, the neat rows of corn, the pretty branches of fruit trees dotting the orchard, the worn little cottage to the left, the big old house to the right. "I've been around the world, Felix. Big Oak is special. It's who you are. Who Rose is. And if it'll have me, it's who I am, too."

I swallowed a lump in my throat when I turned to face him, this man who'd been such a steady presence for most of my life—and since my return. His eyes held more than just their usual sparkle; they were bright and watery with tears.

"Rose means the world to me, and I want to spend the rest of my life proving that to her." My phone buzzed in my pocket again, sending my pulse racing. Surely they were almost here. "I came to see you today because I want to ask her to marry me, and I would be honored to have your blessing." *Buzz buzz.* My armpits were wet with sweat.

He looked me squarely in the eyes, considering my words carefully. A look of approval came over his face, and he stuck out his hand. I grasped it gratefully, his calloused fingers strong despite his seventy-plus years. "Thought you'd never ask. Welcome home."

I clasped his shoulder with my left hand, my right one shaking his vigorously as I let out a whoop of joy. "Thank you. I won't let her down. Ever."

His grip tightened. "Better not, son."

In the distance a cloud of dust billowed in the air near the end of the driveway. "Just under the wire," I said as the Big Oak van approached, the love of my life at the wheel. I had her grandfather's blessing and a smile on my face. I threw my head back and whooped again. Welcome home, indeed.

Rose

"What's going on?" I was happy to see August home early but still surprised. I climbed down from the van, the door squeaking on its hinges as it swung shut. "Wait a minute. Are you crying, Pappy?" I rushed up the steps to the porch.

He swiped a bony finger at a tear on his cheek, but his eyes twinkled with joy, not pain. "I'll leave you two alone." He touched August's shoulder. "Let's go, Fig." He slapped his thigh.

"But where are you—"

The screen door banged shut before I could finish my question.

August came toward me, hands in his pockets, his smile tender. It was late afternoon, and the air held a hazy glow of gold that softened his cheekbones and the hard lines of his shoulders. "You're home." I folded into his embrace like a lunar module docking to its ship. His arms wrapped around me, sure and strong.

"I missed you." His voice was husky in his chest. I nodded, inhaling his smell of salt and sun. He pulled away, tracing his fingers down my arms. "Come with me," he said and tugged me down the steps and into the grass.

He led me to the far end of the orchard, where sun cast shafts of filtered light through the branches of the big Garry oak. He stopped at the top of the rise and turned to face me, both hands now clasped in mine.

"Remember at the farmers market, when Zoe pulled the Wheel of Fortune? I've been thinking about that moment—what she said—a lot. She told me to make the most of the good moments in life while they're in reach—because they could be gone in a heartbeat."

I nodded. How had I thought her foolish when everything she'd said was right?

"At the time I dismissed it, I think because it hit so true. I'm proof of how quickly the good things in life, the things you count on, can disappear. All I've done since I left is dig a hole of pity for myself. Told myself I wasn't good enough—for anyone."

August squeezed my fingers when my eyes blurred with tears.

"I didn't cherish you back then, and I lost you." His voice wavered. "I don't want to lose you again. Ever. I want to marry you, help you grow Big Oak, have a family someday. I don't feel sorry for myself, not anymore. You've shown me what's important. Love. Purpose. Hard work." He dropped my hands and dug in his pocket for a little velvet pouch the color of eggplant.

He loosened the ties and pulled out a platinum-gold ring with diamonds inlaid in a vine. I gasped as he dropped to his knee—both with exhilaration and concern.

He let out a laugh of relief. "Didn't hurt, Rose. Nothing could hurt me right now."

I giggled, wiping the tears from my cheeks.

"So how about it? Will you marry me?"

I reached out to haul him to his feet. I wanted to be standing right in front of him, this man I now realized I trusted in ways I'd never expected to trust again. I touched his chin with my thumb and smiled.

"Yes." It came out as calm as the water in the bay the night we'd swam to the rock. I'd never felt so sure of anything. Then I was enveloped in his arms, and his lips were on mine in a kiss that sent shivers to my toes. When I could speak again, I repeated my answer. "Yes, August Quinn. I'll marry you."

He lifted me in his arms, and I wrapped my legs around him as he spun me, laughing against my ear. When he set me down, I nudged him back until he was against the fissured old trunk of the oak. Now it was my turn to kneel. Knees in the dirt, I unbuttoned his jeans and tugged them down, releasing a cock that was thick and throbbing. He groaned as I took him in my mouth, the taste of him salty on my tongue. He clasped my shoulders, his fingers digging in as he called out my name. But when his cock got so hard I thought he would burst, he gently pushed himself free to step out of his jeans. He sat to the ground in front of me, leaning back on the tree while he nudged open the button on my shorts and unzipped the fly.

I stood and shucked out of them, tossing them with my panties and his jeans. In tandem we slipped off our shirts, too, and I unclipped my bra and dropped it to the ground.

His eyes swept up my body, lingering on the V between my legs, his mouth open, his eyelids hooded. I'd never felt more beautiful, more wanted. More seen.

"Wow."

It was a single word, but it said more than a thousand. August saw me the way I saw him—as my person. We'd lost ten years, but we hadn't lost each other. When we were together, it was with our whole hearts.

I stepped closer, straddling his thighs, his eyes in line with my mound. He tilted his head to look up at me, and I nodded. "Yes," I whispered, tousling his hair.

He pulled me to him. I trembled, ready to beg for his touch, and when he spread my lips open and tongued my core, every cell in my body lit up like a Christmas tree. The world faded away, and it was just me, and August, and the big old oak at the end of the world. I tipped my head back, riding the waves of pleasure that rolled through my body until I could barely hold myself up.

I lowered to his lap, where his erection pressed against my pussy, glistening with precum. "Oh god," he moaned against my lips. 'Fuck me, Rose." Rising to my knees, I guided him into me, his cock splitting me open like the stamen on a bloom. I rocked us, slowly at first, then picking up speed, and he grew impossibly harder, filling me completely as I clenched around him. When he took my nipple between his lips, sending tingles down my spine, I let go completely, crying out his name and pulsing with ecstasy.

His breathing grew ragged, and he clutched my body against him, his head on my shoulder. He thrust deeper, and I closed my eyes, imagining with each throb a fountain of cum shooting into me.

When it was over, we stayed wrapped together, fusing into each other like melted chocolate. The setting sun lit the sky in silky orange, the color of the apricots in the orchard below. When August finally leaned forward, his back etched with the lines of the bark, we pried ourselves apart.

"You're incredible," he told me, buttoning the fly on his jeans while I fastened my bra.

I held out my left hand to admire how the diamonds in my ring sparkled in the twilight. "Sometimes all you need is a second chance," I said, soaking in the love of the magnificent August Quinn.

CHAPTER 24

August

Sunday morning dawned bright and clear, the kind of summer day you dreamed of in the Pacific Northwest. I found myself whistling the song that had been stuck in my head since Rose and I sang it at the top of our lungs—Tom Petty's "American Girl." The sun was warm on my face and the familiar smell of the Pacific filled my head.

It was the day of the wrap party, and I'd driven into Bayview to return Forest's jeep and meet up with Sam and Noah. I found a spot at the end of the docks and sat on the sun-faded cedar, my feet swinging off the end while I waited for them to join me.

"Here you are," Noah said behind me. I turned to see him and Sam approaching, Sam in a blindingly white shirt and jeans. Noah was barefoot, the bottoms of his pants rolled up to his ankles.

They sat down next to me on the dock, Noah leaning back on his palms, his legs spread out in front of him. Sam brought his knees to his chest and wrapped his arms around them.

"How did it go with Rose?" Noah asked, one eye squinted against the sun as he looked me.

I smiled broadly, images from last night flooding my mind. "Fucking incredible." But looking from Noah to Sam and back again, I steeled myself for the conversation I knew we needed to have. "Which means we need to talk."

Sam took off his aviator sunglasses and tucked them into the neck of his shirt, his eyes taking on a serious glint. "I have something I need to tell you, too."

I glanced at Noah again, but he shrugged, as clueless as I was about whatever was on Sam's mind. "You first," I told him.

"These past four years have been some of the best of my life. Meeting you two…" He gazed into the distance, as if trying to come up with the words to describe how he was feeling. "Well, you guys know my family wanted me to join the military. Expected it.

I dreaded it my whole life. Until USERT. You made me feel like I belonged, like I mattered. And you put up with my…fastidiousness."

"Is that what you call it?" Noah belly laughed.

Sam chuckled, then his expression grew serious again. "Anyway. Then the film stuff came along, and we had some amazing experiences, didn't we? But it's time, boys. Time for me to give this acting thing a try."

I clapped his shoulder, hoping to ease some of the worry lining his forehead. "I'm proud of you, man. I'm proud of all of us. I can't wait to see you up on the big screen."

Relief smoothed his features. "Really? You're not mad?"

"No way. Especially not when I tell you I'm staying here on Orcas Island."

We turned in parallel to clock Noah's expression. He just lifted a shoulder and smiled. "So no more underwater filming?" he asked.

"Nah. I mean, maybe as a hobby. But it's farm life for me."

"Huh," he said, rubbing his chin. "Well, not to steal y'all's thunder, but I have a little something up my sleeve myself."

"What's that?" Sam asked.

"Surf photography."

"What?"

"All these years, you didn't tell us you surf?" Sam tried to hide his irritation that after all this time, there was something he didn't know about Noah.

"I don't. Yet." He leaned on his left hand and pulled the phone from his pocket. He tapped to open something and turned it to show me and Sam. On the screen, a video showed a tiny a figure on a Jet Ski driving along the crest of a huge wave, towing an equally tiny figure on a surfboard behind it. I inhaled sharply when the figure let go of the rope and the Jet Ski disappeared behind a giant wall of turquoise. The surfer rocketed down the wave like he'd been shot from a cannon, body bent forward, heading for a bottom that never appeared.

"What the…" I'd never seen anything like it.

"*That's* what you want to do?" Sam asked, dumbfounded.

"I don't want to surf it," Noah explained. "I want to film it."

Rose

After an hour in front of my closet and three different outfits, I settled on an old favorite: a smocked knee-length brown sundress with white polka dots, à la Julia Roberts at the polo match in *Pretty Woman*. My hair framed my face in soft waves, and my mom's drop pearl earrings glowed against my suntan.

Out on the porch, Pappy sat waiting for me.

"Pretty damn good for a farm girl," he said. His party attire looked much the same as his work clothes, only everything was clean, and he'd added what I liked to call his "Big Apple" cap—a floppy newsboy he'd had since I was a kid.

"Pretty good for any girl." Farm girls didn't have a lot of dresses in their closets, but I knew this one suited me.

He crooked his elbow to link with mine, and together we walked to the van. August planned to meet us at the party after his meeting with Sam and Noah. "Moonstone Beach, huh?" Pappy said as he turned onto the main road and headed west. "Haven't been there in…" He seemed to be calculating. "Must be ten years. You?"

I thought back to the moonlight canoe trip with August all those weeks ago. "Oh, I've been once or twice lately," I told him.

He chatted away about the work on the estate house, due to start in a couple of weeks, his wiry frame leaning over the big round steering wheel, his cap adjusted to the side to shade the sun beaming through the window. Oh, how I treasured him.

The side road leading to the beach was jammed with the familiar cars and farm vehicles of our friends and neighbors. It looked like all of Orcas Island was here.

Pappy drove up on a grassy patch instead of fighting for a spot along the gravel. "Ah, it's just old Henry Black's place," he said when I raised an eyebrow. River and Rocky's dad owned half the land on this part of the island.

"You're in charge, Paps." I stuffed my phone in the pocket of my dress and jumped down from the passenger seat. Pappy came around to my side, and we joined arms again to traverse the path, heading past the big boulder to the log stairs.

The beach had been transformed into a boho-chic oasis, with big pots of pampas grass interspersed between groupings of low tables, complete with Moroccan-style rugs and batik-dyed pillows. Lights were strung along poles in elegant rows, and lanterns graced each table and were placed strategically on logs along the beach.

At the bottom of the log stairs, we passed under a driftwood arch decorated with grass fronds and cedar sprigs and were greeted by a dazzling Domino West. "Rose, Felix, I'm so glad you came!" Her enthusiasm was so genuine, it made me doubly glad we were here. "Y'all have been so gracious about me and the crew taking over the island." She gestured behind her. "This'll never be enough to express how grateful I really am, but please enjoy yourselves. Today's about you and this magical place." The sunshine bounced off her shiny dark hair, emanating happiness like an aura around her. I understood even more now what people meant when they said she had "it."

We stepped forward and were swallowed into the crowd of friends. Bluebell and Fern bounded up, drinks in their hands, relaxed and happy.

"What are we drinking, ladies?" Pappy asked, eyes twinkling.

"Moroccan mojitos!" Fern said enthusiastically.

"Whatever that is, I'll take one. You, too, sweetheart?" I nodded as he left my side and made for the bar set up at the top of the beach. My eyes tracked him for a bit before I scanned the crowd to see who was here. Bluebell stared openmouthed while Damon

Mann made his entrance through the driftwood arch.

I spotted River and Rocky Black, heads together near the bar. They were surrounded by folks from Isola, who were preparing food on a series of folding tables covered in batik-print fabric. Forest stood a little way behind Domino, tossing a wave in our direction as his eyes caught mine. Bob and Isa Pease were here, and so were Poppy Willoughby and her mom, Georgia. Tommy and George from the Driftwood chatted with Angela Fletcher next to a big pot of pampas grass, and Mary and Louis Larsen and their son, Freddy, sat on a nearby log. Even Zoe was here with Coco. Crew from *Shore Thing* were in a group by the water, where the red-faced director was holding court, waving his arms around and gesticulating wildly while his assistants shrank behind him.

Pappy returned, his hat still tilted sideways, two frosted glasses in his hands. Leaving him to flirt with Fern and Bluebell, I wandered closer to the water with my mojito, where I sat on a warm log, the ocean turquoise in front of me, the warm breeze in my hair. Footsteps crunched on the beach behind me.

"Well, will you look at that," August said, extending an arm over my shoulder to point out to sea.

Two orcas took turns dipping in and out of the water, sending up big puffs of breath from their blowholes, their shiny dorsal fins gleaming in the sun.

Exhilaration surged through me. "It's a sign, isn't it?"

"It is." He wrapped his arms around me as the whales continued around the curve of the bay, cruising above and below the waves, smooth as silk.

"Think they mate for life?" I leaned back against him.

"They don't." He chuckled quietly. "But we do."

Have you read *The Farthest Star*, book 1 in the Wildflower Romance series? It's available now at all major book retailers.
sallyglover.com/the-farthest-star

Get book 3 in the series, *The Drop*.
sallyglover.com/the-drop

ABOUT THE AUTHOR

Sally Glover is the author of the Wildflower books, set in the Pacific Northwest. She lives and writes on Vancouver Island, a wild little paradise on the west coast of Canada.

Website: sallyglover.com
Instagram: @sallygloverwrites
Facebook: @sallygloverwrites
Newsletter: sallyglover.com/subscribe
Goodreads: goodreads.com/sallygloverwrites
BookBub: bookbub.com/authors/sally-glover